# THE RIVER'S DAUGHTER

PUNITA RICE

RISING GRAINS PUBLISHING

**First Edition**

Rice, Punita C.

*The River's Daughter* / Punita Rice. — 1st ed.

**Summary:** As her arranged marriage approaches, Sahira Raazaan discovers forbidden power tied to the river—and to a stranger who awakens it. She must choose between obedience and the truth in her blood.

**Published by Rising Grains Publishing**

**ISBN (eBook):** 979-8-9987469-0-1

**ISBN (Paperback):** 979-8-9987469-3-2

**ISBN (Large Print Edition):** 979-8-9987469-1-8

**ISBN (Hardcover):** 979-8-9987469-2-5

Cover design and map illustration by Sarah Khan Azamy

Inspired by the legend of Mirza Sahiba
the tale of a woman who loved,
and paid for it with everything she had.

JARAAN
RUINS
TEMPLE OF JARAAN
MARKET SQUARE
MOUTH OF THE SERPENT
ELDER NEFRET'S HOUSE
WAYSTATION
GOVERNMENT COLONY
River Bakki
MEHR'AN CAMP

# PROLOGUE

The water held her.

Sahira, only five years old, was suspended just below the surface of the river, long curls drifting around her like spilled ink. She should have been terrified. Should have been thrashing, lungs burning, desperate for air.

Instead, she floated in perfect stillness.

Light fractured the world around her into impossible patterns of sapphire, emerald, gold. And the river cradled her as a mother holds her daughter: with recognition, with reverence, with love.

Time stretched. Elastic, dreamlike.

Sahira blinked slowly, amber eyes watching bubbles escape her parted lips, up to the shimmering surface.

Through the shimmering membrane above her, she saw her mother's face, her eyes bright with fear and wonder as her arms reached down to her daughter.

Then, just before Ameera's hands broke the surface to pull her daughter into the world of air and voices and boundaries, Sahira heard the river singing to her.

And then the surface shattered.

Sunlight returned, flat and harsh compared to the refracted kaleidoscope of the river.

The voice of the river had faded, but its echo remained.

Sahira's mother clutched her to her chest, her heart pounding against her daughter's cheek.

Sahira smiled up at her as water streamed from her round cheeks, her hair, her clothes, her skin, returning to the river as all water eventually must.

"The river knows me, Mama," she said, her small hands cupping her mother's tear-streaked face.

Recognition flickered across Ameera's features as she looked into her daughter's eyes—a recognition quickly concealed by the careful blankness that women of the Covenant were taught to maintain.

She pulled Sahira closer, her whisper barely stirring the air between them: "Sahira, tell no one about this." Thunder rolled across the valley, and Ameera glanced over her shoulder, where the distant spires of Jaraan rose like accusing fingers against the darkening sky. "Only me. Understand?"

Sahira nodded. Her mother pressed three fingers to her heart. Their sign: *I love you.*

Clouds gathered on the horizon. The first storm of the season was coming.

Ameera's eyes closed briefly, as if in prayer, or as if in resignation. When she looked at Sahira again, her gaze was clear, decided.

"For now, we must be still," she said, the words carrying a weight Sahira wouldn't understand for many years. "But someday you'll understand: the river knows you."

The river pulsed beside them in acknowledgment, its surface catching the last light before the storm.

# PART ONE
# STILLNESS

# CHAPTER I
# SURFACE

Ten breaths in, ten breaths out.

Sahira's knees ached against the wooden floor, which was polished to a mirror shine by generations of unmarried girls before her. She shifted slightly, earning a sharp glance from Elder Margani that instantly stilled her body—but not the restlessness inside.

The floor was hard through the thin cotton of her salwar. Her knees throbbed. Around her, twenty-three other girls sat with ankles tucked beneath them, maintaining perfect stillness. The elder paced behind them, her presence marked only by the creak of the temple's old wood beneath her feet. Sahira's fingers twitched. She flexed them once before forcing them still.

Near the back of the room, a girl shifted position and her hand struck the floor. Immediately, a temple attendant glided forward, placing a firm hand on the child's head—a touch gentle in pressure but unmistakable in meaning: Stillness is salvation. Movement is corruption.

The mark of the Covenant—still water within a perfect circle—hung above the altar at the front of the chamber, like an ever-watchful eye.

"Stillness," came Margani's voice, no louder than a whisper. "Your body is for stillness; your stillness is our peace."

The Covenant of Stillness governed every aspect of a woman's existence in Jaraan: how she moved, spoke, even how she breathed. In public, a woman's voice must never rise above gentle rainfall; her eyes must not meet a man's directly unless he was her relative or betrothed; her body must remain covered and contained. Girls were taught silence, while boys were taught stories where silence saved girls and, in turn, society itself.

Jaraan women were taught to fold their desires, knowledge, and freedom small. And these constraints had been drilled into Sahira since childhood, their weight as familiar as her own skin.

"May Stillness guide you," were Elder Margani's final words when the morning ritual ended.

"May Stillness guide us all," the girls responded in synchronization, and then rose from their knees together in choreography practiced since childhood.

The girls filed out of the women's doors of the temple, into the May morning, just as first light touched the tops of the trees on the eastern ridge. Their assigned doors were narrow, requiring single file entry and exit, and the door frame dipped low enough that it bowed the heads of most girls.

They walked slowly, in order by age, heads and eyes lowered, pausing only to bow one by one to Elder Nefret, the head matriarch among the Samiti Elders, before crossing the threshold that separated the temple from the town.

A twelve-year-old girl, the same one who had shifted during the stillness training earlier, stumbled slightly, disrupting the perfect line. Elder Nefret's gaze snapped to her instantly.

"See that your clumsiness in movement does not become clumsiness in morality." Her voice pitched to carry to every ear. Then, with deceptive gentleness: "Stillness in body reflects stillness in spirit."

The girl—Malsi was her name, Sahira recalled—flushed crimson and straightened her spine, eyes locked on the ground.

"Yes, Elder," she whispered, retreating into formation beside her age group, the largest cohort. Leela, Sahira's cousin, would have walked with the fourteens had her first blood arrived. But until then, she was spared from stillness practice.

Each year's group was smaller than the last; most girls were married off by fifteen. At nineteen, only Sahira and two others remained. But Sahira's status was different—she, at least, was betrothed.

As the girls reached the marketplace and began diverging in their paths, Sahira drifted toward the central fountain. She had always been drawn to the fountain, and to all water—a fact that worried her father endlessly.

After her mother disappeared, this connection only intensified. By twelve, she had learned to hide it, pretending water was merely a resource, nothing more. But some nights, she still pressed against her bedroom window, eyes closed, wishing she could put her hands in the Bakki to their east. A longing she couldn't share with anyone.

The fountain's gentle rippling fragmented her reflection across the water's surface as Sahira approached. Wisps of hair had escaped her long braid, framing her face in a rebellious halo despite her morning efforts at neatness. She tucked the strands behind her ears, frowning at her reflection. With her hair pulled back, her features were too sharp—all angles and edges where there should be softness.

Sighing, she broke the reflection with her fingers and brought cool water to her face. As it touched her skin, a memory surfaced:

She was four, playing by the stream that fed the town's wells while her father tried to catch fish. A frog caught her attention. She leaned too far over the bank, tumbling into water just slightly deeper than her height. But instead of drowning, the water had cradled her. Her father had been close by, and grabbed her quickly out of the stream. She'd tried to explain to her parents that the water had felt like it was holding her. Her mother hugged her. Her father had been angry. Later that night, he had made her drink a bitter tea, and the memory had faded to a distant echo.

Until now.

Her fingers grazed the surface. And for the briefest moment, the water reached back, a thin tendril defying gravity to meet her touch before collapsing. Sahira jerked her hand away, heart pounding. *Had anyone seen?*

She glanced around, but the women nearby were either speaking quietly with heads properly bowed, reading from prayer books, or sitting in silent stillness.

*Water only moves toward those it recognizes.* The thought came unbidden into her mind, its source unclear, and a shiver ran through her body. Goosebumps rose along her arms despite the morning warmth. She shook her head, trying to clear it.

This wasn't the first strange occurrence she'd had with water recently. Just last week, while tending to the garden beds, she'd dropped the watering can, and the water had seemed to hesitate, hovering for an impossible moment, before splashing her skin. A month before that, water in her washing basin had formed perfect concentric circles though she hadn't disturbed its surface. Small oddities she'd dismissed as tricks of the light.

But now she thought of those moments as she gazed into the fountain. And then, she plunged her hands deeper into the water, down to her wrists, shaking off the thoughts.

"Sahira," came a sharp voice.

She turned to find her aunt watching her, eyes narrowed in assessment. Sahira stood up quickly, pulling her hands out of the water, and drying them on her kameez. "Stillness guide you, Tharima Bua."

Tharima ignored the greeting, but moved toward her niece, stopping briefly to reach down, her hand pulling at a plant that jutted out from between the stones. Its root held tight. "Burdock," she said, shaking her head. "It's hard to pull once it roots. You have to kill it early."

She dropped the plant and dusted off her hands. "Your plait is crooked," she said, reaching to adjust the gray ribbon that bound Sahira's long, dark, and always loose braid. "The knot must be neat. Women with loose ribbons can cause storms."

Sahira's throat tightened as several women by the fountain paused their quiet conversations to watch the interaction. She was well past the age when most received such corrections, but as an unmarried woman still in her father's house, she remained under the close supervision of his widowed younger sister. A reminder of her highly unusual position: not a girl but certainly not a fully accepted woman.

Her aunt noticed. "Never mind them," she said, motioning for her niece to stand and move with her. "I have news." Her face brightened. "Tavin is back. He and the whole Daraio family are coming for dinner tonight." She looked giddy with delight. "And there's more. Your marriage petition has been approved for exactly eight days from today. No more waiting."

Something caught in the pit of Sahira's stomach then, though she kept her eyes properly lowered and her expression neutral.

"Well, aren't you excited?" Tharima asked, her voice still appropriately quiet for a market conversation, but not concealing her enthusiasm.

"I've been waiting," Sahira answered, offering a small smile for her aunt's benefit.

Six years of waiting, to be precise.

The memory of sitting stiffly beside her father as he and his childhood best friend Dafar Daraio signed the betrothal contract flashed through her mind. The documents that promised a then-thirteen-year-old Sahira to a then-seventeen-year-old Tavin.

Tavin Daraio, the golden boy of the community.

In the good days before Sahira's mother disappeared, the Raazaans and Daraios spent a great deal of time together. In the privacy of the old Government Colony, the gated community where descendants of Jaraan's oldest families lived in grand ancestral homes, Tavin had always helped Sahira look for dandelions and butterflies, played pretend with her, helped her fly kites. Everything was simple. They had gotten to be children together.

Those memories lived separate from what came later. As Tavin matured, he had begun to ignore her publicly, but at gatherings in Government Colony, when no parent or aunt was looking directly at them, Tavin would wink at her, or slip her small flowers he found in the grass.

He became a favorite of the town elders as he grew older. Besides being a Daraio, he was studious, and as his charm evolved alongside his intellect. Sahira's childhood fondness for him had also evolved as she grew older, into a growing infatuation. By the time their fathers signed the formal betrothal contract, she could have squealed with excitement.

But then, Tavin had been awarded by the town elders the rare honor of permission to leave Jaraan for his studies. Dafar Daraio had gently requested—and Sahira's father, Tahir Raazaan, had, of course, agreed—that Tavin should complete his studies abroad before returning to marry Sahira.

Tavin's long absence, and the extended delay of their marriage that resulted, marked Sahira as different, and she was subjected to whispers that followed her through her teenage years and cast an uncomfortable shadow over her adolescence.

Her once-rosy excitement at becoming Tavin's wife gradually degraded in the years that passed. In the years after his departure, she became more aware of being a woman in Jaraan meant, and it stripped down her fantasies. The town's scrutiny only sped up the process.

Not that the scrutiny of the town was itself unfamiliar.

As if reading Sahira's thoughts, her aunt said, "I know our family name has carried a shadow since… your mother." She rarely spoke of Sahira's mother. Her voice lowered. "This alliance with the Daraios isn't just marriage. It will redeem us, Sahira." Her hand tightened on her niece's shoulder. "Everything must be perfect. Do you understand?"

Sahira nodded, but her fingers trembled as she adjusted her sleeves, discomfort crawling up her neck. She understood.

The Raazaan family had long stood apart in Jaraan, the subject of gossip even before Sahira's delayed marriage gave them something new to talk about.

Tharima's smile was sad. "The Raazaan name has endured much. Your Baba has endured much."

Sahira's eyes remained downcast. "I won't disappoint Baba. Everything will be perfect." This alliance with Jaraan's most respected family would remind the town that Tahir Raazaan still was, despite his wife's disappearance, an important man; he married his daughter to the Daraios' only son, after all.

"I've pressed your formal salwar kameez," her aunt continued, as if they had been discussing clothes all along. "The one with the silver embroidery at the cuffs. Modest, but suitable for the importance of the occasion."

"Thank you, Bua," Sahira said. But she felt blood rushing in her ears.

A curious heaviness was spreading through her chest, as if some tethered part of her were straining to break free. She pressed her hand against her ribs, willing the feeling to subside before her aunt noticed.

"Come along," Tharima said, walking briskly.

As they crossed the square, they passed a group of young girls seated in a semicircle around Elder Laal, her wrinkled hands gesturing emphatically as she delivered the weekly history lesson. Sahira caught some of the words as they passed.

"The perversions of the Old World…" the elder was saying to the gathered children. "Women did not care for their husbands, their children…"

Sahira had heard this lesson countless times. Women had grown selfish and abandoned their duties; they had taken up using magic to serve their own interests and pleasures; society collapsed under the weight of women's selfishness and excesses.

Then came a series of great windstorms and earthquakes; panic followed as hundreds of thousands of people lost homes, lost families. And then, systems began to fail: wells ran dry, crops failed. And towns quickly descended into confusion and violence, neighbor turning on neighbor.

After that came The Flooding Years.

Entire towns drowned, and as hundreds of thousands of people desperately tried to move inland, the violence grew worse. Entire communities were killed. Sahira had seen old maps in her father's study. Vast territories that were now marked as Reclaimed by the Sea.

According to the elders, only the Covenant of Stillness, established by men like her own great-great-grandfather, had saved humanity from complete destruction.

"From this chaos," Elder Laal was saying now, "our Covenant arose. Stillness. Order. Purpose." The older woman raised one finger, as she finished her lesson. "Remember this, children: The foundation of Jaraan is the stillness of girls and women. Still your bodies, so that we can have order."

Tharima nodded approvingly as they walked past. "A necessary reminder," she murmured, "especially with so much restlessness these days."

Sahira said nothing, but sometimes she wondered if these histories told the complete truth. But such questions remained safely locked away behind her downcast eyes.

As THEY WALKED, they passed one of the town's western boundary markers: a tall pole topped with a chipped statue of an empty vessel. Far in the distance, the ruins of the Old World thrust from the earth, their skeletons slowly turning to dust.

Sahira and her aunt made their way across the middle of the

market square, Sahira's attention on the distant ruins. And then her eyes moved east, to the Bakki, curling around the valley's edge. Sahira stopped walking, staring in its direction.

"Sahira, are you listening?"

She startled, realizing her aunt had been speaking to her.

"You're drifting," Tharima said, disapproval etched in the lines around her downturned mouth. And then, more quietly: "Just like Ameera used to." Twice in one day, she had mentioned her mother. And the comparison stung, as it was meant to.

Sahira thought then of the private language she and her mother had shared. The spring when Sahira was nine—the last full season before her mother disappeared, abandoning Sahira forever—she and Ameera had developed a secret language of gestures. It had begun innocently enough, with her mother teaching her the traditional hand signals women had once used in the marketplace to negotiate prices without speaking above a whisper—now, women could at least speak in a normal volume when completing their weekly shopping.

"Like this," Ameera had demonstrated, forming her fingers into an arch that meant too much. "The Covenant teaches that our voices should be soft, but our hands can speak volumes if we're clever."

What started as a practical lesson evolved into their own private code. A touch to the wrist meant "quiet now." A particular tucking of hair behind the ear asked "are you alright?" A subtle brush of fingertips along the cheek: "I am fine." Three fingers pressed briefly to the heart: "I love you."

They would communicate across crowded rooms this way, mother and daughter exchanging thoughts no one else could hear. During temple ceremonies, when silence was mandatory, Ameera would catch Sahira's eye and scratch her nose with her pinky, a secret gesture that meant "this is not the full truth," and Sahira would feel less alone in her questions.

One evening before bed, as Ameera brushed her daughter's hair, she had taught her a sign Sahira had never understood.

"This one is special," her mother had whispered, keeping her voice barely audible even in the privacy of Sahira's room. She placed her palm over Sahira's heart, then drew her fingers away in a flowing motion. "This means: remember what flows in your blood."

When Sahira asked what she was supposed to remember flowed in her blood, Ameera had smiled mysteriously. "When the time comes, your body will know." She'd pressed her forehead to Sahira's then, their breath mingling in the quiet moment.

And Sahira had nodded solemnly, not understanding what her mother was preparing her for.

One year later, Ameera was gone.

And the Covenant elders forbade mention of her. Sahira's father had burned most of her possessions, and her aunt had systematically eliminated any visible trace of her from their home, save for a nearly empty leather jewelry box given to Sahira. In their house, it was as if Ameera had never existed.

Yet the hand language remained, preserved in Sahira's muscle memory. Sometimes, in the market or temple, she would catch herself almost forming one of their signs before she forced her hands still. Sometimes, she would wake from dreams where her mother's hands told her things about water and memory and power that her waking mind couldn't grasp. And sometimes, when she was alone and certain no one could see, Sahira would place her palm over her heart and draw her fingers away in a flowing motion. *Remember what flows in your blood.* She still didn't understand the message, but she remembered her promise.

It had been ten years since then, and still sometimes Sahira would catch a trace of how her mother smelled—jasmine and river silt—and her throat would close with a grief and an anger she couldn't express.

The elders said her mother had abandoned her. That she had gone mad and then drowned herself in the Bakki. But in Sahira's dreams, her mother hadn't drowned. And in her waking life, Sahira sometimes wondered if she hadn't even gone mad.

Now, Sahira bowed her head at her aunt. "Sorry Tharima Bua."

Her aunt shook her head, but then patted Sahira's shoulder gently.

As they reached the center of the marketplace, Tharima handed Sahira the family's signed market ledger that served as both a shopping list and chit. "I'll need to go have Maru press the table linens, and then start the dinner preparations. You fill the shopping for this evening's dinner," she said, handing Sahira her straw basket. "And then you meet me at home so you can also look over the food. We'll want to show your future mother-in-law you can manage kitchen servants." Her aunt smiled, and then her mouth turned down again. "And listen, when you get to the spice vendor, get the small container of saffron threads—not the ground nonsense—the real threads."

Sahira nodded obediently and accepted the ledger and basket from her aunt, before turning toward the stalls.

Before she completed the dinner shopping, Sahira stopped at the fabric merchant's stall, her fingers brushing over the materials on display. They lingered on a silky fabric she had never seen before but now could not stop touching. How soft, how sinewy, how like water it was, how unlike the stiff cotton of her own kameez. She closed her eyes, imagining the feel of such fabric against her skin.

The town's economy had been closely regulated for as long as she could remember, but restrictions had tightened in the last decade. Around the time Sahira's mother disappeared, three girls had run away together. The elders believed they had followed the river north. Investigations revealed they had purchased food, cloth, and multiple pairs of heavy-soled shoes before their departure, likely with coin stolen from their families.

Since then, purchases not recorded on a family's ledger weren't explicitly prohibited, but they raised questions. A woman buying herbs not listed in her family's inventory—was she hoping to sedate a relative? A woman seeking shoes with thicker soles than was typical—was she preparing for an unauthorized journey? Merchants were expected to only make sales when an item was on a woman's family ledger, and to document any transaction that was not pre-approved. Men, meanwhile, remained free to use coin without documentation.

Still, most traders would look the other way if a woman paid with enough coin or gold.

In the Raazaan household, Tahir often signed blank ledgers, allowing his sister to fill in their shopping needs on her own, saving time.

Sahira longed for fabric that felt like this, like the river flowing under her touch. But there was no need for such extravagance, and certainly no approval for it on her ledger.

"Stillness guide you," the fabric merchant greeted Sahira.

"May stillness guide us all," Sahira responded automatically, withdrawing her fingers from the fabrics.

"Any fabric on your list, my dear? Your marriage is soon, Karam hears, you must be excited."

Sahira shook her head, blushing. "Nothing for me ma'am."

"Not even a ribbon on that list, dear? Perhaps Karam can offer something for your trousseau?" the woman, who must have been Karam, continued.

Before Sahira could answer, she caught the scent of citrus, leather, and soap, a scent that was expensive and foreign. A shadow fell across the fabric display.

"Surely a ribbon will be necessary," came a low voice beside her.

Sahira's heart jumped. She knew that voice, though it was deeper now, more assured. She turned slowly to find Tavin Daraio, who she hadn't seen in six years, standing close enough that she could see the fine weave of his traveling clothes.

Her pulse quickened, and she didn't know if what she felt was an urge to throw her arms around him, which would be impossible, or to run away, which would seem highly unusual.

Tavin Daraio. Her husband to be. In eight days.

Her mouth went dry and she found she couldn't speak. And something flickered under his confident exterior too. A moment of hesitation as his eyes took her in, seeing her for the first time in six years. Seeing her as a woman for the first time.

She blushed.

Tavin smiled widely at Karam. "Stillness guide you, ma'am. Please, won't you offer a lovely green ribbon to my betrothed?"

The woman's face grew bright, and she began rummaging through her drawers and baskets, nearly humming with excitement.

"I don't need a green ribbon," Sahira said, trying to stop the smile spreading across her face.

"But you do. It's the Daraio family color. Choose one in a fabric you like." He was effortless.

And somehow more handsome than when he had left. The roundness of his teenage years had been chiseled away, revealing a square jaw and high cheekbones, and his gray eyes seemed to glow as if lit from within. He was smart, charming, and beautiful, and ready to take on the mantle of community leadership his father held in wait… And he was going to become Sahira's husband.

Sahira shook her head. "It wouldn't be right."

Tavin frowned, an eyebrow raised. "Is it not my right as your future husband to give you a gift when I desire?"

Sahira's cheeks felt hot. But she pretended to be unaffected. "It is," she replied, trying to shrug. "But it is my right to not accept it."

At this, Tavin laughed. "Then choose a gift you'll accept, Miss Raazaan," he teased. "And do hurry, I'll not wait forever." The jest carried a subtle edge. Laughter, concealing a command.

Sahira didn't know how to respond. Instead, she looked to Karam, who now stood with an armful of green ribbon spools in various materials, watching their exchange with furrowed brows, clearly anxious about losing the sale.

Sahira nodded to the woman, assuaging her worry. "Thank you, ma'am, the dark one at the top of the pile looks perfect." Sahira glanced at Tavin.

Karam smiled broadly. "Such a lovely choice. And such a lovely match!" she exclaimed. "A proper girl marrying a proper man." She set down the armful of ribbon, unspooling the dark green velvet Sahira had selected.

She cut a standard ribbon length, tied it into a bow, and then pressed it into Tavin's right hand. "And will this go on your family's ledger, young man?"

"No, I'll pay with coin," Tavin said, and the woman's smile grew even wider.

"Just five coin," she told him, preening. "And Karam offers congratulations to the lucky bride to be."

"The lucky one is me, ma'am," he responded with a grin, and dropped the requested amount of coin into her hand before accepting the ribbon.

"Stillness guide you," the fabric merchant said.

Tavin pressed the ribbon gently into Sahira's hand.

"Thank you," she said, suddenly feeling shy. "It's lovely." She hugged the ribbon to her chest before slipping it into her kameez pocket.

"Anything for my bride to be," he said so quietly that only she could hear.

"I have to pick up spices now," she said, almost stumbling over the words, feeling for all the world like a shy little girl. "Stillness guide you," she backed away, moving toward the spice vendor's shop.

"See you tonight," he answered, his eyes twinkling.

When she turned to leave the stall, and him, she heard him laughing behind her.

ONCE HOME, Sahira went straight to the kitchen to help with the preparations for dinner. She spent two hours with her aunt as together they supervised the servants, and added their own touches to the evening's food.

Maru, the elderly servant who had been in their home since even before Sahira was born, stood close at hand, the red-checked rag that always hung from his shoulder covered in tomato paste and turmeric. He gave a toothy smile of approval as Sahira added a heaping spoonful of cumin seed to the marinade for the fish.

When she reached for the salt, he slid it toward her without being asked. Quiet and watchful, the way he always was with Sahira.

After the bulk of the dinner preparation was done, Sahira went into her bedroom to change out of her market clothes. She emptied the contents of her kameez pocket onto her dresser.

The green ribbon from Tavin lay beside the market ledger, a tangible reminder of the life she was about to enter. The weight of the evening ahead pressed against her chest. *Eight days.*

Her eyes fell on the jewelry chest she kept on her dresser.

The small leather jewelry chest was all she had of her mother. Most of the jewelry it once held had been melted down over the years, though a few pieces were saved for Sahira's dowry. She opened it carefully, running her fingers along the edges.

And somehow, she noticed for the first time, a small slit along the inside of the lid, where the felt lining separated from the hard shell. Her brows knit together as she slid her fingers along the slit. And then discovered a folded paper tucked inside.

Her heart raced as she drew the out the delicate paper. She unfolded it carefully, fingers trembling.

*There are truths the Covenant cannot teach, powers they will not name. The river's call is one. Love that defies their rules is another. You are the product of both.*

*When they tell you your awakening is corruption, remember: Some things are inexplicable to those who have never felt them. You are exactly as you were meant to be.*

*I love you forever.*

Sahira stared at the letter, at this evidence of her mother's descent into madness. Her mouth grew dry.

A memory came, unbidden: A night from the summer before her mother disappeared, when Ameera had woken nine-year-old Sahira.

*"Come,"* she'd whispered. *"There's something I need to show you."*

*They'd slipped through darkened streets to the river's edge, where moonlight turned the water silver. Ameera was never naked in front of her daughter, but on this night, she undressed completely.*

*And in the moonlight, as they waded into the water, Sahira had seen blue, swirling markings bloom like ink beneath her mother's skin.*

*They hadn't been there a moment before. Her mother had said, "They only appear when the river remembers us."*

*"Will I have them?" Sahira had asked, mesmerized.*

*And Ameera had only smiled. "If you allow your awakening," she had said, and then extended a hand to her daughter. "Come. The water won't hurt you. It's been waiting for you."*

*They swam in the river, Ameera teaching Sahira to float, to listen to the water's music. "They will try to make you forget this," her mother said as they dried on the bank. "But this is your birthright. The river will always remember you, even if you forget it."*

For those stolen hours, Sahira felt truly free. And when her mother disappeared weeks later, the freedom was gone, the memory buried deep beneath resentment.

## CHAPTER 1

Sahira shook her head to clear away the memory, and then folded up the letter, and slid it carefully back into its hiding place.

She rinsed her face in the wash basin, then went to her bathing room where servants had already drawn three buckets of water.

After she was clean and had wrapped herself in a long towel, she carefully combed out her hair, and opened her window to let the wind dry it.

Once it was mostly dry, she rebraided it, weaving the new velvety green ribbon through her strands as though it were part of her hair, tying it into a neat bow at the bottom.

As promised, the salwar kameez with the silver embroidery hung on the outside of her closet door.

The scent of cardamom and ginger wafted up from the kitchen below. Sahira dressed carefully. It was almost time.

She pressed her stomach, willing the flutter away.

AT SUNDOWN, the air in the Raazaan house was thick with anticipation and the scents of the lavish meal that had been cooking since midday. Servants moved efficiently around the room, placing steaming dishes on the table as her father's smile spread wide across his face.

The Daraio family entered their home, bringing the sound of merriment with them. Tahir Raazaan had greeted his old friend Dafar Daraio with warmth Sahira hadn't seen in her father's face in over a decade. Without a glance in her direction, the two men had hugged, talked, and laughed, their voices joyful as they discussed details of the coming marriage ceremony. Even Tavin's mother, Neelma Daraio, a regal looking woman with angular features that looked as though they were never used to smile, had looked almost happy.

"Let us seat the family properly," Tahir instructed one of the servants who nodded quickly before pulling out chairs for the guests. "This night is one of great honor for us all."

"The fish looks excellent," Tavin's mother remarked to Tharima, who beamed with pride though she had merely supervised its preparation. "You've taught your niece well."

"She has always been an attentive student," Tharima replied, glancing approvingly at Sahira as she took her place at the far end of the table.

The meal progressed through multiple courses—roasted potatoes and spinach, lamb and vegetables in curry, roasted fish from the Bakki, chicken pulao with saffron.

Throughout, Sahira felt Tavin's eyes on her.

Each time she sensed his gaze, her cheeks warmed. He felt both foreign and familiar. His jawline was sharper and his shoulders were broader, yes, but his gray eyes still held that glint of mischief she remembered from when they were children.

After dinner, Sahira kept her head lowered as she served tea to her soon-to-be family. Her hands trembled slightly as she poured for Tavin's father first, then his mother. She was careful not to spill a drop.

When she reached Tavin, their fingers brushed as he accepted the cup. The brief unexpected contact sent a shiver up her arm, and she glanced up involuntarily, finding his eyes already on her. He offered a smile—private, almost conspiratorial—before she lowered her gaze and drew back.

"Eight days from now," her father announced proudly, raising his water cup, "the Raazaan and Daraio families will join, God willing."

*Eight days.* Sahira sat down and stared at the floor. In eight days, Sahira's room would be exchanged for a chamber in the Daraio household, where her mother-in-law's eyes would replace her aunt's in evaluating her every movement. Her days would revolve around her new family's routines: when they woke, how they took their meals, how they spoke to their household servants. Everything that awaited would be different. Everything that awaited was unknown.

And despite his presence across the table, Tavin himself remained something of a mystery, their childhood connection too distant to rely upon with certainty. The stories of his studies spoke of a brilliant scholar, one whose mind had been shaped by exposure to ideas beyond their valley. When he spoke of his learning to her father, his vocabulary included words she didn't recognize, concepts that made the men at the table nod with approval. Certainly, the Tavin who had once helped her search for butterflies was not the man she would be marrying.

Would he expect a wife who matched him in thought? Or would he prefer the stillness his family, their community so valued?

In a matter of days, she would find out. She would belong to him completely. Her life, her body, her very self, would be transferred from her father's authority to her husband's.

She had been preparing for this reality her entire life. Yet now, here with her future husband and future in-laws, the weight of these thoughts pressed against her chest like stone.

"The ceremony will be in the temple courtyard," her father continued, helping himself to more sweet rice pudding. "Elder Nefret has agreed to perform the ceremony herself."

"A great honor," Dafar Daraio agreed. "Elder Nefret performing the ceremony herself," he tilted his head, smiling approvingly. "It speaks to the importance of our families' union, and of your wonderful daughter."

Sahira felt every pair of eyes on her. Tavin's smile, her aunt's approving nod, her father's satisfied gaze.

Only her younger cousin Leela, Tharima's daughter, watched Sahira with something more somber in her eyes.

After the main course had been cleared away, Tavin's mother presented Sahira with a small lacquered box. As Sahira opened it, she suppressed a gasp. Inside lay a ribbon of deepest green, in the exact material her fingers had lingered on at the fabric merchant's stall, but this one had golden thread woven in intricate patterns along its length that caught the light from the oil lamps.

"It is silk. For your hair at the marriage ceremony," Neelma explained, her voice formal, but pleased. "A Daraio tradition. Every bride in our family has worn such a ribbon since my grandmother's time."

"Thank you. It is beautiful." Sahira bowed her head, and resisted the urge to run her fingers over the fine embroidery.

"Green suits you," Tavin said softly when his mother turned to speak with Tharima. "Our family's color has always brought out your amber eyes." The intimacy of the observation sent an unexpected warmth through her, soothing her uncertainty, just slightly.

AFTER THE DARAIOS LEFT, after many exchanged bows and warm wishes, Sahira stood alone in her room, the green ribbon laid across her open palms. The ribbon's silky fluidity in her hands made her think of water: flowing, unconstrained. Unlike the life that awaited her.

*Eight days.* The number rang like a bell in her mind. Eight days until the end of one life, and the beginning of another.

She turned her head toward the windows that faced east toward the Bakki. She couldn't be sure, but she felt like she had heard something. And it felt like something was listening.

# CHAPTER 2
## MARKETPLACE

The next afternoon, the town square was buzzing with midday activity as Sahira made her way along familiar paths between market stalls. Her market ledger was tucked safely in her pocket, and her basket hung from her arm.

It was a day of transition for Sahira. That morning's stillness practice—which still lingered in her aching knees, in her shoulders that were stiff from maintaining perfect stillness—was her last. There were seven days until her marriage ceremony; tomorrow would mark the start of the six auspicious day period, the period during which a girl stopped being considered an unmarried girl but instead a true bride-to-be.

No formal acknowledgement of this was made during stillness practice, but as Sahira moved toward the women's door to leave, Elder Nefret had quietly wished her congratulations. Sahira knew she meant for the coming marriage ceremony, but privately, Sahira was celebrating her freedom from the chains of stillness practice. She smiled to herself.

And then almost immediately, her smile faded. She was free from one prison but would soon enter another. Seven days from today, golden thread would bind her to Tavin Daraio and to the role of wife, forever.

The sun seemed to hang low, lower than it should at this time of day, at this time of year, gilding the fabric stalls and casting long shadows across the marketplace. She looked around, wondering if anyone else noticed. But no one seemed to.

At the north end of the market, a horse spooked, rearing and almost pulling away from its rider's grip. A child to the west screamed, then fell silent as someone admonished her.

Sahira slowly made her way to the cobbler's stall, waiting in the queue to deliver shoes that needed reheeling before her marriage ceremony—she couldn't come to the Daraios' home with an unpolished wardrobe.

As she waited in line, the wind changed slightly, making her skin prickle. She shivered, and looked over to the well in the center of the market.

There, at the stone lip of the well, where no one from Jaraan would dare rest, sat a man. His clothing was unusual. Rather than the fitted kurtas and achkans favored by Jaraan men, his kurta was long, thin and loosely-fitting, river-blue, and rippling in the breeze. It looked like something a man might sleep in. A leather cord hung from his neck, holding a small gray stone at his chest.

In his long, slender hands, he held a stringed instrument, curved and made of wood and wire. His face was framed by dark curls that fell around deep, dark eyes. And intricate blue markings glowed on his forearms with every movement, hinting at Old magic.

A note slid from the instrument's body as he moved something like a stick across its strings. Low, resonant, almost wet with weight. The sound pulled at something deep in Sahira's belly.

And then, their eyes met. For an instant, the sounds of the marketplace faded, and she heard only the rush of her own blood, alive with a memory it shouldn't possess. Something thrummed in her veins, like the river itself coursing through her. It felt like a key turning in a lock.

His eyes, dark as the deepest part of the river, widened slightly. As if he'd felt it too.

A few years earlier, when she was fifteen, Sahira had suffered a fever that lasted three days. In her delirium, she'd thought a boy stood watching her from the corner of her room, humming a melody that cooled her burning skin. When she'd told her aunt about the imagined visitor, the house had been cleansed with sage and salt, and Sahira had been forced to drink special tea for a week after her recovery. She didn't know why she now thought of that boy, of that fever-dream.

The man began to play a new melody, but almost immediately, his music faltered—a single missed note. His expression changed, a flash of recognition crossing his features.

"Stillness protect you," whispered a woman beside Sahira, looking scandalized. "That Mehr'an man is looking at you."

Sahira quickly lowered her gaze, her cheeks burning.

So he was of the Mehr'an. One of the river worshippers from beyond the valley. The elders taught that they were dangerous; corrupted by water-worship. Even speaking to one of them could unravel your mind.

Once the woman was gone, Sahira's eyes wandered back to the Mehr'an man. His eyes were on his instrument now—he played louder, his fingers flying across the strings as his other hand moved the stick over them in a challenging melody that felt directed at her alone.

Then Sahira noticed the water in the well beside him. A single droplet rose from the water, just for an instant, before falling back into stillness. Sahira blinked, certain she had imagined it.

And then he abruptly stopped playing and looked directly at her, as if somehow, through the crowd, across the market, he knew exactly what she had seen.

The briefest of smirks passed over his lips before he turned away.

Only when her chest began to ache did she realize she had

been holding her breath. When she exhaled, the air left her lips like it belonged to someone else.

"Dear woman, please," the merchant was saying, calling her attention back to the forgotten cobbler's stall.

"Sorry, what?" she blurted out, the words escaping before she could contain them.

"What will you be needing today?" the merchant asked, impatient.

She looked at him vacantly, her breath caught in her throat. She couldn't remember why she was here. But she remembered how the Mehr'an musician's eyes had found hers.

She glanced back toward the well. He was still there, his fingers moving slowly over the strings now, but he was no longer looking in her direction. He played quietly now, his music barely audible through the market's bustle.

She realized that some part of her had hoped he would still be there.

The cobbler working at his table behind the merchant clucked. "River worshippers," he muttered, shaking his head.

The words brought Sahira back into her body.

She shook her head as if waking from a dream, and then turned back to the merchant, remembering her purpose. "I'll need these shoes re-heeled please," she said, handing over the shoes and her market ledger for marking.

After, as she turned to leave, she cast a final glance toward the well. He was gone.

As Sahira walked away from the cobbler's stall, her body hummed with an awareness that felt foreign. She had almost reached the path that led to the community's neighborhoods, when she heard a weathered voice beside her.

"The river's daughter returns to us."

Sahira turned to find Dasha, the herb seller, staring at her. She didn't live in town, but she had sold herbs and remedies here for as long as Sahira could recall. She was also eccentric enough that people remembered her—and knew to avoid her.

"Returns to us, returns to us, the daughter of the river returns!" Her voice rose and fell in a rhythmic cadence. Her collection of bangles, adorned with small river stones hanging like charms, clanged together wildly as she clapped her hands. And then she laughed, a tinkling sound emerging from her wrinkled mouth.

Sahira made as if to back away, but Dasha caught her wrist with surprising strength. The old woman's gaze sharpened. "You have your mother's eyes," she whispered. "She liked to wear jasmine oil. Said it reminded her of the river at night." Her eyes grew unfocused again, and her head tilted, bird-like. "The river at night, the river at night, the jasmine of the river!"

"You knew my mother?" Sahira couldn't mask her surprise.

But Dasha's attention had scattered like leaves in wind. The old woman twirled once, her long kameez flaring over a long patchwork skirt that twirled with it. She stopped, her eyes tracking something invisible in the east. "The mouth opens soon," she sang softly. "Opens soon, the serpent's mouth. The river's daughter will go!"

Sahira's heart was pounding, and she glanced around to see if anyone was listening. "The river's daughter returns," the old woman said again gleefully. Then she turned clumsily on her heel, waiting for no reply, and hobbled away, humming to herself as she went, leaving Sahira alone, gaping after her.

SAHIRA PASSED the fountain at the center of the market, still getting her bearings from the disorienting conversation. A few girls sat on benches nearby, hands resting neatly in their laps, eyes lowered. The only sound was water and cloth shoes on cobblestones.

Sahira considered this stillness. *What if women's corruption hadn't caused the collapse of the Old World?*

And then a more unnerving question rose in her mind. *But then, what purpose did their containment serve?*

She was still considering this when she saw Elder Malik, a curious old man, and one of the town's few remaining knowledge keepers.

Elder Malik maintained what little written history had survived the Great Correction, and was one of few people in Jaraan who answered questions asked of him instead of deflecting with Covenant teachings.

He sat alone by the broken fountain, thumbing through fragile pages protected in waxed cloth, the scent of tobacco clinging to his weathered clothes. She was overcome by an urge to ask him about the Old World.

"Stillness guide you, Elder Malik," she greeted him with a bow.

He glanced up, his milky eyes somehow seeing more than those with perfect vision. "Daughter of Ameera," he said, using her mother's name rather than her father's. "Stillness, yes," he said, his voice trailing. "Ah, but you have questions swimming behind your eyes."

Sahira hesitated, then knelt beside him. "I do."

"It's been too long since anyone asked me anything worth asking," he said, with a conspiratorial wiggle of his brows. "So ask, child."

"I hoped you might share some things with me about the Old World."

Elder Malik squinted at her, and then back at his book. "Questions, questions," he muttered, flipping pages seemingly at random. "Always the daughters ask the questions the fathers won't answer." He paused on a page, tracing something with his finger. "Or can't answer. Or shouldn't answer." He laughed. "Which kind of question do you have, Daughter of Ameera?"

Sahira hesitated, unsettled. "I… I'm not sure."

"Ah!" He clapped once, delighted. "The best kind! The kind that doesn't know it's dangerous yet." He leaned closer, lowering his voice. "The stories of the Old World are full of holes, you know. Like a fishing net. Plenty of holes for things to slip through." He made a gesture of something slipping between his fingers.

"Magic, connection, all the same really. Until the waters rose and the threads... snapped." He made a breaking gesture with his hands. "Everything gets washed clean."

The Flooding Years. Sahira nodded.

"Yes, floods wash things clean. Clean slate, clean history, clean conscience." His fingers smoothed the pages of his book. "Funny how the cleanest stories are always written by the dirtiest hands." He shook his head. "Your great-great-grandfather was a man who valued cleanliness."

"Did you know him?" Sahira asked in a whisper.

Elder Malik laughed riotously. "Oh, I am old, but I was just a child when *his* son was born. But to be honest," he said, leaning forward, "they were all the same. A long line of men, all the same."

Then, he turned a page, and motioned for Sahira to look: a sketch depicted a woman floating above the river, water rising around her like blades of grass. Sahira gasped.

Something was trying to untangle itself inside of her as she stared at the image. "Elder, are you saying—"

"I'm saying nothing!" he said cheerfully, snapping the book shut. "Just an old man rambling about old things. Although..." He smiled. "The water does remember what we've tried to forget. Rivers have very long memories, you know."

Sahira stayed silent, staring at the cobblestones beneath her feet. And then she nodded and folded her hands. "Thank you for talking with me."

"Ah, I'm just a crazy old man, who can say if I even know what I'm talking about?" the elder replied, his eyes crinkling.

"Your mother had the same kinds of questions you do. Even the ones you don't ask."

Sahira turned her face up to look directly at him then. His eyes were twinkling.

"Go on then, leave an old man to rest in the sun," he said by way of dismissal. Sahira bowed her head before rising.

LOST IN THOUGHT, Sahira didn't notice anyone approaching until a familiar voice broke through her reverie.

"I've always wondered who talked to that crazy old man." Tavin was now walking beside her, the sun catching in his dark hair, glinting off his gray eyes.

"He is wise," she said defensively, suppressing how startled she had been by his unexpected appearance.

"And you are kind," he replied. "You leave impressions on people, Miss Raazaan, even after years away."

Sahira said nothing, but glanced up to find him looking at her thoughtfully. She could think of nothing to say.

A noise from a nearby alley distracted them both—a child running past, chased by another.

Tavin's eyes darted around the square, noting the people nearby, the watching faces. "I need to speak to you privately. There are many ears here," he said quietly. "Come with me." He motioned for her to follow him, and then slipped into a nearby passageway before she could protest.

She looked around. Her instincts told her that to follow him into a passageway was highly improper.

But how could she refuse her betrothed? To ignore him, to walk away could be an insult to both of their families. And part of her did want to know what he had to say that couldn't be spoken in public.

She looked around one more time, and then took a deep breath before slipping into the passageway behind him.

Tavin stood leaning against the wall. Even as she pressed back against the opposite wall, they were too close.

"When I was gone, I saw things," he said, without preamble. "Unusual things. Women with unbound hair. Women and men speaking openly in public spaces. Touching in front of the world." His tone held both fascination and revulsion.

Sahira swallowed. "What was it like... to see such freedoms?"

"I'd hardly call them freedoms," he scoffed. "It was unnatural. The Covenant protects us from such chaos."

She glanced up at his face, and saw that his eyes were studying her face intently. Her mouth felt dry. The space was too narrow.

"I thought of you often when I was away," he murmured, stepping away from his wall, closing the already too little distance between them further.

Her face flushed and she looked down to the damp cobblestone. She reached up to tuck a loose strand of hair behind her ear, and his eyes widened as they fell on her left wrist, where a green thread—faded and fragile—was tied. "You still have it."

She glanced down in surprise. "I do—it's like a part of me," she admitted, holding out her wrist.

Pride bloomed in his face. He reached forward, his thumb brushing the thread before quickly pulling away again. "I remember. I gave it to you the day before I left for my studies."

The words unlocked a memory: the day before Tavin departed for his studies abroad. How they had stolen away to his father's storage shed as twilight painted the sky amber and gold.

"We shouldn't be here," thirteen-year-old Sahira had whispered, though she made no move to leave. At seventeen, Tavin stood tall, his shoulders already broadening into manhood, while she remained caught between childhood and the woman she would become.

"I leave tomorrow," he'd said simply.

The shed was filled with trade goods: bales of fabric, sacks of grain, and in one corner, sheer curtains meant for a merchant in another town. Tavin had pulled one free, its gauzy material catching the last golden light that streamed through the shed windows.

"I want to try something," he'd said, his voice uncertain, vulnerable. "Before I go."

And he'd hung the curtain between them, before draping it over Sahira's face and head, the translucent fabric transforming her into a shadow-self. Through the veil, she saw the nervous working of his throat as he swallowed.

"The elders say a man and woman shouldn't touch before marriage," he'd said. "But they never mentioned curtains. We can touch those."

Sahira had laughed then, the sound surprising them both. "I don't think that's what they meant."

"Probably not." His smile was visible even through the sheer fabric. "But I thought... maybe just this once..."

And he'd raised his hand, caressing the fabric from his side. The fabric dimpled beneath his touch, creating a perfect impression of his fingers.

"We're promised to each other," he said softly. "And I'll be gone for so long."

Understanding flooded her. He just wanted to share a special moment together. It wasn't transgression, not really. It was sweet. A moment of connection that honored the boundaries set before them while honoring their future. Honoring their love.

Slowly, hesitantly, she raised her own hand, smaller than his, and touched her fingers against the fabric from her side, against his jaw. The gauzy material warmed instantly against her fingertips, the only barrier between their skin thin enough to feel the heat of him, yet present enough to keep them feeling safely within the Covenant's rules.

"I can feel you," he whispered.

Through the curtain, his face moved closer, and she found herself mirroring him until only inches and sheer fabric separated them. His hand shifted from the curtain to her face, the fabric dipping slightly with the proximity of his fingers. The curtain kissed her cheek first, then the warmth of his hand through it. She leaned into the touch, feeling the contours of his palm through the veil.

"When I return," he promised, "we'll begin our life together. As the Covenant intends."

Sahira brought her face nearer to his, the fabric separating their lips. His eyes closed at her nearness, his breath catching. For that suspended moment, the boundary between them felt like a sacred space where longing could exist without trespass.

Then, he pulled back and reached down into his pocket. "I got you this," he whispered, his hand unfolding to reveal a thin green braided thread.

Her eyes went up to his, and then slowly, she lifted the gauzy veil between them enough to offer him her hand. He reached down and tied it around her wrist with careful precision, his fingers lingering against her pulse.

"I'll wear it," she'd whispered. "Every day until you return."

"Now everyone will know," he said, a gleam of pleasure in his eyes.

When they put away the curtain, the setting sun had painted the shed in a deep gold, transforming the ordinary space into something hallowed. They had touched without touching, connected without transgression.

As they slipped back to their separate homes, Sahira had felt the weight of the green thread around her wrist—a tether across distance, a promise preserved.

～

Now, in the market passageway, with his eyes on the thread, with so little space between them, it felt even more like a tether than it had all those years ago.

"Seeing it on you now… it feels like you're still mine," he breathed. And then his hands moved from the wall to her waist, and he closed the distance between them. He turned his face down toward hers, his lips close to hers.

Sahira's heart hammered against her ribs. *What if someone saw them?* She wanted to draw back from him, but she was pressed to the wall. And at the same time, something in her body made her yearn for him to touch his mouth to hers.

His eyes darkened. "I've thought about this since I returned," he murmured.

"We shouldn't—" she whispered against his lips. But even as she spoke, her body betrayed her, and she leaned into him.

The moment stretched across time. And then his lips gently touched hers.

But almost as soon as the kiss started, he abruptly pulled back again. "No," He said, shaking his head as if clearing it. "You're right, of course." His hands remained on her waist, contradicting his words, but he used them to push her body away. "We shouldn't. It's not appropriate for you to feel this way…"

At this, confusion and shame burned Sahira's cheeks.

His expression softened. "It's alright. Don't feel bad, you couldn't have known," he said, straightening his achkan's sleeves, and offering her a smile. "You can always come to me. If you're… confused."

Sahira, utterly bewildered now, pressed her lips together tightly and nodded.

His eyes held pity. "It's hard to understand the difference between proper obedience and… want."

*Want.* The word sent a shiver through her. So that's what she had felt. That rush of sensation that had momentarily overwhelmed her. That was what he'd said was inappropriate for her to feel.

Tavin reached forward and tenderly tucked a loose strand of hair behind her ear, his touch lingering longer than necessary. "I'll teach you the difference," he said, his voice low with promise that sent contradictory shivers through her. "May stillness guide you," he murmured, before slipping out of the passageway.

Sahira stayed where she was. A sick loneliness crept in as she watched him go.

So this was what a kiss felt like.

She smoothed her kameez and blinked back tears, and then stepped away from the wall, and back into the late afternoon light, blinking as if waking from a dream. She began slowly making her way home.

She felt very aware of the thread on her wrist.

SAHIRA FELT unsettled even hours later.

By late afternoon, her stomach was still churning as she made her way back into town, first stopping at the tailor's, then continuing on to deliver clothes she'd had stitched to Elder Nefret's residence for approval. They were part of her dowry demonstration: proof she possessed the domestic skills required of a Covenant wife.

As she moved through the marketplace, holding her bundle of stitched garments, her mind returned again and again to the encounter in the passageway, trying to make sense of what she'd done wrong.

And that's when she saw him again. The musician from the well. This time, standing inside a merchant stall with an older Mehr'an woman.

Her unease evaporated. Sahira drifted closer, pretending to examine pottery at a nearby stall.

He no longer held an instrument, but instead some kind of curved, elegant object, unlike anything she'd ever seen before. He poured a brown liquid into its mouth, and Sahira watched from behind the display as it trickled through the device and emerged clear into a clay bowl on a table in front of him.

The Mehr'an woman beside him ruffled his hair and said something with an approving smile. Sahira edged closer, pretending to examine a shelf of bowls, trying to catch their words.

"—the deeper channels stay cleaner," it sounded like he was saying.

The woman, likely his mother judging by the easy affection between them, adjusted something on the device. "And they'll install it?"

"They have agreed to try it. If it works..." He shrugged, but Sahira caught the hope in his voice. "Clean water means fewer children lost."

Sahira stared, mesmerized.

The woman in front of her at the stall finished her purchase and moved away, leaving Sahira exposed, but she didn't notice until the pottery merchant spoke.

"Miss, you've been standing in front of that bowl for five minutes," he said, amused. "Planning to buy, or just admire?"

Sahira startled. "Oh! I—sorry, I was just—" She began backing away.

But as she turned, she couldn't help glancing back—and her heart jumped.

The musician was leaning against a column, arms crossed, one brow raised. The metal water contraption sat forgotten on the table.

He had been watching her.

A slow, knowing smirk creased his face.

Sahira, cheeks burning now, turned and rushed across the square, hugging her bundle of garments to her chest, all the rest of the way to Elder Nefret's house, not daring to look back.

THE AFTERNOON SUN HAD SHIFTED, casting longer shadows as Sahira made her way south through the market, eyes lowered, pace measured. By the time she reached the southernmost edge, the sun was near setting, and Elder Nefret's residence loomed in the dusky light.

The elder was already outside as Sahira approached, as if though she'd been waiting for her arrival. "Were you looking at someone just now, before you got here?" Elder Nefret asked in lieu of greeting, her voice cool, unreadable.

Sahira's brows knit together. "I—" she began, then faltered. If Elder Nefret was asking, she must have seen something. Lying outright felt dangerous.

"There was a man," she said instead. "He was holding some kind of object, some kind of makeshift tap, maybe. I'd never seen anything like it." The half-truth fell convincingly from her lips. "I was trying to determine what it was."

"Ah," Elder Nefret said, expression easing. "Curious about the river man's strange contraptions." She stepped in closer. "You should know… the Mehr'an," she spat, "are only permitted to trade here only because their people are supposed to be implementing a water filtration system for us."

"Water filtration?" Sahira frowned.

Elder Nefret sighed. "Some of the Samiti claim the Mehr'an's filtration methods saved the northern towns during a fever season. But… their ways are… " she hesitated. "Different."

"Different how?" The question slipped out before Sahira could stop it.

The elder's brows rose slightly at her directness. "They worship the river as a deity," she said slowly. "They tattoo their skin with symbols from the Old World." Her voice dropped. "They believe their women can hear the water speak."

A tightness bloomed in Sahira's chest. "That's impossible."

"Of course," she agreed. "But impossible things have always

attracted the corrupted. They are dangerous people—everyone knows to fear the Mehr'an stranger. Their water-craft is their one redeeming quality."

The older woman turned her attention then to the bundle Sahira carried. She examined each garment with meticulous precision, her fingers grazing fabric, noting every choice of color and pattern.

*They believe their women can hear the water speak.* With the elder's attention turned to the garments, Sahira found her mind wandering to strange childhood memories: rainwater forming shapes on window glass; well water rising to meet her bucket; the way storms had always calmed her rather than frightened her. And hadn't she just imagined the river was listening to her the night before?

"Your selections are tasteful," Elder Nefret finally said. "The Daraio household should find these adequate."

"Thank you, Elder," Sahira replied, bowing slightly.

Elder Nefret was still watching her. "Your mother had fine taste as well. Before her affliction."

Sahira's heart quickened. "Thank you," she said again, quieter.

"You favor her," the elder continued thoughtfully. "The Zaroun women often have these strong family resemblances."

A chill prickled Sahira's skin. "I wouldn't know much about family traits, Elder."

Elder Nefret's expression was one of cool assessment. "No, I suppose you wouldn't," she murmured, reaching forward and adjusting Sahira's kameez at the neck. "That's good. Your father has been selective about what family history he shares." Her fingers drifted idly over one of the garments. "The Daraio men also understand... discretion. It's one reason of many why this match is so suitable."

Sahira swallowed, and then gathered her composure. "Elder, my father and aunt asked me to thank you," she said, keeping her voice steady. "It's an honor to have you preside over the ceremony."

"Some bloodlines require very particular handling," Elder Nefret said, more to herself than to Sahira. Then, catching her tone, she smiled thinly. "It's my honor. The binding ceremony will ensure... proper stability." Elder Nefret's smile didn't reach her eyes. "The Covenant protects us all, especially those who might otherwise find themselves... vulnerable to certain influences."

A chill crept up Sahira's spine. This marriage wasn't just about family alliances or her future happiness or her father's reputation. It was also about containment. About preventing whatever had happened to her mother from happening to her.

"We'll be observing your marriage preparations with great interest, Sahira Raazaan," Elder Nefret said, her tone formal now. "The binding of a new generation brings stability to the community."

The words felt weighted with meaning beyond their surface, a warning wrapped in ritual phrasing. Sahira bowed her head, eager to escape.

AFTER SHE FLED Elder Nefret's house, the woman's voice echoed still in her mind.

Sahira paused at the market's edge, breath shallow. The sunset painted the western sky in dark rose and crimson shades. The eastern horizon—beyond Jaraan's boundaries—deepened into to an inky blue, where below, the Bakki rose as if in answer to her silent questions.

The contrast pulled at something in Sahira's chest—the division between where she was expected to be and where some part of her longed to go.

Behind her, the temple bells rang, as if in warning, and she pressed down the desire to look to the river.

And in that very moment, the ribbon she had woven in her hair unraveled on its own, the white strip of material whipping in the wind of a coming storm.

She turned to go home.

She didn't know she was being watched.

THAT NIGHT, Sahira tossed and turned in her bed. She pulled the coverlet tighter around her shoulders, trying to ignore the strange restlessness that had followed her home.

Just as she began to drift into dreams, a melody floated through her window—faint and almost imperceptible, but there, cutting through the night's stillness. Her eyes flew open. The tune rose from the direction of the river itself, carried on wind that shouldn't have been able to reach her room.

She sat up, heart racing, drawn to the sound like water to lower ground. She looked to her window, drawn by an urge she couldn't name, as if the water itself were calling to her.

She shook off the thought and forced herself to lay back down.

But the air in her room somehow felt different now.

When sleep claimed her, she dreamed of blue markings beneath her skin, of water that moved in strange patterns at her touch, and of dark eyes that seemed to recognize her across an impossible distance.

She dreamed of a stranger who somehow wasn't strange at all.

# CHAPTER 3
# STORM

There were six days until Sahira would become Tavin's wife.

Each remaining morning brought a new ritual, another test of readiness. Today's was to deliver an empty clay pot to the temple, a symbol of herself as a vessel for the Covenant and for its future children.

The impending marriage had sparked economic opportunity for the town. Merchants sold white flowers for guests to weave into their hair, sandalwood oil for blessings, floating candles for the central fountain.

Sahira moved through it all in a waking haze, the clay pot pressed to her stomach, her thoughts drifting to the river. To her mother.

Until she snapped into lucidity at the sight of Elder Malik seated as always near the eastern fountain. In his old age, the elder tended to excuse himself from town affairs, preferring to keep his own rhythms. But he noticed more than he let on.

"I knew you would come," he said, sensing her approach without turning to look. "Funny thing to be carrying that vessel, when you are such a curious one yourself." He chuckled, amused by his own riddle. "Well, then. What are your questions today?"

Sahira bowed her head but dispensed with the formal greetings. "I came to ask you about my mother. You knew her. I know you must know things… others don't. Please."

The old man was silent for so long that Sahira wondered if he'd fallen asleep with his eyes open. Then his weathered fingers began tracing patterns in the thin sheen of moisture on the stone bench—flowing lines like river currents.

"Ameera," he murmured. "The Covenant's cautionary tale." He looked up at the sky. "Did you know, daughter of Ameera, that the day your mother was born, it rained for the first time in months?"

Sahira shook her head.

"Some say that's why the river noticed her. One raindrop, falling at just the right moment…" his voice trailed off. "The town forgets that rain. They only remember she was river-touched."

"What about you?" Sahira said softly. "What do you remember?"

"I remember a woman who heard what others could not." His fingers stilled. "She knew the voice of water in her blood. She knew stillness was not her salvation." He turned to Sahira and raised his brows.

She clutched the pot tighter. "They say she went mad," she whispered, "that the river made her mad and that's why she… why she abandoned me."

"Do they? That's a nice, clean story." He tilted his head. "Perhaps that's why they tell it. Perhaps the real story is a dirtier one."

Sahira drew back, unsettled.

"What if the madness was never hers?" His fingers traced another pattern on the bench, swirling, spiraling. "Your mother's only sin was understanding water. She listened to the river."

Elder Malik's eyes were distant, fixed on something beyond the visible world. "And the river remembers."

EVERYTHING FELT SHARPER after Sahira's conversation with Elder Malik. The breeze on her neck, the rhythmic clatter of a potter's wheel, the scent of spice and fresh bread wafting from the baker's shop.

She continued toward the temple. Nearing the central fountain, she heard the sound of drying beads clanging in the wind to the east and instinctively turned her face toward it. As she did, a soft breeze carrying river scent caressed her cheek, and then, she heard a melody she hadn't thought of in years. One her mother used to hum when she was a child.

But it wasn't a memory. She turned back toward the central fountain, and there he was again—the Mehr'an musician.

He sat casually on the fountain's stone edge, his strange instrument balanced on one knee, his dark curls falling into his eyes. His fingers moved with unthinking ease, coaxing the familiar song from the strings. He plucked a single note, then another. Even at a distance, each one untangled something inside her she hadn't known was knotted.

She should have continued walking. Should have lowered her eyes, quickened her pace, and completed the morning's ritual. Instead, her steps slowed, and she found herself drifting toward the edge of the square where a narrow alley let her watch him without being so exposed.

And then, he glanced toward the alley and his eyes found hers instantly, as if he had been waiting for her. This time, he didn't smirk, or give her a knowing smile. He only looked, his gaze deliberate and unwavering.

The connection was almost tangible in the morning air as their eyes held.

And then, his head tilted slightly—so subtly she almost thought she imagined it—toward the east side of the market.

Toward the path that led to the river.

She looked away quickly, letting her eyes fall to the cobblestones, tightening her grip on the clay pot as heat rose to her cheeks, spreading down her neck and chest.

She dared not look at him again as she stepped forward out of the alleyway, back onto the proper path.

As she turned toward the temple, intent on completing her ritual, she saw that someone was watching. Across the square, at the temple's entrance, stood Elder Nefret.

And she had been watching Sahira watch the musician.

Watching the musician watch Sahira.

And this time, her expression was not unreadable. Her eyes narrowed, calculating.

Sahira's feet refused to move. For a moment, she stood as if rooted to the earth itself. She willed herself to walk, silently begging her feet to unfreeze. Then—one breath, then another—she forced herself forward, face blank, stomach roiling.

She reached the temple steps, and swallowed hard, forcing her face into a mask of nonchalance. She bowed low when she reached Elder Nefret, holding the clay pot above her head in offering.

For a moment that stretched into eternity, the elder said nothing. Sahira slowly lowered the pot, willing her face to remain expressionless.

"You may deliver it inside," Elder Nefret said flatly.

Sahira nodded, her throat dry, and stepped into the temple's shadowed chambers. She placed the pot on the waiting altar.

And left as quickly as she could.

THAT NIGHT, Sahira couldn't sleep. After tossing beneath her coverlet for what felt like hours, she gave in to wakefulness.

If she couldn't rest, she might as well be useful. She rose and crossed to her desk to finish editing her father's market report. No woman needed to understand economics, of course, but copy editing was a valued skill for the daughter or wife of a Samiti man.

Her gaze landed on the green ribbon, still lying where she'd left it. She almost reached for it, to pick it up, put it away. Instead, she took a charcoal pencil and pulled her notebook toward her.

"Monsoon market patterns" was written at the top in her father's neat hand. "Merchant categorization; sales data prior to monsoon; sales data on day 1…" She read and reread the words, unable to focus on their meaning.

As she stared at the page, her hand moved the pencil absently, sketching in the margin. She remembered the feeling she had in the alley. The one that came before the shame. The feeling of want. Something bloomed inside her, deep in her body.

She looked down at what she had drawn.

Eyes.

Her eyes widened and she reached for the eraser, scrubbing frantically at the eyes until they vanished from the paper. But even erased, she could still see them.

She pushed herself away from the desk, tossed down the eraser, and turned toward the window where she could see the distant outline of the river, silvered by moonlight.

It called to her.

The pull toward the river made sense—she was to be married soon, and the river had always called to her during moments of transition.

When her mother vanished, leaving her shawl hanging from a branch at the river's edge, Sahira had sleepwalked three nights in a row, always waking to find herself headed eastward, toward flowing water. Her father had made her drink a special tea, and the wandering had stopped.

A few years later, during her first bleeding, the river called again. She'd made it halfway to the eastern boundary before she was found. The guards had returned her home, her father gave her the same tea, and again, her wandering stopped.

Now, for the first time since her first blood, for the first time as a woman, she wondered what would happen if she simply... went there.

The house was silent. The night outside, still.

And suddenly, the urge to go to the river became unbearable.

Sahira moved as if in a dream—slipping on her shoes, out her door. Her feet carried her through the hedges behind their house that would let her leave Government Colony through a loose fencepost, without passing through the main gates or meeting a district guard. Through silent streets and sleeping gardens, past the town's boundaries and into the forest beyond, deeper and deeper into the trees, the forest rising around her, moonlight filtering through the leaves, her every footfall defied the boundaries she'd been taught not to cross.

Her mind raced, and her feet carried her forward on their own toward the river. When she regained control of her limbs, she was kneeling at the water's edge, breathless and dizzy.

How had she let herself come here? Was it every small rebellious thought she'd ever had, every question she'd ever swallowed? Had they all been leading to this moment, where her body made decisions her mind refused to claim?

She reached forward, intending only to cup water in her hand and drink from the river. But as her fingertips touched the surface, the water paused in its flow for just a moment, curling up against her skin like a living thing seeking contact.

And then, a voice. Not heard with her ears but felt in her blood. A voice both strange and achingly familiar.

*"Sahira."*

She jerked back, heart pounding. That voice... it couldn't be.

*"My Sahira."*

The sound was impossible. Not quite words, not quite music.

Memory given voice through water, like something desperately reaching across an impossible distance.

"Mama?" she whispered, the word escaping before she could think.

The river rippled in response, forming patterns, for just an instant before dissolving back into ordinary current.

The rational part of her mind rejected what was happening. She was imagining things. People didn't become water. Dead women didn't speak through rivers.

Yet the sensation was too real, too specific to dismiss entirely. Something was calling to her through the water. Something that knew her name, that recognized her blood. Something that felt impossibly, inexplicably, like her mother.

Her heart was beating so hard she thought it might break through her chest.

She strained to hear the voice again, but then in the distance, a flicker of light caught her eye, distracting her.

Across the river, partially hidden by reeds and willow branches, a light moved. Then another. And then another. Too steady to be fireflies, too purposeful to be random.

People. People moving near the water at night.

She pulled back into the shadows, holding absolutely still as figures emerged from the tree line on the far bank. Women, she realized. Seven of them, each holding a lantern, moving with the confidence of those who knew their path well.

These were not women of town. These women stood tall, hair unbound, voices murmuring together without the careful modulation of Jaraan speech. Instead of the salwar kameez worn by Covenant daughters, they wore fabric draped in the old way—wrapped around their bodies, and blue patterns with points of glowing light swirled over their bare arms. They carried baskets and bottles, gathering at the river's edge under moonlight, without hesitation, without fear.

Mehr'an women.

One of the youngest laughed—a full, unrestrained sound that would have earned correction in town.

Sahira watched, transfixed, as they performed a ceremony, dipping vessels into the current, sharing water among them, marking patterns on each other's hands with clay from the riverbed.

When they finished, they departed the way they had come, but one remained. An older woman with silver streaking her dark hair. She stood absolutely still, gazing across the water directly toward Sahira's hiding place, where she should not have been able to see her.

"Daughter of the River," the woman called softly, in a voice Sahira should not have been able to hear at this distance. "We know you're there. And we will be here when you're ready."

Before Sahira could decide whether to flee or respond, the woman bowed her head and turned away.

Sahira remained frozen, trying to unscramble what had just happened.

And then, the rain began. At first, a soft pattering. And then, without warning, the sky tore open and within seconds, she was soaked through.

BY THE TIME she found shelter beneath a rocky overhang, the woman across the river had vanished, leaving Sahira to wonder if she had imagined the entire scene.

She ducked under the overhang, pressing deeper into the shallow cave to escape the downpour.

Only to realize the space was already occupied.

"The Covenant daughter ventures out alone." A voice came from the shadows behind her.

Sahira nearly retreated back into the rain, but a flash of lightning changed her mind. "I didn't know this place was claimed," she said stiffly.

A second flash illuminated the face the voice belonged to. The musician.

"It isn't," he said, a hint of amusement in his voice. "Nature belongs to no one."

He shifted, making more space for her—the overhang was barely large enough for them both. Another flash of lightning illuminated his features, and Sahira chanced a glance at him.

The blue patterns on his arms seemed to glow in the darkness.

She stood close the edge of the overhang, rain soaking her back, debating whether getting drenched was preferable to this forced closeness.

"I'm surprised your elders allow you out after dark," he said over the sound of rainfall. The words themselves were mocking, but his tone was not unkind.

Of course no elders allowed her to be out at this time. But she said, "I don't need their permission to seek shelter," and she stepped further inside.

Their shoulders almost touched in the cramped space, and she was acutely aware of how close they were. She could smell wild herbs, earth, and smoke on his skin.

A particularly loud crack of thunder made Sahira flinch involuntarily, and her shoulder brushed against his. The thin fabric of their rain-soaked clothes did little to diminish the heat of his skin.

He shifted slightly, recreating the space between them. A gesture of respect she should have appreciated. Instead, her body wanted to close the gap between them. The thought shocked her the moment it formed.

Lightning flashed, and she saw that he was watching her.

"Why are you out here, daughter of the Covenant?"

"I wanted to see the river," she admitted, seeing no point in lying.

"But not to hear it, I imagine." His tone was dismissive, as if she'd somehow fallen short of his expectations.

"What does that mean?" she demanded.

He shook his head. "You Covenant women are all the same. You look at water but never listen to it. You go to the river but fear getting wet." His eyes flicked to her sodden clothes, and he smirked.

"You don't know me," Sahira said quietly. "You think you do just because you've seen me in town. Do you always stare at strangers in the market?" She surprised herself with her own boldness.

His laugh was unexpected, warm. "Only those the water recognizes." When she looked confused, he elaborated. "The fountain's surface changed when you approached. Just a ripple, but I noticed. Then I noticed you."

Silence fell between them.

Then thunder cracked overhead, and Sahira's mind went back to the river, to the voice she'd heard. *Had she imagined it?*

The musician shifted beside her, and she turned, only to realize they were mere breaths apart. She froze, caught between the instinct to pull away and the inexplicable urge to lean closer.

The space between them was alive with energy, a tangible current.

A single droplet of water slid from her hair down her temple. His eyes tracked its path, and then his fingers rose as if to catch the droplet, but he stopped just short of touching her skin.

The droplet splashed down her cheek.

"What would happen," he asked softly, lowering his hand, "if you allowed yourself to truly feel the water?"

Sahira exhaled. "You know nothing about me." Her voice was sharper than she'd intended.

He smiled. "Perhaps. Or maybe I see more than you wish to show."

And then they fell into silence, waiting as the storm passed.

As the rain slowed to a trickle, Sahira turned to leave, but stumbled on the uneven ground. The musician reflexively caught her wrist to steady her. And the contact ignited something electric between them.

His fingers were warm against her wrist, and her pulse fluttered wildly beneath his touch. Slowly, giving her every chance to pull away, he turned her hand in his, palm upward, his thumb tracing a curved mark she hadn't noticed before.

"You're changing," he whispered, almost in reverence.

She started to turn away, but he still held her wrist gently.

"Wait," he said, reaching his other hand into his pocket, and then opening his palm to reveal a small, blue stone with a spiral pattern etched into its surface. "Take this. It's a river token. My people carry them to find their way back to water when they're lost." He gestured to his own gray stone that hung from a leather cord around his neck.

"I can't—"

"Then I'll leave it here," he said, releasing her wrist. He placed the stone on a flat rock at their feet. "The river will return it to me if you don't claim it."

The rain had stopped completely now, and without a word, Sahira backed out of the overhang.

And then, she ran.

She ran without looking back, ran as fast as her legs would carry her. By the time she reached the hedges that would allow her to sneak back into her father's home, she was seeing the night more clearly. *What had she been thinking going to the river?*

She peeled off the damp clothes, hanging them on a hook in her closet to drip dry. She dried her hair on a towel, dressed quickly in her night clothes, and slipped into her bed, trying to slow her breathing.

She shook off as much of the night as she could.

But the memory of the musician's nearness lingered on her skin like a ghost.

# CHAPTER 4
# DREAMS

*S*he was standing in the river, water swirling around her waist, her hands transformed into something fluid, neither flesh nor water but both. When she looked up, the Mehr'an musician watched from the bank, playing a melody that commanded the current.

Sahira woke trembling, breathing slowly to calm her thundering heart.

The melody from the dream lingered, humming through her body like a remembered touch. Droplets of water were beading on her arms. She blinked, and they vanished. And then she realized she was holding something. She unfolded her hand and her eyes widened.

There, nestled in her palm, was the blue stone the musician had tried to give her.

She had no memory of taking it.

She slipped from bed and opened the leather jewelry chest on her dresser, dropping stone into one of its empty compartments. Her fingers brushed against the slit that concealed her mother's letter, and she thought again of the voice she'd heard last night.

She shook her head and closed the chest again. In five days, she would be married. This was no time for voices, or letters or river tokens.

Just then, Tharima entered the room, carrying a spool of white thread. The ritual for this morning was one Sahira had been particularly dreading: she would have her hands bound together until her mother-in-law unbound her, as a symbol of her dependence on her new family.

Tharima sat at her niece's bedside and wordlessly waited for Sahira to hold out her hands. When she did, Tharima pressed her niece's hands together, and wound the thread tightly around them, an approving smile on her face.

The final step of the ceremony was to place the end of the thread into Sahira's mouth, symbolizing her deference to her future in-laws.

Sahira opened her mouth to accept the thread, and her aunt pressed it between her lips. As Sahira clamped her lips down around it, something twisted inside her uncomfortably. If the thread fell, with her hands bound, she would have no way to retrieve it, so she couldn't speak. She felt helpless.

And that was the point.

Soon, golden thread would bind her to Tavin Daraio forever. It wouldn't be so different than this.

"Five days," Tharima said, smiling at her niece. "And then you'll take your rightful place in the Daraio household." She sighed.

Sahira, who sat immobilized with bound hands and lips pressed tight around the thread, felt an ache expand inside of her, like water pushing against a dam.

"You'll keep your hands and mouth this way until we get to the kitchen, and your soon-to-be mother-in-law will unbind them for you." And Tharima left the room, leaving Sahira staring after her.

Sahira slowly climbed from her bed, walking to her bathroom in her bound state, and then stopped in frustration. She wouldn't be able to wash her face, or brush her teeth, or even adjust her clothes. It was a revocation of any independence.

She passed the mirror and felt bile rise in her throat. The

sight of herself—lips clenched around thread that tethered to her bound hands—filled her with revulsion. A puppet on strings.

She quickly made her way to the kitchen, unable to bear being alone with her reflection.

~

THARIMA WAS MEASURING rice with practiced precision when Sahira entered the room. The woman's eyes shone with pride. "Your mother would have been proud to see this day," she said. Sahira sincerely doubted that was true, though she kept the thought carefully contained behind her thread-sealed lips.

"Your new life begins soon," came the voice of her father, rare approval warming his voice as he entered. But he drew back slightly when he saw the thread, and glanced at his sister. "Can you remove those now?" he asked, clearly uncomfortable.

"Her mother-in-law is meant to do it," Tharima told her elder brother, the pride evident in her voice. "It's tradition."

Moments later, Neelma Daraio arrived, flanked by servants from the Daraio household bearing trays of gifts and sweets for the Raazaans.

"Ah, the binding day," Tavin's mother said, her tone breezy as her eyes swept over Sahira like a merchant appraising livestock.

Sahira nearly whimpered at the thought of freedom, but held her stillness. Neelma took her time, circling slowly, inspecting every detail, while Sahira tried not to squirm or let the thread slip from her mouth.

"Her coloring favors the deeper tones," she observed, tapping her chin. "She is not very fair, but the ceremonial red should stand out well against her skin."

Tharima nodded. "No real sun damage to mar the effect."

Sahira's restlessness was growing. She silently willed Tavin's mother to release her, but the woman's movements were slow and unconcerned.

Over the next several hours, the two women flitted around Sahira, draping material against her skin, discussing her as if she were an object to be appraised. They debated colors, textures, and fabric weights, ignoring her growing thirst, her need for air, for release.

And through it all, Sahira remained perfectly still, though her jaw ached from clenching the thread.

When Tavin's mother finally unbound her, starting with her wrists and only pulling the thread from her mouth at the very end, Sahira could have wept with relief.

Instead, she met Neelma's cool, appraising gaze with steady eyes. The woman only raised an eyebrow. Then she finally left, satisfied with her measurements and assessments of her future daughter-in-law.

Sahira took the deepest breath of her life.

She exhaled slowly. But the weight of the morning still pressed her into the earth.

A STORM BEGAN as Tahir Raazaan returned home that evening. Shaking off his raincoat and hanging it by the door, he moved into the central room of the Raazaan home.

Sahira greeted her father, and offered him a drink. He ignored her, and took a seat in one of the room's armchairs.

"Have a seat, daughter." Tahir Raazaan's face was troubled, his hands clasped tightly before him.

Tharima came in, taking in the scene. "Tahir?"

"You too, Tharima," he gestured to the cushion across from his chair.

Sahira and her aunt obeyed, eyes lowered in deference.

"Elder Nefret visited me today at the office," he began without preamble. "She expressed... concerns."

Sahira's pulse quickened, but she kept her expression neutral. "Concerns, Baba?"

"About your readiness for the Daraio household. About certain… observations that have been made."

"Tahir, her ritual this morning went exactly as planned, what is the problem?" Tharima asked.

But Sahira's mind jumped to the previous night, to the river. Dread crept beneath her skin.

Tahir sighed, a sound heavy with expectation and worry, then looked to his sister. "She was seen watching a Mehr'an man in the market. More than once. With inappropriate… interest."

The accusation hung in the air between all of them. Inwardly, Sahira exhaled. It was not the most serious transgression a woman could commit, but still—curiosity was dangerous in Jaraan.

"I was only surprised by the man's strange instrument," Sahira said, thinking quickly. "I had never seen its like before."

Tharima exhaled with relief, but her father shook his head. "Interest is a luxury you cannot afford. Especially in this family."

The last words carried a particular weight that made Sahira look up, meeting his eyes directly for the first time. "Because of what happened with Mama," she said.

It wasn't a question, but he answered anyway. "Your mother's… affliction began with small transgressions. Questions. Interests in things beyond her proper sphere." His face broke slightly—a rare glimpse of the grief he usually kept carefully contained. "I cannot lose you as I lost her."

Something inside Sahira softened at this. She had so many questions. About what happened the night her mother disappeared, about the madness that claimed her.

But there was no room for her questions in this house. And she said nothing.

"The marriage ceremony is in five days," her father continued. "See that you avoid giving into your… curiosities until then. There is no need for interests."

"Yes, Baba," she responded automatically.

As he left the room, satisfaction evident in the set of his shoulders, Sahira remained seated, her thoughts racing.

~

As Sahira prepared for bed that night, she caught her reflection in the small mirror atop her dresser.

For a moment, her amber eyes held a strange shimmering light, like moonlight on the surface of water.

She blinked, and it was gone. But it left her with an uneasy feeling. A sense that something was there, awakening inside her. Something that had always been there, waiting.

~

That night, it stormed again. Sahira and Leela fell asleep in the same bed, as they often had during childhood storms.

In the strange realm between waking and dreaming, their breaths synchronized, falling into a matching rhythm. And Sahira dreamed of water again.

*She stood waist-deep in the river, the water alive against her skin. It rose around her, embracing her.*

*Across from her, Leela watched from the shoreline, her eyes wide with both fear and fascination.*

*Sahira raised her arms, and the water reached up with them, curling around her fingers like a living thing.*

*"Didi, it recognizes you," Leela called from the shore, her voice echoing strangely. "It knows you."*

*A third figure appeared. Familiar, though she couldn't place him at first.*

*The Mehr'an musician, but different. His eyes glowed with an inner light. And he was standing between them, on the water's surface.*

*"Where are we?" she asked, looking around at the vivid dreamscape.*

*"This is the in-between. Where water meets memory," he said, his*

*voice somehow both distant and intimately close. "You've been here before."*

*"This isn't real," she insisted, though the water felt more substantial than the waking world had ever been.*

*"Not yet," he agreed. "But it will be."*

*Leela stepped carefully into the water then, gasping as it swirled around her ankles. "Didi, it's speaking to me too." Her eyes were wide. "I can hear it."*

*The musician extended his hand across the impossible distance between them. Without understanding why, Sahira reached back.*

*Their fingers didn't touch, yet something unnameable and ancient passed between them. And then he brought his palm to his chest, and drew his fingers away in a flowing motion.*

*And then Ameera was there. Not the mother Sahira remembered from her childhood memories, but as a woman with long and flowing hair, and outstretched arms, who was somehow also the river itself. "The water remembers," her mother said, turning to face Sahira. "And so will you."*

*And then it was the musician's voice again. "Remember," he seemed to say, but it was the river who spoke. "Remember what flows in your blood."*

Sahira woke shaking, catching her breath.

Beside her, her cousin was still asleep.

But when Sahira looked down, both hers and Leela's fingertips were pruned.

# CHAPTER 5
## SHED

Only four days remained until the marriage ceremony. Four days until Sahira's life narrowed to the confines of the Daraio household. Four days until the final bindings made her the property of Tavin Daraio forever.

And today was the Ritual of Submission.

She moved through her duties as if in a waking dream. Even as she oversaw the morning's cooking and cleaning, she felt detached. She was watching herself from a distance, her body going through the motions while her mind slipped elsewhere. To her dream. To the river. To her mother.

To the musician.

"You're distracted," Tharima accused sharply as Sahira dropped a bowl of lentils and they scattered across the floor. "This is not the time for carelessness." She gestured sharply for Maru to clean it up. "Your marriage is days away."

"I'm sorry, Tharima Bua," Sahira murmured, kneeling to gather the lentils. "I didn't sleep well."

Maru appeared, with a hand broom, his red checked rag hanging as always from one shoulder, and gently nudged Sahira aside, making quick work of the mess.

Tharima's eyes didn't leave Sahira. "Dreams?" she asked. Dreams, especially those involving water, flight, or magic, were a problem. Girls were trained to suppress them before they took root.

"No," Sahira lied. "Just... thoughts about the ceremony."

Tharima's expression softened. "It's natural to feel apprehension. Marriage is quite the transition." Her gaze drifted, as if remembering something from long ago, but then snapped back to Sahira. "The Daraio household is respected. Tavin will be a good husband. Firm, but not cruel."

The words were meant as reassurance. Instead, they settled in Sahira's stomach like stones. Firm but not cruel. Was that the best she could hope for? A cage with comfortable bars?

"Thank you, Tharima Bua," she said.

She swallowed the lump that had formed in her throat. Her aunt was right, of course—she was distracted, and not only by her dreams. But by the thought of the ritual that awaited her today. The thought of which filled with a quiet, mounting dread.

SAHIRA KEPT her head low as she and Tharima walked to the temple for the ritual. On the way, they stopped at the tailor's shop to check the fit of her bridal lehenga.

"The Daraio bride!" the tailor had exclaimed when they entered, her weathered face creased with approval. "Only a few days until your marriage ceremony. You must be eager for the waiting to end."

The tailor leaned closer to Tharima then, her voice dropping to a whisper. "They say young Tavin has prepared a home that would make the elders themselves envious."

Tharima gave the woman a demure smile, and Sahira nodded politely, the appropriate response to such fortune. But something was clawing at her insides, desperate for escape.

The next hour went by in a blur of measuring tape and safety pins as the tailor checked and rechecked Sahira's waist, bust, and arms. Sahira's mind drifted—to the river, to the musician—anywhere but the reality of the ritual awaiting her.

"I'll need to adjust your kameez for the ceremony as well," the tailor said, turning to Tharima. "Do you have time?"

"Actually, we should be getting to the temple," Tharima began.

"Please, Tharima Bua, go ahead," Sahira said quietly. "If it's alright, I'll sit outside for a moment. Just to get some air before the ritual." She kept her voice soft, and trusted that her aunt wouldn't refuse such a modest request in front of the tailor.

Tharima hesitated, then nodded. "Very well. But stay close."

The tailor's eyes flicked between them, her face unreadable. "Just so we can easily find you," Tharima added, glancing at the tailor.

Sahira nodded and stepped outside.

ONCE OUTSIDE, Sahira inhaled deeply, then exhaled as if purging the tailor's shop air from her lungs.

A thin girl, a few years younger, brushed past her. "I apologize," the girl murmured—but as she passed, she slipped a folded paper into Sahira's sleeve.

Kaya.

That was her name. Sahira nearly called after her, but the girl vanished into a narrow passageway before she could.

Sahira glanced around. Too many eyes. She slid the paper from her sleeve into the pocket of her kameez, her fingers trembling.

Just then, an old woman approached.

"Sahiba?" she said, her voice trembling. She wasn't dressed like the townspeople. Her garments resembled the long drape of the Mehr'an. Her eyes were wide, frantic.

"I—no, my name is Sahira," she responded, puzzled.

"You look so like your mother…" the woman whispered. "You have her face." Her fingers twitched at her sides.

"You knew my mother?" Sahira asked, brows drawn tight. Why had she called her *Sahiba*?

"I knew her. And she wasn't mad—she—" The woman stopped short as Tharima exited the shop, slowing at the sight of her niece with the strange woman.

"Some waters run too deep to be contained," the old woman finished quietly. Then she turned and hurried away before either of them could stop her.

"Why was she speaking to you?" Tharima demanded, eyes narrowing.

"I—I don't know," Sahira said earnestly, glancing at her aunt.

Tharima clucked her tongue. "Madwoman. I don't know why someone doesn't banish her from the market. Mind's been drifting for years." She shook her head. "You'll find plenty like her near the river, I'm sure."

Sahira turned and watched the woman disappear down the street.

IN A SMALL ROOM inside the temple in town, Sahira knelt on a small embroidered cushion, back straight, hands folded precisely in her lap. A circle of seven married women surrounded her.

Elder Nefret approached, a silver chain strung with tiny bells jingling with each step. She draped the chain over Sahira's open palms.

"Repeat after me: I surrender my body to my husband's discipline."

Sahira swallowed. "I surrender my body to my husband's discipline," she echoed. The women repeated the vow, their voices harmonizing with hers.

"I will obey without question, for his authority is absolute."

"I will obey without question, for his authority is absolute."

"My will is subordinate to his command."

"My will is subordinate to his command," Sahira repeated.

"I will submit to him, for I will belong to him."

Sahira's throat constricted, but she forced the words out. "I will submit to him, for I will belong to him."

Elder Nefret wound the chain loosely around Sahira's wrists, forming a fragile circle she would have to consciously maintain.

"You offer your will," the elder said. "Your obedience, and your submission." She smiled beatifically.

Sahira didn't move.

"Repeat it child: I surrender, I obey, I submit."

"I surrender. I obey. I submit," Sahira breathed as she worked to keep the chain still.

Each of the seven women stepped forward to add a small bell to the chain before filing out, leaving Sahira alone.

The vows she'd spoken echoed in her bones.

"You will hold this position until sunset," Elder Nefret instructed. "The chain must not fall. If it does, another hour will be added." She paused at the door. "Keep your mind on your duties: surrender, obey, submit."

The door closed.

The chain rested in her open palms. They were not truly binding her, yet they felt more restrictive than any physical restraint.

Outside, shadows lengthened. Inside, Sahira sat perfectly still, wrestling for control of her own body.

The hours blurred in a haze of discomfort that turned into pain, and pain that turned into fog. By the time Elder Nefret returned, Sahira's limbs were numb and hypersensitive all at once. Standing sent bolts of pain through her joints.

The ritual was over, but something inside her had curled in on itself. Stillness had left its mark.

~

It was dusk when Sahira finally walked home from the temple.

Her body moved mechanically, still caught in the trance-like state the ritual had induced. Her wrists retained the phantom sensation of the chain's weight, and the vows she'd been forced to repeat echoed in her mind with each step: *I surrender, I obey, I submit.*

The words had seeped beneath her skin, tightening her movements, as if she were already rehearsing the diminishment expected of her.

Her arms still ached as she reached the gate to Government Colony.

Waiting at the steps, holding a lamp that had long since gone out, was Tavin, handsome in a fitted kurta and trousers. He stood as she neared, the extinguished lamp forgotten.

Seeing him, a strange mixture coursed through her: relief, because he was familiar, known; and dread, because it was to him those vows belonged. To him, she would surrender. Him, she would obey. To him, she would submit.

"I waited for you," he said gently.

"Here I am," she replied. *Surrender. Obey. Submit.*

"It's nearly the hour of dreams, and you're not in your bed."

"It was the Ritual of Submission," she said softly, watching his face. He understood. She saw it in the way his brow furrowed with concern.

"Are you alright?"

In the warm light of the street lamps, he looked like safety. Like childhood. *To him, she would surrender.*

"I'm alright." Her voice barely carried. "Tharima Bua will be expecting me. I should get home."

"Or," Tavin said, something shifting in his eyes as he watched her, "we could check that everything is secure in my shed. She doesn't know exactly when to expect you. You could be a little late." *Him, she would obey.*

The suggestion hung in the air, loaded with meaning she couldn't fully understand but sensed nonetheless.

After hours of ritual submission, Sahira's instincts were raw. The chain might be gone, but its logic still pulsed in her bones.

A proper Covenant daughter would politely thank him for inviting her to help him, and then continue to her own home. But a proper bride-to-be would listen. Would not resist.

She nodded.

Some part of her rebelled at the automatic gesture—but the larger part, the quieter, wearier part, simply followed.

And then, without another word, he guided her toward the gate.

The district guard was new. He looked between them. "Late to be escorting a young woman, isn't it?"

"I am to be her husband in four days time, my good man," Tavin said smiling easily.

The guard raised a brow at this, and the ghost of a smirk appeared before quickly vanishing. "Be sure she gets home," he said, unlatching the gate.

Something in the exchange made Sahira's skin prickle uncomfortably. There had been something in the look the two men had shared that felt like a conversation she wasn't privy to.

Tavin's smile lingered as they passed into the residential district. At the turn, they turned toward the Daraio property. For a moment, she considered turning back, the flutter in her stomach turning to something heavier.

His family's grand house came into view, but they turned, moving behind hedges that shielded the Daraios' shed from the road.

His hand rested at the small of her back, gentle but insistent.

She felt unable to turn back. *To him, she would submit.*

The shed door came into view, and she thought suddenly of Tharima's voice: "women with loose ribbons cause storms."

She touched her braid self-consciously. The ribbon at the bottom had fallen away somewhere. And the braid was loosening, as though it could unravel at any moment.

THEY WALKED in silence as they reached the shed. Tavin unlocked the door and gestured for Sahira to enter.

She stepped inside, remembering the last time she'd been here with him. How they'd hung gauzy fabric between them, tracing each other's features through the translucent barrier.

Intimacy without transgression.

The boldness that had brought them here suddenly wavered, and she saw uncertainty flash across his face too. He gestured toward the settee, and she sat.

In the quiet, he found matches and lit the lamps one by one, then slid the door's lock shut.

When he turned to her, lamplight caught the hollow of his throat, the curve where neck meets shoulder. Her heart pounded.

He stepped closer, then joined her on the settee, sitting beside her. "Do you remember the last time we were here?"

She nodded.

He reached for her hand, and guided it to his face. "Then touch me," he whispered. "Like you did before I left."

Hesitantly, Sahira let her fingers trace his jaw.

"I've waited so long," he murmured, and then put his own hands on her face, pressing his forehead against hers, his breathing heavy.

Sahira froze, her hand still on his face. Tavin slid his hands into her hair, and her already loosened braid came fully undone.

His mouth found hers, and she froze momentarily, unprepared for the sensation.

*I will surrender. I will obey. I will submit.*

She returned the kiss.

He pressed her back gently against the cushions, the kiss growing deeper. And then his body was half-covering hers, and his hands were sliding down from her hair, to her neck, to her arms, to her waist. He held her body to his while they kissed.

It felt good.

He pulled back just long enough to murmur against her lips, "this is what a husband does with his wife."

Sahira's worry about the wrongness of what they were doing was being quickly overridden by a physical sensation growing inside her, as his kisses grew in urgency.

She arched slightly toward him, an unfamiliar feeling fluttering through her body—the same feeling she'd had in the passageway.

And then panic rushed in. Tavin had called that feeling want, and had said she wasn't meant to feel it. Something warned her that this, whatever it was, was improper before their marriage ceremony.

And then the ritual's words cut through the conflicting thoughts: *"I will obey without question."* Her body followed the script she'd been rehearsing all day, even as confusion clouded her thoughts.

And then, Tavin slipped one hand beneath her kameez, and pulled her salwar loose. Sahira froze, her mind screaming warnings her voice couldn't form. His lips continued crushing hers as his other hand held her steady.

And then without warning, his fingers found her, invaded her.

Protest caught in her throat. Almost as quickly as he had started, he removed his fingers, and his weight shifted suddenly as he repositioned himself.

And then: pain. Sharp, unexpected, intrusive. She tried to cry out, to push him away, but he held her tightly, restraining her movements, and her voice emerged only as a muffled sound against his mouth, easily ignored.

Her body was no longer her own. Just as she had promised. The ritual's final vow twisted mockingly in her thoughts: *"I will submit to him, for I will belong to him."* Her mind fractured.

His movements were hurried. Forceful. Hard. Nothing like the tender kisses that had started this encounter.

*This wasn't supposed to happen.*

And then, with a heavy grunt, it was over.

Tavin pulled himself off of her body. "You shouldn't have done this," he groaned, refastening his trousers.

Sahira lay frozen, unmoving. Her body was still processing the intrusion, and her mind was a jumble.

*She* shouldn't have done this?

He'd brought her here… he'd kissed her… and then he'd guided her body, and he'd done this… thing.

"What did I do?" Sahira's voice was barely audible.

He reached over and pulled Sahira's kameez down over her salwar—she hadn't even noticed it had been hiked up around her waist.

Then he sat at the far end of the settee, adjusting his sleeves, gaze fixed on the door. "You came here willingly. You wanted me to…" His voice trailed off. "What did you think would happen when you followed me here?"

"I wanted…?" she echoed, dazed. Her thoughts felt slippery, incoherent.

"You shouldn't have come," he muttered, something between remorse and disgust curling in his tone. "Now you're… not pure."

The words struck like a slap. A hot flush bloomed in her cheeks and chest, and her stomach turned.

He stood up and walked to the other side of the shed, leaving her where she lay, disheveled and burning with shame.

Sahira pulled herself upright, dazed. She waited—desperately—for him to laugh, to say it had been a mistake, a misunderstanding. A horrible joke. That he would say he was sorry he'd scared her, sorry he'd hurt her. That he wished they'd only just kept on kissing, and that he could everything else back.

But he said nothing.

A moment passed. The shed felt too hot, the air too thick with the horror of time that couldn't be unwound.

Sahira pulled herself to her feet shakily. Tears blurred her vision, but she blinked them back, refusing to let him see.

But her lip trembled.

He glanced at her then, and something in how she looked made him soften. "Don't worry," he said gently. "I'll still marry you."

The words should have been a comfort. Instead, her stomach roiled, bile rising in her throat.

"Th— thank you," she managed, willing herself not to be sick in his shed. "I should get home."

He nodded, unlocked the door, and stepped aside without meeting her eyes. And as Sahira stepped out into the night, she left the girl she'd been all her life behind in that shed.

HER BODY FELT FOREIGN, wrong. Each step away from the shed was painful—physically, but also in some deeper way.

Worst of all was the confusion. How had it all changed so quickly? One moment, they were kissing, the next…

And then the blame.

She tried to piece it together, tried to find where she had gone wrong. But the pieces wouldn't fit together no matter how she arranged them in her mind.

She would tell no one, she decided.

What was there to tell? She had followed him. She had kissed him. And now she was no longer pure. Her aunt would blame her. The elders would say she had tempted him. Even she wasn't sure where her consent had ended. And the shame would kill her father.

Beneath the confusion, something else now began to rise.

Anger. Not only at Tavin, but at the town that had made this possible. At Jaraan. At a world where his promise to still marry her was something she was expected to be grateful for.

The anger cut through the fog of shame. And then suddenly, she was desperately thirsty. Not for drink, but for cleansing. For washing away everything that had just happened.

And before she could stop herself, her feet were already turning, carrying her forward. Not toward her father's house, but away from Government Colony.

Toward the river.

SAHIRA HAD SLIPPED through the hedges behind the shed, and taken the secret path that bypassed the guards, before she realized what she was doing. Without knowing why, she only knew that her hands needed to touch water.

She ran. She ran as hard as she could, the movement making her aching joints cry out, but the pain and the effort at least distracted her from the shock and confusion she was feeling.

She ran until the ground beneath her feet changed from packed dirt to soft sand. Ran until she stumbled to the riverbank, her breath coming in ragged gasps, knees buckling as she fell to the river's edge.

And then she plunged her hands into the river. Almost instantly, calm spread through her body, flowing from fingertips to chest, easing the places inside her that had been torn open.

For the first time since dawn, she wasn't fighting—not fighting to hold still, not fighting to get free, not fighting back tears. She exhaled a slow shuddering breath. "Foolish girl," she pressed her wet palms to her eyes. "Foolish, foolish girl."

"Not foolish," a voice said from the darkness. "Never that."

She jerked her head up, and found the musician standing just a few paces away.

His expression was unreadable in the moonlight, but his posture was carefully nonthreatening, hands open at his sides, no sudden movements.

"Did you follow me?" Her voice trembled. Had he somehow sensed her sorrow? Had he—an unbearable self-loathing rose within her—somehow witnessed what happened in the shed?

"No," he said quietly. "I come here most nights. The river speaks more clearly after dark."

She should leave immediately. If she'd been caught alone with Tavin in his shed, that would have been bad enough. But being caught alone with this man, in the moonlight, by the river —it wouldn't just mean shame. It would be unforgivable; it would destroy her family.

But she was exhausted.

And maybe it was because of this, or maybe it was the trials of the day, or maybe it was something in his voice, or the careful distance he maintained…

She didn't want to leave. Not yet.

"You're trembling," he observed. "Are you cold, or afraid?"

"I'm not afraid of you." It surprised her to realize it was true.

"Perhaps you should be." But it didn't sound like a threat. He crouched down and set a small, leaf-wrapped bundle on the sand. "River-root. For pain."

She stared at him. How could he possibly know?

The gesture, the consideration, broke something open in her. A sob escaped before she could contain it.

He didn't move. He made no move to comfort her, or to close the space between them. He just stayed. A steady presence in the dark, as she struggled to gather her composure. She brought the river-root bundle close to her face, and slowly her breathing evened. The scent soothed her nerves and dulled the ache in her body.

"Do you need me to take you home?" he asked. "I can stay in the forest so I'm unseen. I can walk you to the edge of town."

She shook her head, her breath calming. "I'll find my way."

"I know." He rose to his feet, and then paused. "You aren't alone, Zarouni girl." He turned to go, but stopped when she spoke again.

"Why did you call me that? Zarouni—Zaroun was my mother's family name."

For a brief moment, something like longing passed over his face. "Because the river recognizes its own," he said softly.

Then he was gone, melting into the darkness, leaving Sahira with the river-root bundle and the faint sense that despite everything that had happened today, something essential had just been returned to her.

WHEN SAHIRA RETURNED HOME, the house was already asleep.

That night, she dreamed.

*She stood in rushing water that reached her waist, the current strong but strangely supportive. Across the flow stood the musician, his hands extended toward her though too far to touch.*

*The dream shifted. She was still in the water, but it wasn't the river she knew. It felt wider, darker. A man stood on the opposite shore, playing a curved instrument she recognized from the marketplace.*

*But he wasn't the musician. This man was older, with lines around his eyes and silver at his temples, but something in his eyes was familiar.*

*"Cross to me," he called.*

*"I can't," she said.*

*"Your mother tried," he said, his voice carrying across the water. "She nearly reached me."*

*Behind her, the sound of shouting voices and horses pounding through the shallows, distracted her, made her turn.*

*And when she turned back, the river man was gone, and only his voice remained, haunting and insistent, like a song: "Go and tell Sahiba that her beloved Mirza calls for her."*

*Sahira reached out—and the current pulled her under.*

Sahira awoke with a ragged gasp as if surfacing from water. Her night clothes were soaked through. The night was dry, but the sound of rushing water lingered in her ears.

CHAPTER 5

*Mirza.*

The name swirled in her mind and made her head throb.

She looked across the room, and for a heartbeat, she could have sworn that water in the washing basin rippled. Though no breeze stirred the air.

She didn't go back to sleep.

# CHAPTER 6
# TETHER

Three days remained until Sahira's marriage ceremony.

Cool air drifted through the window. She opened her eyes to a sunrise obscured by dark clouds.

She was so tired. Sleep had come in fitful bursts, and she had woken repeatedly, from dreams in which her voice vanished when she tried to scream.

She turned toward the window, letting the breeze cool her skin.

And then she remembered the shed, and a wave of nausea overtook her.

She had bathed the moment she had gotten home, scrubbing her skin raw. Still, she felt unclean.

She lay still in her bed, trying to steady her breathing.

Ten breaths in, ten breaths out.

And then she remembered Kaya.

Outside the tailor's shop yesterday, the girl had slipped Sahira a note. It had been so strange.

It had felt significant.

But then everything that followed had pushed the moment from Sahira's mind, and the note remained, forgotten—still tucked in her kameez pocket.

But now, she remembered.

Yesterday's kameez was hanging on a hook inside her bathing room. She dug into the pocket and withdrew the folded scrap of paper and unfolded it.

*Your betrothed is not a good man. Be careful.*

Sahira's heart lurched.

She read it again, and again, and felt panic rising inside her like bile. The room tilted. Blood roared in her ears. Her breaths shortened. Ten breaths in—she couldn't breathe.

She dropped the note, doubled over, trying to force air into her lungs. Ten breaths—she was panicking.

*I have to burn it.*

The thought was a lifeline, the resolution letting her breathe again. She gasped as air returned to her body.

She steadied her breathing, and then, with shaking fingers, struck a match, and lit the candle on her dresser.

She held the note to the flame, and her heartbeat slowed back down as the note blackened, curled, and turned to ash. Then she blew out the candle, and took a deep breath.

But the words were burned into her mind's eye.

*Your betrothed is not a good man. Be careful.* Restlessness prickled under her skin. She twisted her hands together to keep them still.

And that's when she noticed it.

The green thread that had bound her to Tavin for years had frayed overnight.

She stared at her bare wrist. She hadn't removed it; it was just… gone. Dissolved like sugar in water, leaving behind only a faint stain.

TODAY WAS the Ritual of Household Direction.

Another ritual to prepare her for her marriage to Tavin.

*Your betrothed is not a good man. Be careful.*

Sahira shuddered, pushing the words from her mind. She steadied her shaking fingers, weaving her hair into a perfect braid.

She dressed in the yellow kameez Maru had pressed and left in her room.

Sahira turned to the mirror. The yellow garment's brightness was a mockery of how she felt inside. The face staring back looked haunted. It was her own, but her eyes looked different; they shimmered with something just beneath the surface. Something dark and shifting.

Leela stood silently in the doorway, watching.

Her eyes full of quiet worry.

As Sahira made her way down to the Raazaan courtyard for the day's ritual, she passed the garden fountain and paused. Ripples were forming, without wind or touch.

"Is someone… there?" she whispered, feeling foolish even as the words left her lips.

Nothing happened.

She extended a hand above the surface.

For a heartbeat, a single droplet rose from the surface before falling back in. As if it had reached for her.

Sahira snatched her hand away, heart pounding.

She reached the courtyard, where Tharima stood, waiting with Elder Laal, who held a ceremonial ledger. Behind them stood the Daraio family's twelve household servants in a line.

"You must understand the work of running a home in order to properly direct the help," Elder Laal explained. "The Daraio household employs twelve servants; you must command their respect, and uphold your husband's family's standards."

Sahira nodded obediently.

"You will now instruct each servant in her duties," Elder Laal continued, "and you must correct errors without impatience. You must praise, but not indulge. Flawless command is necessary."

Throughout the morning's ritual, Sahira moved numbly. She noted every test she was meant to: salt instead of sugar in the tea preparation, miscounted coins, stitches out of line. When Tavin's old wet-nurse carelessly handled a doll meant to represent an infant, Sahira corrected her with an even tone, though the sight made her feel sick.

Elder Laal nodded approvingly. "Flawless command."

As the servants were dismissed, Sahira clasped her hands tightly to hide their tremble.

She closed her eyes. Breathed in. Pressed down the rising tide of panic. All of this. All of these rituals. All of it was so she could become Tavin's wife.

AFTER THE RITUAL ENDED, Sahira could hardly contain the urge to escape. The desire to breathe air untainted by expectation became the only thing she could think about.

"I'll gather lavender for your tonics," she called to Tharima as she passed through the kitchen. "The temple garden was depleted yesterday."

Her aunt nodded, distracted by directing servants in preparing food, too busy to question her. "Take Leela with you."

"I think she's already out running errands," Sahira replied smoothly. "I'll be quick."

She followed the main path that led north toward the market and the temple. But instead of turning toward the temple gardens, she turned toward the eastern boundary where trees met water.

And she slipped into the forest.

The clouds had begun to part, and sunlight filtered through the canopy in shifting patterns. Sahira told herself she was searching for herbs that grew in shade, but her basket remained empty as she pressed deeper into the trees.

She followed the sound of water against stone and moss, though she wasn't near the Bakki yet. A hidden stream. Water that ran where it shouldn't.

And then, she heard the rustle of leaves, and a branch snapped somewhere to her left. She whirled toward the sound.

And there, through the moss and the leaves, she could see a tall silhouette. A man stood among the trees, something blue and faintly glowing on his forearms.

And she knew who it was, before he even stepped forward.

The Mehr'an musician.

"You shouldn't be here," he said, but he looked at her like he had been expecting to see her.

He stepped forward, dappled sunlight revealing him in fragments. Dark curls. Dark eyes that returned light with unsettling intensity. Swirling blue patterns that glowed across his forearms.

Her body tensed, instinctively bracing itself in a way it hadn't needed to before last night. But the distance he maintained, the absence of entitlement that it implied, kept her rooted in place.

"Are you following me?" she blurted out, surprising herself with her own boldness.

"These are Mehr'an paths," he countered, and he took another step closer. "You're the one trespassing."

Her stomach tightened as he moved toward her, but she didn't feel afraid. "Nature belongs to no one," she said, echoing his own words from days earlier. "Or is that only true when it suits you?"

Something like amusement flickered across his features. "You remember my words but ignore their meaning."

"And you speak in riddles instead of truths."

Suppressing a smile, he reached toward her face, and then immediately froze when he saw her flinch. He reached again, more slowly, as if trying not to frighten an animal, and plucked a small twig from her loosening braid.

"You're unraveling, daughter of the Covenant," he said, showing her the twig and the strands of hair wrapped around it. "In more ways than one."

She lifted her chin and met his gaze.

The shadow of a smile pulled at the corners of his mouth. "Did you come here for me?" he asked softly.

"No," she said too quickly, taking a step back. "And I should return before I'm missed."

"Always running back to your cage," he murmured.

"It's not a cage." The words felt hollow.

"No? Then why does your body lean toward freedom even as your mind pulls you back to confinement?"

She hadn't realized it but she had been leaning toward him. "You don't know me," she said, standing up straighter.

"I know what you could be, if you weren't afraid."

She was about to protest, but then he gestured for her to follow him.

Fleetingly, her mind went to the last time she'd followed a man where he'd wanted her to. But the musician tilted his head, gesturing again for her to follow.

And against all wisdom, she did.

SHE FOLLOWED AND MOMENTS LATER, the hidden stream revealed itself, a ribbon of silver cutting through moss-covered stone.

The musician crouched, scooping water in a cupped palm before letting it spill through his fingers. "You're far from the permitted gathering grounds," he remarked, looking up at her.

"I'm collecting herbs," she answered, the lie smooth on her tongue. "For my aunt's tonics."

He glanced at her empty basket. "Tonic herbs don't grow this deep," he said, a curve of amusement in his voice. "They grow in the edges, between forest and field."

A flush of heat touched her cheeks.

He reached further into the stream, shifting large, round river stones just slightly. She blinked. For a brief moment, she thought that the current had somehow changed, flowing around the rocks' new positions. She opened her mouth to ask what he was doing, but he spoke first.

"You're betrothed to Tavin Daraio."

"I—Tavin?" she startled.

"Is he not your betrothed?" the musician asked flatly.

"What about him?" Her mouth was suddenly dry.

"My people may live outside your walls, but we hear things." His eyes held hers. "In town, they say he's a good match. Devoted to the Covenant." The words were spoken like an accusation, though she couldn't tell toward whom.

"We have known one another since childhood. His family is respected." Sahira crossed her arms.

"Respected," he echoed dryly. "Did he behave respectably toward you before you came to the forest last night?"

Sahira felt shock run through her body and she looked at him sharply.

*How could he know anything had happened?*

She opened and then closed her mouth.

"What did he do to you?" His voice was quiet, but beneath it ran a current of intensity that made her shiver.

She shook her head. "I—nothing." She swallowed. "Nothing."

Without being able to say how, she felt that the musician knew everything.

She thought of the night before. Of the river-root.

"Do you want me to kill him?" His voice was so quiet she almost missed it.

Her eyes widened. "What?"

He didn't respond.

"I don't understand your idea of humor," she said slowly, though she wasn't confident he was joking.

Something flickered in his eyes. Something heavier and older than anger. "Men like him... they take what isn't offered. They call it their right." His jaw clenched, and a muscle flickered under his skin. "My parents were killed by men like him. Covenant guards, who thought awakening women were theirs to cleanse—or claim."

The admission hung between them.

"Your parents…"

He stood, shaking water from his hand. "They died believing women should choose their own fate." His eyes bore into hers.

The intensity of his gaze unnerved her.

She turned away, plucking a leaf from a low branch and changing the subject. "So how does a Mehr'an man know about gathering practices?"

"You know me to be Mehr'an?" he said with an easy smile.

She glanced at the cord around his neck that held his gray river token. "Everyone knows to fear the Mehr'an stranger," she recited, flushing with embarrassment as he raised an eyebrow at the offense.

"You know of my people, but don't know that our men do the gathering alongside our women?"

Her cheeks burned.

"Fear the Mehr'an stranger," he repeated with a smirk. Then he stepped closer. "I am called Syfir. And there, I am a stranger no more."

She turned, and began walking alongside the stream. "I'm Sahira," she said quietly, avoiding his gaze.

"I know." He fell into step beside her, and they walked together in silence, moving deeper into the forest.

The morning sunlight was golden but dim under the trees, and they were cocooned in a private world of gold and green. She glanced over. His eyes were so dark, and yet they somehow seemed to be lit from within, as if reflecting candlelight.

"I'm sorry for what I said," she said, tugging at a thin branch from a tree as they walked. "They say it in Jaraan. That the Mehr'an are dangerous."

"And what do you say?" He stopped, turning to look at her.

She avoided his eyes, instead letting her gaze fall to a deep scar that wound around his forearm. "I think sometimes what they say isn't always true." She pointed to the scar, avoiding looking too closely at the blue patterns it ran through. "How did you get this?"

Something flickered in his expression that made her think of him as a young boy. "Maybe Jaraan's guards are more dangerous than the Mehr'an."

"Fear can keep you safe, but it can become the walls of your prison." He stepped closer.

Then he reached his arm slowly around her body.

She held perfectly still, following his arm with her eyes.

"But you can choose to feel the fear, and move forward anyway." Then he snapped his hand shut, and she yelped in surprise.

He uncurled his fingers. A wasp lay dead in his palm.

Sahira exhaled as he dropped it onto the forest floor, looking at him gratefully.

And then he stepped closer, peering down into her eyes. "Is it fear you feel now, Zarouni girl?"

She swallowed. She thought about lying, but then decided against it. "Yes."

His eyes searched hers. "Of me?"

She shook her head, but held his gaze.

"Of how I make you feel?"

She had no answer. She turned away, heat rising in her cheeks.

"I watch you in town," he said. "And you watch me."

"I don't watch you—" she began, turning back around.

"Don't do that," he interrupted. "Don't say what isn't true."

She didn't respond. He held her gaze, and for a moment neither of them moved.

But then a mischievous smile broke across his features, and he shook his head, moving past her and back toward the stream.

SYFIR CROUCHED beside the flowing water, his brows knit together in thought. "I want to show you something," he said, glancing over to Sahira.

She stepped closer, and watched as he carefully rearranged a series of stones in a pattern along the stream's edge. "What are you doing?"

"Shh." He shifted another stone. "Listen." A moment later, the stream's whisper changed pitch. Where water had been turbulent moments ago, it now flowed calmly. He smiled at his handiwork, then turned. Sahira's eyes were wide.

"This is water shaping," he said. "The stones guide the flow without forcing it."

"Is this old magic?" she breathed.

"No." He smiled. "Would you want to see old magic?"

"Yes," she said without thinking.

"Show me your hand," he said softly.

She hesitated, then set down her empty basket, and extended her right hand.

He shook his head. "The other one."

Behind her back, her fingers had been absently tracing a faint blue swirl on her left palm. She thought she had seen something there earlier, but it was so faint she'd told herself it was just a vein.

She knew now, as she extended her left hand, that it wasn't. The mark curled from wrist to palm in a delicate spiral, glowing faintly.

He nodded, as if confirming something. "Maybe you've already seen old magic," he murmured.

She looked at him with wide eyes.

"They should fade when you're far from the river," he said, touching her wrist. Then he stood, too close, and looked down at her. "Why did you come to the forest?" he asked softly.

She opened her mouth to answer, but he interrupted gently. "Not the lie. The truth beneath it."

Something in the question, and in his face made a painful lump form in her throat. And she found herself answering with words she hadn't known lived inside her. "I came because the walls are too close." She swallowed. "I came because in town, I can't hear myself."

*"I came because last night I was made to feel like property, and I don't know if I can live the life I'm supposed to live,"* she almost said, the words rising like bile before she swallowed them back.

"And what does Sahira Raazaan hear when she listens to herself?"

She looked at him blankly. What did she hear when she listened to herself? Her confusion? Her anger? Her shame?

Or something else? Something that had been waiting long before last night's violation?

"I don't know," she said quietly.

"The Mehr'an believe a person's destiny is like water. It always finds its path." His eyes twinkled. "Now destiny, that's powerful old magic. It's like desire. You can divert it or dam it— but eventually… it breaks through."

Sahira couldn't think of anything to say.

"You should return before they notice your absence," Syfir said, motioning west. "It isn't safe for you to be here alone."

"You're here," she pointed out.

The smile that curved his mouth was quick, enigmatic. "Maybe that's why it isn't safe."

Yet despite the warning, despite his earlier offer—joke?—to kill Tavin, she felt no threat from him. He stood close enough that she could take in the scar at his temple, the curve of his lower lip, the way his lashes cast shadows on his cheeks.

*What does Sahira Raazaan hear when she listens to herself?*

She didn't know. But in this moment, she knew only that she wanted to continue standing close to him.

The space between them remained intact, but it suddenly felt charged with possibility. For a heartbeat, she almost imagined that something might happen…

Then he spoke, his voice barely a whisper. "I wonder how your betrothed would feel about your being here."

Sahira took a half step back. "Do you plan to tell him?"

Syfir laughed, and held up his hands in apology. "I only wondered if it would offend his virtue."

She crossed her arms, indignant. "And what virtue do the Mehr'an teach?"

His smile faded. "Want."

The word breathed between them, dangerous and alive.

His eyes dropped briefly to her lips, then back to her eyes, a glance so quick she might have imagined it.

Yet her body responded to that glance as if he had reached out and touched her. Her lips parted slightly of their own accord. His pupils dilated, further darkening his already night-dark eyes. She briefly imagined drowning in them.

For one breathless moment, the forest around them disappeared. There was only this man, this electric space between them, this hunger neither was supposed to feel.

And then he took a deliberate step back, increasing the distance between them, breaking the spell.

But she saw the way his hands flexed at his sides, and realized that this stepping back cost him something.

He wanted but chose not to take.

"The river teaches patience," he said, his voice rough.

Sahira released a breath she hadn't realized she was holding.

"Go back, Zarouni girl," he said quietly, his eyes darkening. "Don't return until you're ready."

"Ready for what?" she asked, voice catching on the words.

He hesitated, then took another step back. "There's a place where the river runs shallower. South of here." His voice dropped lower. "You'll know it by the pale stones. If you ever need to cross."

He only held her gaze for one breath longer before he stepped back into the shadows.

And Sahira stood frozen as he disappeared.

Then she shook herself back into the present. She retrieved her basket, and made her way back toward town.

As she walked, her fingers drifted to her palm, tracing the mark that had already begun to fade with each step away from the Bakki.

And a single word had risen to her lips.

*Want.*

WHEN SAHIRA RETURNED HOME, she placed the gathered lavender that she had thankfully remembered to pluck on her way back from the forest, down on the table in the central room. Then she went to the kitchen—and froze.

There stood Tavin, speaking with her father and aunt.

"May stillness guide you, Sahira," Tavin smiled.

The memory of the shed flashed through her, and her mouth went dry. "And you," she managed. She forced a polite smile.

His eyes went straight to her wrist. "Your thread," he said casually. "It's gone."

*Your betrothed is not a good man. Be careful.*

"Oh! It must have broken in the night," Sahira replied, fighting to keep her voice light. "I'll look for it."

"Strange," he said, stepping closer. "I tied that knot myself." His fingers hovered around her wrist, not quite touching her skin. "Are you sure you didn't remove it?"

*Be careful.* "Why would I do that?" she asked with a small laugh. Her heart was hammering against her ribs.

"I wondered the same." His smile lingered, but his eyes had hardened. "Maybe there's something you're not telling me."

Tharima's sharp intake of breath cut through the tension. "I'm sure it simply wore through," she said briskly. "Six years is a long time for a single thread."

"Yes, you're right," Tavin agreed, still looking at Sahira. "I anticipated this might happen. The closer we come to our ceremony, the more... strange things become."

He turned to Tharima, smiling again, and reached into his pocket. "Thank goodness I have something special to replace it with." He drew out a velvet pouch in deepest green and withdrew a solid gold bangle, its surface inlaid with emeralds.

His face broke into a warm smile.

Everyone in the room seemed to exhale, the tension replaced with sounds of quiet approval.

Tavin reached for Sahira's wrist again. "Allow me."

She extended her arm. The bangle caught the morning light as Tavin slipped it over her fingers.

But it didn't fit over the rest of her hand.

His brows furrowed.

He squeezed her fingers together, trying with deliberate precision to slide the too-small bangle onto her wrist.

"Oh," Tharima clucked, "it's tight for her. It's no matter, I can take it to the jeweler and have them—"

"No," Tavin interrupted sharply. "It's her size. She needs to squeeze harder."

Pain shot through Sahira's hand as he forced the bracelet over it, his knuckles white with effort.

As she winced, a drop of water appeared on her wrist, though the room was dry. Then another.

"What is this?" Tavin muttered, wiping at the moisture. Then, with a brutal shove, the bangle slid into place.

It sat against her wrist like a manacle.

"There," he said, stepping back. "A better tether. Now you'll always remember who you belong to."

Around them, her family made sounds of approval.

Tavin's eyes locked on Sahira's. And they were full of warning.

# CHAPTER 7
# FOREST

Sahira lay in her bed that night, feeling heavier with the new bangle. She felt its weight on her wrist, around her throat, around her future, around her very self.

Her father had retired early, and her aunt's door had clicked shut. Leela slept in her own room.

The house was still.

Only Sahira lay awake, listening to her own heartbeats.

*"Now you'll always remember who you belong to."*

She turned over. The room suddenly felt suffocating.

*Your betrothed is not a good man.*

She turned again. She needed more air. *Be careful.*

She sat up. She had to get out of here.

Without letting herself stop to think, she slipped out of bed. Within moments, her shoes were on, and she was moving through the back hedges and out through the loose fencepost. She went before she could even name where she was going, or who she hoped to find.

THE MOON CAST silver light on the path to the river, breaking through the clouds in brief, flickering intervals.

Sahira moved through the forest, her heart pounding in her chest. She hadn't let herself admit it, wouldn't let herself name it, but something deep inside knew: She wanted to see Syfir.

But when she reached the riverbank, he wasn't there. She scanned the trees, suddenly self-conscious.

And then, she heard it. A melody. Haunting, familiar, like something from a half-forgotten dream. She turned toward the sound, and followed the bank south, walking until she came to where the river grew thinner.

And then she saw it—the place he had told her about. The cluster of pale stones. The shallows. She slipped off her shoes and stepped barefoot across the worn boulders.

Syfir sat on the other side of the bank, coaxing song from the strings of his instrument. His fingers stilled when he saw her.

"Hello, Zarouni girl."

"I shouldn't be here," she said, even as she moved closer. The words were just a ritual now. An acknowledgment of a boundary already crossed.

"Yet here you are." His voice was calm.

"In three days I'll be married."

"I know." He set his instrument aside.

Her breath caught. "Did you think I would come tonight?"

"I prayed you would come tonight," he answered, with a steadiness that unsettled her. Then he rose, fluid as water, and stepped toward her.

His gaze fell to the gold bangle at her wrist. And then, to the faint bruising forming around it. His jaw tightened. "And your people call the Mehr'an uncivilized."

Sahira moved her hand behind her back, and he looked away. He exhaled slowly, and when he met her eyes again, his expression had softened. "They call us that because we worship the river." He began walking along the bank. "Do you know why?"

She shook her head and fell into step beside him.

"The Mehr'an tell a story," he said. "From the First Age, when the river was still a goddess who walked the land. She loved a mortal man. But during a great drought, the sky gods demanded a sacrifice in exchange for rain."

His voice took on a rhythmic cadence. "They chose the man she loved, claiming his beauty was irresistible to the gods. And they took him from her."

Sahira listened, spellbound.

"In her grief, her rage, she opened her mouth wide," he widened his jaw in an exaggerated gesture that made Sahira laugh, "and swallowed herself. Gave up her body. Became the river."

Syfir stopped walking and turned to look into Sahira's eyes. "The Mehr'an believe the river goddess chose certain bloodlines to carry her power. And when those bloodlines are threatened, the river rises to protect what's hers."

Sahira's throat tightened. "Do you believe that?"

He nodded slowly. "I do. There are many tellings of the story. In some, after her beloved was taken, she became the river itself. In others, she became the serpent mother—a protector and destroyer. But in the oldest stories, they're the same. The river is the serpent, and the serpent is the goddess. She shed her skin and became water. And she waits in the river, guarding what remains of her line."

He paused. "I know this: there are women who can still hear the river." His gaze held hers. "Your mother could. That's why the town feared her."

"My mother?" The words knocked the air from her lungs. She swayed, and Syfir instinctively reached to steady her, his hand catching her elbow. "What do you know of my mother?" she asked, barely above a whisper.

"My people know a great deal about your mother." At her stunned silence, he added, "I'll tell you what I can."

He led her to a smooth boulder beneath a tree and knelt, sweeping a patch of dirt clean.

"Your mother was born during a storm," he said, voice low. "The women of Zaroun have always been called to the water. But the rain marked her before she ever saw the river."

He began to draw.

"Hers is the tale of the river and the rain," he said, tracing two figures on either side of a flowing line. "The Mehr'an chief who fell in love with a town girl. Forbidden, like all great loves. I called him uncle. But the valley called him Mirza of the Waters. Your mother only called him Mirza."

Sahira gasped, remembering her dream. "I had a dream about… this can't be real," she murmured.

"Can't it?" Syfir tilted his head. "Her family, the Zarouns, refused the match. Her brothers were furious. They said they'd kill Mirza if she married him. They wanted her to marry a man with better prospects." His fingers drew a path that split off into two. "So they locked her in the house, and arranged her marriage to Tahir Raazaan."

Sahira's mouth parted, her eyes shifting between the drawing and Syfir's face.

"Your mother agreed to the marriage, thinking if she did, then her brothers wouldn't have any reason to hurt her beloved. Marrying Tahir Raazaan would spare Mirza's life." Syfir added a third figure in the dirt, circling it with her mother's.

"But Mirza learned of her plan. The night before your mother married Tahir Raazaan, Mirza swam the entire length of the Bakki, from its mouth in the mountains, all the way to the north end of Jaraan." Syfir's fingers traced a long curve. "He swam through the entire night. He came to take her away."

He paused, meeting her eyes.

"But she knew he would come. And she knew what her brothers would do if he made it to town. So on the morning of her wedding, she came to the river before dawn, before Mirza arrived, and she begged it to hide Mirza. She thought she was saving him."

Sahira gripped the rock beneath her.

"The river listened. But rivers don't stop halfway. It kept him hidden—because it pulled him under."

Sahira clapped her hands to her mouth.

"Your mother didn't know the goddess would keep him."

Sahira couldn't help the sob that escaped her lips.

"The same day she married Tahir was the same day Mirza was claimed by the river. And your mother was left behind. A bride who felt like a widow."

Sahira's eyes stung with hot tears threatening to spill over.

"In town, they called it river madness. But your mother was never mad. She could talk to the river. Just as some of the Mehr'an do. Just as some of the Zaroun once did." And then, his voice lowering to a reverent whisper. "And in the end, she was reunited with her love. She was claimed by the river."

She knew he spoke truth. She felt it in her bones, in her blood. Her tears came freely now.

And as she cried, a tingling bloomed in both her wrists. Patterns reemerged beneath her skin, still scarcely visible, but unmistakable.

She thought of her mother, who had suffered so much for love. And in her grief, the patterns flared brighter.

Syfir reached out, gently brushed one of her tears away. He touched it to his own cheekbone. "I share your sorrow," he said.

Sahira didn't recognize the gesture, but something deep inside her understood its meaning. She looked up into his eyes, her vision blurred with tears.

And he stayed close, gazing at her in shared silence.

With Tavin, proximity had felt like being cornered in a trap disguised as desire. But with Syfir, the nearness felt expansive, like she was growing larger in her own skin.

He stood and then offered his hand to help her rise. She took it, and they rose together, eyes locked, like they had been in the marketplace that first day.

"Why do I want to stand so close to you?" she whispered.

He stepped close enough that his breath stirred the loose strands around her face. "It's why we're here."

Sahira knew she should step back, break this before it became something more dangerous. But she didn't.

And then he reached and gently touched her bruised wrist, his gaze dark. She looked down, and watched as his fingers traced the marks with a tenderness that made her heart ache.

And then, his hand moved. His fingers traveled slowly up her arm, to her shoulder, and then to her throat, to her face, his touch so light she might have imagined it if not for the heat it left behind.

His thumb brushed her lips, sending a current through her body that made her think of the storm they had sheltered from together.

And then his hand cupped her cheek, tilting her chin so that his eyes could fix on hers. His gaze was dark and deep as the river, and she felt herself being pulled into their depths. Her heart was beating so loudly that she worried he might hear.

The river beside them stilled to perfect glass, holding its breath.

He brought his face closer. "I want to touch my lips to yours," he said, his voice low. "Do you want that?"

Sahira's heart pounded so loudly she thought he would hear it, would feel it through his fingertips where they rested near her pulse. "Yes."

Then, his lips were on hers, soft, and filling her entire body with warmth.

And she knew, with a certainty she couldn't explain, that Syfir would never shame her for this. Where Tavin had shamed her for her desire, Syfir seemed to revel in it.

The kiss deepened. Her body arched toward him without conscious thought, as if it recognized something her mind was only beginning to understand. Her hands found his shoulders, solid and warm beneath the thin fabric of his kurta, anchoring herself as the world tilted.

He pulled back just enough to murmur, "Some people say that serpents eat their own skin."

She had no idea why he said this, and yet images flashed in her mind: Transformation. Rebirth. Shedding what no longer serves. Becoming what you were meant to be.

And then their lips met again, and it wasn't soft. It was the shattering of a dam, it was water finding its path to the sea.

And then he pulled back, and there was laughter between them, soft and breathless and quiet.

But as the silence returned, Sahira's smile slowly faded. A shiver ran down her spine.

Was she repeating her mother's fate? Was she, too, destined to love someone she could never keep? To bind herself to the wrong man, the wrong life, and lose the one who made her feel most alive?

When she looked down, the faint blue patterns were no longer faint. They were glowing unmistakably now, curling along her forearms like living river serpents. They coiled and shimmered, shifting with her pulse, alive beneath her skin.

She looked up, and Syfir was already watching her, unafraid.

"What's happening to me?" she asked. Her voice was steady despite the wonder unfurling within and around her.

"You're remembering what flows in your blood," he said.

Her breath caught.

*Remember what flows in your blood.* Her eyes widened.

And as if in response, the river pulsed beside them, waves lapping the shore in recognition.

Sahira walked home that night barefoot, changed in ways that couldn't be undone.

Her body felt different. Looser, more fluid, as if her bones had softened and reformed into something truer to her nature.

She slipped through the back door, quiet as shadow.

In the hallway mirror, she caught a glimpse of herself, and for a moment, didn't recognize the girl staring back. There was something different in her eyes. A hunger.

Her heart still raced with the memory of Syfir's kiss.

She had just opened her bedroom door when a sharp intake of breath in the corner made her freeze.

"Where were you?"

Sahira's heart jumped. Leela sat in the corner, knees hugged to her chest, eyes wide.

"You should be asleep," Sahira hissed.

At fourteen, her cousin was caught between childhood and womanhood—old enough to understand the Covenant's restrictions, young enough to still question them privately.

"So should you." Leela stood slowly, and moved to Sahira's bed. In the dim moonlight, her expression was more curious than accusatory. "Where were you?"

Denial rose automatically to Sahira's lips. The instinctive response of a woman trained to hide, to diminish, to deflect. But something in Leela's gaze stopped her.

"I went to the river," Sahira said quietly.

Leela's eyes lit up. "I knew it," she squealed, climbing into the covers.

"Shh." Sahira shut the door and motioned for Leela to get into the bed.

"I knew it," Leela squealed. "I knew it. You're different now. It's like... you've woken up."

Sahira swallowed hard. That was exactly how she felt. As if she'd spent her life half-dreaming and was now fully conscious for the first time.

"Leela," she began carefully, moving to sit at the edge of her bed, "what I did tonight, going out alone. It breaks Covenant law. If anyone found out—"

"I won't tell," Leela interrupted. "I swear."

Relief flared, but so did worry. "Why were you watching for me?"

Leela hesitated. "Sometimes I watch you. You're doing everything right… but you still feel different." Her voice softened. "I worry."

Goosebumps prickled along Sahira's arms. Did others see what Leela saw?

"What about you?" she asked, deflecting attention from herself. "Are you different too?"

Leela pulled the covers up around her body. "I have dreams."

"What kind of dreams?"

"Water. Sometimes you're in them. Sometimes Ameera Mami, too, even though I barely remember her."

Sahira's heart thudded.

"She always wore long sleeves, I remember. But in my dream, she pulled them up, and her arms…"

Sahira knew what her cousin wanted to say. Her arms were marked with blue swirling patterns.

The admission hung between them.

"You haven't told anyone," Sahira said. It wasn't a question.

Leela shook her head. "They would say I have the river sickness."

"The Covenant calls many things sickness that aren't," Sahira said, sitting beside her. "Sometimes… they're memories. Things we've been taught to forget."

Leela took a deep breath, as if gathering courage to share a secret. "When I was really little, before Baba passed, he took me to see his mother. She was so old," Leela paused. "Baba left me alone with her, and I remember being scared she would die right in front of me."

She hesitated, then continued. "She told me a story about a woman who became a serpent."

Sahira turned toward her, suddenly alert.

"She said the serpent woman wasn't evil. She was from the Old World. A Naga. She could shift between woman and water-serpent."

"What happened to her?" Sahira asked.

"Men tried to cage her. That's when she turned. But before she vanished, she left marks on her daughters." Leela's voice dropped. "Patterns that coil like snakes. Or like river currents."

"She said the serpent woman flowed into every river, and every stream, and even into woman's tears, waiting for the day her daughters would remember how to transform too." Leela's eyes gleamed in the darkness. "The story scared me so much. I was terrified the serpent goddess would mark me."

She reached forward suddenly, touching Sahira's wrist where a faint line had begun to appear beneath the skin—a subtle change Sahira herself hadn't yet noticed.

"Something's happening to you, isn't it?" Leela whispered. "What the elders fear."

Sahira should have pulled away, should have denied it, should have reminded her cousin of proper Covenant beliefs.

Instead, she nodded once, the simple acknowledgment feeling like both confession and declaration.

"Are you afraid?" Leela asked.

"Yes," Sahira whispered. "But I'm not afraid of the change. I'm afraid of what they'll do when they notice."

Leela was quiet for some time after that. And then she laid her head down on Sahira's pillow, pulling the covers up around herself.

Sahira slid out of her salwar and kameez and pulled on night clothes before sliding into her bed and laying her head down beside Leela's. She touched her forehead to her cousin's.

Leela took a deep breath. "Didi, can I say something?"

Sahira nodded, but her eyes were closed.

"Didi... I don't think you should marry Tavin."

Sahira startled and her eyes shot open to look at Leela, but her younger cousin had turned her body away, not wanting to make eye contact after the admission.

"Go to bed," Sahira said gently.

Leela didn't respond for a long moment. But then she finally spoke. "Be more careful next time you go to the river. They can punish us for anything. Without even proving it."

And then she didn't say anything else.

Moments later, her breathing steadied into sleep, leaving Sahira awake to ponder the ally she had found in her wise young cousin. An ally who was undergoing her own awakening, finding her own path to the water that called to them both.

# CHAPTER 8
# PURITY

The next morning, Sahira woke with the memory of the river still clinging to her skin.

A knock at the door made her jump, and roused Leela awake.

"Get ready," Tharima called. "All women have been summoned to the temple for the Purging."

Sahira sat up. "But the Purging isn't scheduled until the solstice—"

"They say it's urgent," was Tharima's curt reply.

Leela was already scrambling to dress. Sahira followed, her fingers clumsy as she fumbled with a white kameez.

"What about the ritual for today?" Sahira asked, voice low.

"Just the Reading of Wifely Duties," Tharima said, waving it off. "We'll do it after temple."

Sahira said nothing, relieved to have only two rituals remaining.

~

"ELDER NEFRET IS in a particularly stern mood," Tharima said as they left the house and out of Government Colony.

"What's going on?" Sahira asked, walking beside her aunt as she motioned for Leela to keep up.

Tharima's voice dropped, a hint of fear in her words. "There are rumors... inappropriate behavior. It's one of the younger women. The elders are concerned."

Sahira's heart stopped. *Had someone seen her at the river?*

And then an even worse thought: *Did someone know what happened in the shed?*

She forced her face to remain neutral as they made their way toward the market square, toward the temple.

"It's the Purging," Tharima reminded the girls, "so cover your heads." Sahira and Leela quickly pulled their dupattas over their heads.

"We're ready," Sahira said.

THE TEMPLE COURTYARD was crowded with women of all ages. The air felt charged, electric with anticipation and dread.

Sahira and Leela followed Tharima into the temple's main hall, where the smell of incense hung heavy. They took seats near the stage.

Elder Nefret stepped onto the stage.

At her side stood Elder Varden, the only man in the room. He was small and pale, with dark eyes set too deep in his face.

The Purging began.

The Elders lifted their arms. A low groan rose from their throats, deep and guttural, symbolizing the purging of wrongness, disobedience, unclean thoughts.

In unison, the women in the room joined in the groan, one by one, until the room shook with sound.

The collective groaning built to a cacophonous crescendo, until Elder Nefret raised one hand, and silence fell.

She scanned the room and her gaze landed on a girl only a few seats from Sahira:

Kaya.

Sahira's mind flashed back to the note. *Be careful.*

"Step forward," Elder Nefret said, pointing one finger at the girl.

Kaya stood slowly, her hands shaking. She glanced around nervously and walked toward the stage.

"Come," Elder Nefret said, her voice deceptively soft. "Tell our congregation, my dear, what is your name?"

"Kaya Muktan," the girl whispered. Her voice cracked.

"Kaya Muktan," the elder repeated, savoring each syllable. "And Kaya, do you know why you've been summoned today?"

Kaya's chin quivered. "I—I don't know."

Elder Nefret stepped closer, her voice still velveted with false kindness. "Do you think it wise to shirk the questions of an Elder, Kaya?" she asked in a voice that was like honey.

Sahira's stomach tightened.

"No, Elder. I—I truly don't know," Kaya said, curling slightly inward, as if bracing against unseen wind.

"Kaya, you are here today because this is not just a Purging." Elder Nefret turned to the congregation. "It will also be a Ceremony of Purification."

Gasps rippled through the courtyard. Something in Kaya's expression shifted. Some glimmer of hope that was now gone. Sahira's eyes darted to Leela, whose eyes were wide.

"Kaya, what were you doing in the market last weekend?" Elder Nefret asked, her voice now syrupy and slow.

This jolted something in Kaya because she took a few steps back, her hands moving up to her opposite arms protectively. "I —just the weekly shopping," she stammered. "Nothing else."

But the tremble in her voice betrayed the lie.

Elder Nefret looked at her thoughtfully, head tilted like a predator considering its approach. "Get down, on your knees, girl," she said, her voice softer now.

Kaya's eyes darted around as she hesitated.

Elder Nefret stepped closer and hissed, "Come now, I'm certain you're familiar with what I ask."

Kaya knelt now onstage, trembling visibly, looking everywhere except at Elder Nefret.

The silence in the temple was absolute.

"This woman," Elder Nefret said to the gathered women, her voice growing louder with every word, "was seen in a market alleyway last weekend, with a man whose trousers were on the ground, kneeling, just as you see her kneeling before you now, with her lips on his loins!" She kicked Kaya with her left leg, shoving her to the ground as the girl cried out in protest.

Every woman in the room gasped in unison. Sahira's fingers found the edge of her seat, gripping so tightly her knuckles turned white.

"I didn't," Kaya sobbed. "He forced me—"

But Elder Nefret reached forward and grabbed the girl's face in one hand, startling the girl into silence.

Sahira's mouth went dry and her stomach clenched so violently she thought she might be sick. The shed flashed through her mind. Its darkness, the press of his hands.

*Your betrothed is not a good man.*

Had Tavin…

Sahira tried to steady her breathing, her vision blurring. And onstage, Elder Nefret's fingers forced Kaya's mouth open for the watching women.

"Look into the mouth of this woman who has been made impure," she announced to the room, her voice rising. "She has been infected with the disgusting, morality-rotting poison of *want*." And then, the elder shoved her fingers forcefully into Kaya's throat, before pulling them back out and pushing Kaya's face to the floor.

Sahira watched, frozen in place, as Kaya lay on the stage, tears streaming down her face.

Sahira looked away, and caught the look on Leela's face. Her cousin's face was pale, her eyes wide with horror.

Elder Nefret looked to the congregation now. "Come now, everyone. Should we banish her, or should we cleanse her?"

The room was quiet. Someone cried softly in the corner of the room.

"Cleanse her," called a voice. A pause. "Cleanse her," called another. More murmurs of agreement sounded, a chorus of complicity.

"Ah, yes. Good. Let us cleanse her," Elder Nefret said with a warm smile that didn't reach her eyes. "And let us hope to God she is forgiven."

And then she was kneeling down beside her, stroking Kaya's hair with a mockery of tenderness. "Stillness is peace," she said with a soft smile. "Stillness is our freedom."

The congregation repeated the words in unison, their voices creating a hypnotic chant. "Stillness is peace. Stillness is our freedom."

Sahira found her mouth forming the words automatically, though inside she was screaming.

Elder Nefret nodded, satisfied, and stood up, addressing the crowd now. "Stillness is peace, indeed. Stillness is freedom from desire. Freedom from the thing that man and beast must suffer: *want.*"

"Can you imagine living with want?" she asked, and several women responded, no. "With hunger? With lust?" she asked more loudly now, and more voices expressed their disapproval, their disgust.

She moved closer to Kaya again, and the girl whimpered, a small, animal sound of distress.

"When a woman is pure," the elder said, looking at Kaya with disgust, "she is safe from want." The crowd tittered in agreement.

And then Elder Nefret reached down and grabbed Kaya's hair, pulling it toward her. "But when a woman is not pure, she will sin, again and again, and again!" She was screaming now, pulling Kaya's hair so violently that several strands came loose in her hand. The girl wailed.

Elder Nefret released Kaya's hair, and Kaya's body thudded on the ground, racked with sobs.

A woman in the audience let out a stifled cry.

Elder Nefret was looking at Kaya now with a softened expression. "Thank the river you are still young. We can still save you."

Elder Nefret knelt down now next to Kaya, who had curled her body into a ball, making herself as small as possible, trying to disappear.

The elder reached her hand out and caressed the girl's face.

"Rise, child," she said, helping Kaya from the ground. Then to all of them, "Come, women, let us come together, let us cleanse the evil from inside of this child. Let us, once again, make her pure."

Elder Nefret held Kaya's arms behind her back, and motioned to a gray-haired woman in the front row. "You there, come here." The woman hesitated only a moment before stepping forward and climbing on stage. "Remove her garments," the elder commanded, pointing to Kaya's kameez.

The woman glanced at Elder Nefret, and then at Elder Varden, as if confirming she had heard correctly. And then she began unbuttoning the back of the girl's kameez.

Kaya's face was slick with tears and snot, burning with shame.

Elder Varden watched silently, his expression unreadable.

Elder Nefret motioned to a second woman. "Help her," she commanded.

Two acolytes stepped forward, carrying between them a wooden box. Elder Nefret opened it with reverent care. Inside lay ancient tools, their exact purposes opaque, but their threat unmistakable.

She removed a small vial filled with cloudy liquid. "Blessed water from deep within the temple," she announced. "Infused with tonics to purify what has been defiled."

The acolytes held Kaya's arms as Elder Nefret paused before her. "Repeat after me: I will embrace stillness."

Kaya opened her mouth, but only a whisper came.

"Louder, child," the elder demanded.

"I will embrace stillness," Kaya said, voice trembling.

Elder Nefret gripped her by the hair and tilted her head back, pouring the vial's contents into her mouth. Kaya gagged as the liquid burned down her throat.

"The body must be cleansed from within," Elder Nefret intoned calmly, still holding Kaya's jaw shut. "To purge the poison of desire. Of shamelessness."

But she wasn't finished.

She turned to the assembled women. "The final cleansing will require witnesses." Her finger moved through the crowd. "You, and you."

Two middle-aged women Sahira didn't recognize stepped forward reluctantly. "And you," Elder Nefret said, pointing directly at Neelma Daraio. Neelma stood with undisguised satisfaction.

"You'll help hold her head still," Nefret said. Neelma nodded, stepping onto the dais.

Then Elder Nefret returned to the box and drew out a slender metal rod with a circular end; the Covenant's symbol: still water inside unbroken lines.

It was a branding iron.

"Today, we mark Kaya with the symbol of her cleansing."

One of the acolytes brought forward a small brazier of glowing coals. Elder Nefret placed the metal end into the heat, her eyes never leaving Kaya's trembling form. Sahira's eyes widened in horror as she understood what the tool was for.

"In the time before the Great Correction, women lived without shame," she declared. She raised the glowing iron. The air around it shimmered. "Never again!"

Sahira's stomach lurched. She wanted to look away, but couldn't. Elder Nefret approached Kaya with the glowing brand. Leela reached out and grabbed at Sahira's hand fumbling desperately to clutch it tight.

"Let this mark be a reminder to us all, of the importance of shame. The importance of purity. The importance of stillness."

Kaya began to struggle and the acolytes and two women held her limbs tightly. Neelma gripped her head.

And with deliberate, terrible precision, Elder Nefret pressed the heated iron to Kaya's shoulder.

A sickening sizzle. Then Kaya's scream.

Sahira gagged, hand clamped to her mouth as bile surged.

When the iron lifted, it left behind a dark circle. Still water inside unbroken lines.

"The mark of cleansing will remind you and all who see you that some stains cannot be washed away, only contained."

She turned to the congregation, smiling beatifically. "You are all dismissed."

Sahira rose on trembling legs, following the others. But before the room emptied, she saw Kaya being led away, through a door behind the altar, into the inner sanctum. The door closed behind them.

Finally, slowly, the assembled women began to disperse, no one speaking above a whisper. Some looked troubled, while others looked relieved it hadn't been their daughters or sisters. Most simply looked down as they walked.

Had ceremonies like this happened before? The memory of her mother rose unbidden in Sahira's mind. Had they forced bitter liquid down her throat, pressed hot metal to her skin?

As she and the other women filed slowly out into the temple courtyard, Sahira overheard two much older women whispering.

"Disgusting girl," one was saying.

"No, the girl said she was forced," her companion admonished.

Sahira froze in her steps, and thought of the shed. *Your betrothed is not a good man.*

"Men have always claimed what isn't theirs to take," the first woman hissed back. "She was foolish to let it happen so publicly."

The second woman shushed her companion hastily.

Sahira swallowed hard. If they ever found out—about Tavin and the shed, about Syfir about what flowed in her blood—would they strip her bare, too? Would they brand her flesh and call it purity, too?

When Sahira, Tharima, and Leela came home, it was immediately time to prepare for the Ritual Reading of Wifely Duties—dinner would have to wait.

Sahira was taken to her room and dressed in white linen, and then brought to the central room in the home, where Tavin's mother sat before Sahira, and Tharima and Leela sat silently behind her.

The four women waited in silence for Elder Nefret's arrival.

What felt like a long while later, they heard knocking at the door, and Maru escorted in Elder Murat.

Maru nodded encouragingly at Sahira before bowing and leaving the room.

"I'm afraid Elder Nefret cannot join us this evening," said Elder Murat, an elderly woman with a regal air about her. "The temple purification ceremonies… require her personal attention well into the night." Something in her face betrayed distaste. "But I am here, and I will conduct this ritual reading in her stead."

She withdrew the Covenant Book of Matrimony, its leather binding worn smooth by generations of similar ceremonies.

"Two days hence, Sahira Raazaan will cease to exist," Elder

Murat announced, her voice echoing in the vaulted central room. "In her place will stand Sahira Daraio, who will be bound by sacred duties to her husband, his family, and the Covenant that governs us all."

Sahira glanced briefly at Leela, who was already watching her with worry.

Elder Murat opened the ancient book, its pages yellowed with age. "Today, we read aloud the expectations that will shape her new life, so that she may enter her marriage with clarity of purpose and acceptance of her role." She passed the book to Tavin's mother, to read the first duty.

"The Duty of Body," Neelma read, her voice precise and unyielding. "A wife's body belongs first to her husband, then to his children, and finally to his household. She dresses modestly, revealing only what is necessary for her duties. She maintains its cleanliness, its health, and its readiness to serve. She yields it without hesitation when required, whether for labor, for child-bearing, or for her husband's pleasure."

She returned the book to Elder Murat, who handed it next to Tharima.

"The Duty of Voice," Tharima read carefully. "A wife speaks only when necessary, and then with gentle tone and careful words. Her voice never rises in anger, complaint, or excessive emotion. She expresses no opinion contrary to her husband's wisdom. She speaks well of him in his absence, and falls silent in his presence unless invited to contribute."

One by one, the remaining duties were read in turn by Tavin's mother and Tharima. Each detailed specific expectations, permissions, and prohibitions that would govern Sahira's life from the moment of her marriage forward.

The final page, sealed with black wax, was opened by Elder Murat herself. "The Duty of Memory," she read, her eyes fixed on Sahira rather than the paper. "A wife remembers her place and forgets that which does not serve her purpose. She remembers her husband's preferences and forgets her own desires. She remembers proper behavior and forgets impure impulses. She remembers the Covenant's teachings and forgets questions that lead to corruption."

Throughout the reading, Sahira remained perfectly still, her face a careful mask of acceptance.

When the ritual ended, each woman in attendance came forward to place grains of rice in Sahira's outstretched palms, symbolizing the many small duties she would carry without complaint.

"Remember what you have heard today," Elder Murat concluded, placing her hand on Sahira's head in a gesture that was both blessing and warning. "For these duties will define your existence from this day forward."

As the women filed out, Sahira remained kneeling, her hands still extended and carrying the weight of her these new expectations.

THAT NIGHT, after the ritual was complete and Sahira lay in bed staring at the ceiling, she overheard her father and aunt whispering in the hallway.

"The elders are concerned," Tharima was whispering. "They don't want girls' inappropriate behavior to spread."

In her bed, Sahira turned over, thinking of Kaya.

She buried her face in her pillow. After some time, the voices in the hallway faded away, and her door opened and Leela slipped in.

"Didi," she whispered, climbing into her cousin's bed. "I need to ask you something."

Her urgency made Sahira look up. "What is it?"

"You know the musician in the market?"

Sahira froze.

"The one with the strange instrument?" Leela's voice was anxious. "Have you... have you ever heard his music?"

Sahira turned to face her, her body tensing. "Why do you ask?"

"Because I've been dreaming of it." Leela's words tumbled out in a rush. "A melody I've never heard before. Except... I have. Somehow, I know it. And last night, I saw you in my dream, standing in the river. The water was... moving strangely. Like it was alive."

Sahira felt a flutter of panic.

"Dreams are just dreams," Sahira whispered. But the words rang hollow. After what happened to Kaya, even dreams felt dangerous.

"But what if they're not just dreams?" Leela persisted.

"I don't know," Sahira said. Her eyes didn't leave her cousin's. "But you can't talk about this to anyone else. Only to me."

Leela's lip quivered. "But you'll be gone soon."

"I know," Sahira whispered. And she pulled her cousin into an embrace. "You can't ask these questions after I'm gone."

It wasn't just her own awakening she needed to protect now.

Whatever was stirring inside Sahira was reaching others now, flowing outward like the river.

And she wasn't sure how much longer she could contain it.

THAT NIGHT SAHIRA dreamed of standing at the temple threshold, moments before becoming Tavin's bride.

*A single blue flower bloomed in Sahira's hands. And then, golden binding thread twined her wrists together.*

*As she stepped forward to meet Tavin, water began seeping through the temple floor, rising around her ankles. The elders continued their chanting, ignoring the flood, while Tavin's smile grew fixed and desperate.*

# CHAPTER 8

*"It's too late," he said, though his lips didn't move. "The river has already claimed you."*

She woke gasping, her bedsheets inexplicably damp though the windows were shut, and the night was clear.

# CHAPTER 9
# INSPECTION

Dawn broke on the final day before her wedding.

The house thrummed with activity. The air smelled of lavender, rosewater, and expectation.

Today was the Ritual of Inspection. The last rite before Sahira became Tavin's wife.

"The bath ceremony begins soon," Tharima called from the kitchen.

Sahira's mind drifted to Syfir's kiss. And then to the shed. And then to Kaya's scream. The memories blurred together, and Sahira's stomach turned.

She picked up the white robe she was meant to wear, but couldn't make herself put it on.

Leela entered, took the robe from her hands, and helped her into it with quiet care. "You don't seem… alright," she whispered.

Sahira flinched. "What do you mean?"

But before Leela could answer, Tharima swept in with the ceremonial flower-jewelry. Sahira was decorated with white roses that were hung from her ears. More were twisted into her hair. More were tied around her neck like a necklace.

Or like a noose.

Leela, unmarried, and Tharima, widowed, weren't permitted to participate, but they walked Sahira to the courtyard.

Maru passed as they made their way, the red-checked rag still slung over his shoulder. He paused just long enough to hand Sahira a cup of warm water before disappearing into the house again.

She accepted it gratefully, sipping to calm her nerves as her aunt and cousin led her to the center of the courtyard, where a stone basin waited. The bride's bath.

Neelma Daraio arrived, trailed by married women from her side of the family.

They were strangers to Sahira, yet they all stared as Sahira removed her robe.

The Ritual of Inspection began.

When she raised her arms to shield her chest, the women gently pulled them down. Their hands were soft, but their eyes were clinical. Evaluating.

Leela hovered at the courtyard gate until Tharima quietly drew her away.

One woman pried Sahira's lips open to examine her teeth. Another lifted her hair, inspecting her scalp. A third circled her slowly. "Her hips are narrow," she remarked.

Fingers pressed along Sahira's collarbones. Her skin prickled. She checked her palms. The faint blue patterns weren't visible. She was far enough from the basin that the marks remained dormant—just skin and memory.

The same helplessness she had felt in the shed was back.

After the inspection of her body was complete, Neelma reached for her hand to guide her toward the basin—then stopped.

Her eyes went to Sahira's hand as it neared the water.

"What is this?" she asked sharply, turning Sahira's palm

128

toward the light, where a blue swirl had just barely begun to surface under her skin.

"A birthmark," Sahira said too quickly, drawing her hand back.

Neelma's eyes narrowed. "I've known you since childhood. That wasn't there."

Sahira said nothing.

Neelma's voice dropped to a whisper. "I've heard of such marks. These... swirls. They show up just before a woman is... claimed."

Sahira's blood ran cold. "I don't... know what you mean."

Neelma's eyes were hard now. "I would imagine your mother had a mark like this." The warning in her voice was unmistakable.

Sahira could think of nothing more to say.

"Let us start," one of the other Daraio women tittered, breaking the tension.

The strangers guided Sahira up the steps that led into the basin. When Sahira hesitated, hands immediately pressed her forward, forcing her in.

Sahira gasped and pulled back—the water was ice cold.

"Hold still," Neelma commanded when Sahira flinched.

The women gripped her shoulders and began reciting blessings: for fertility. For obedience.

Sahira said nothing. But inside, something cracked. A single thought rose in her mind: *I am not supposed to be here.*

"Chin up. Turn left. Now right." The commands came one after the other as various oils were applied to her hair.

All the while, Sahira kept her hands submerged, curled into tight fists. She could feel the patterns tingling now. She pressed her arms to her sides.

Her breath quickened and panic flared inside her. *Please,* she begged silently. *Let something pull their attention. Let this be over.*

And then, as if summoned by her desperation, a loud crash sounded from the front of the house.

Shouted voices. The clatter of something breaking. Maru's voice rising faintly in the distance, apologizing for dropping a tray.

Neelma cursed under her breath, and then snapped, "go see what that was," to the youngest relative, who hurried away.

Sahira seized the moment.

"I'm cold," she said too sharply, and stepped backward toward the basin's edge. "I think I need to come out."

"Let her out," one of them muttered. "She's shivering."

Hands reached to steady her as she climbed out of the basin, still keeping her palms turned away, her arms close.

The women around her clicked and hissed their disapproval as Sahira pulled on her robe.

And through it all, Neelma Daraio watched her.

Sahira didn't meet her gaze.

She slipped back into the house.

HOURS LATER, Sahira sat in the courtyard with Leela, waiting for her bridal mehndi to dry. The henna artist packed up her tools just as Elder Nefret arrived to finalize the next day's preparations with Sahira's father.

"Bridal mehndi all done?" she asked Sahira with a smile that didn't reach her eyes.

"Yes, Elder," Sahira replied, eyes lowered.

"Squeeze lemon juice on her hands today," Elder Nefret said to Leela, her gaze never leaving Sahira's face. "Darker mehndi means a happier marriage."

Leela nodded politely, but wondered how Sahira's marriage to Tavin could ever be a happy one.

Elder Nefret's eyes narrowed, and she looked at Sahira's face, her gaze lingering a moment too long. "You seem… different, Sahira."

Her mouth went dry. She lowered her eyes further. "Perhaps it's my joy, Elder. I await the ceremony with great anticipation."

"Mm." Elder Nefret's lips thinned as she cocked her head to the side. "The Daraio family is honorable," she continued, "and Tavin has always been such a good boy. He deserves a bride who rises to his family's standards." She paused, the silence thick. "A true daughter of the Covenant… I trust that's what you are."

Sahira nodded respectfully.

But a chill ran down her spine.

As evening fell, Sahira still sat beside Leela, who was now stringing flowers for the ceremony, when Tavin appeared.

She felt it instantly. That rising tension that bloomed in her chest whenever she even thought of him now.

"Hello, ladies," he said. The smile on his face didn't match the worry in his eyes. He barely glanced at the mehndi or the garlands.

"Can we speak?"

"Of course," Sahira rose carefully, taking care not to let her dried henna rub against anything. "I'll be back," she whispered to Leela, whose eyes instantly mirrored her own unease.

They stepped aside into the shadowed edge of the courtyard.

"Do you like my mehndi?" she asked, raising her hands.

He didn't look. "Sahira, I don't want my father to dissolve our betrothal."

"I—what?" Her breath caught. The ground felt suddenly unsteady beneath her.

"There've been rumors," Tavin said, his voice quiet. "Someone reported seeing you at the river. At night."

His gaze was sharp now, urgent. "Tell me it's not true. Tell me you haven't been—"

"I haven't—" she started, then stopped. Lowered her hands.

What had they seen? If it was just her slipping out alone, that was bad enough. But if they knew about Syfir… or the blue marks that were appearing under her skin when she neared the river…

Then Tavin wouldn't be standing here. The elders would.

"You haven't been… touched by…" His voice trailed off.

Sahira stared at him, a chill spreading through her. Her mind swam with possibilities. None of them good.

"Touched by the river," he finished. His face looked haunted.

She exhaled. "I haven't."

He let out a breath, visibly relieved.

"Has someone officially reported this claim?" she asked.

"No," he said, too quickly. "And I'll make sure they don't. But I needed to hear it from you."

"It isn't true," she repeated, the words dull in her mouth.

He nodded. "You can tell me anything, you know. It's just… you've seemed far away lately."

Lately.

Since the shed.

"Are you alright?" he said, peering into her face carefully when she didn't reply.

His concern might have moved her once. Now it only made her feel sick inside. "I'm fine," she said, forcing a smile. But her hands betrayed her, wringing together as flakes of dried henna crumbled and fell to her feet like ashes.

She turned to gesture toward Leela. "Do you want to help with the flowers?"

"No," he said with a faint smile. "Just wanted to talk to my bride-to-be."

Her smile froze for half a beat before she recovered. "Thank you," she said softly.

He smiled.

She turned and walked back to Leela.

Tavin watched her go, thoughtful and silent.

∿

As the final preparations for the marriage ceremony were underway, Sahira found herself alone in her room for a fleeting moment.

She sat on a chair in front of her dressing table, and allowed her mind to wander to a night she never allowed it to go. The night before her mother disappeared.

*She'd awakened in the night to find her mother sitting by the window, staring toward the river, her unbound hair seeming to move though no breeze stirred the room. "Listen," her mother had whispered, taking Sahira's small hands in hers. "The river is calling. It knows our name, our blood."*

*She pressed her lips to Sahira's forehead, and for a moment, Sahira heard it too—a melody too beautiful for human voice, words in no earthly language, yet they resonated in her bones like ancestral memory.*

*"Someday," her mother had promised, "you'll remember what I've had to help you forget. When that day comes, don't be afraid."*

That very night, Ameera Raazaan had walked into the river and never returned. And Sahira, in her grief and anger, had locked away the memory of water singing her name.

Sahira looked up at her reflection in the mirror, barely recognizing the woman staring back. Her eyes held a flicker of something wild, something untamed.

Suddenly, a drop of water landed on her cheek.

She looked up. No leak. The ceiling was dry.

Then another drop. And another.

As each tear-like droplet touched her skin, she felt the pull of the river calling to her. The same force that had drawn her mother.

In the water, she saw a fleeting image: her mother, standing in a rushing river, her face radiant.

A voice, not her own, echoed in her mind: *"The river remembers. And so must you."*

The water vanished as quickly as it had appeared, leaving

behind only a dampness on her skin and an unshakable resolve in her heart.

Tomorrow she would stand before the entire community and promise to be someone she was no longer capable of being.

Sahira turned to the window in her bedroom, and before she could think better of it, she unlatched it. The night air rushed in, carrying the scent of jasmine and river silt.

And she knew, with absolute certainty, she had to go to the river.

She had to see him. One last time.

CHAPTER 10

# NIGHT

The full moon was a witness, painting the world in shades of silver and shadow. The forest held its breath, waiting.

Sahira followed the river south, to where the pale stones rose from the shallows. Smooth, glinting faintly in the moonlight.

She crossed barefoot, as she had once before, but more quickly this time—as if the very act of crossing the river might keep her from unraveling.

She was going to him. One last time.

On the far bank, Syfir stood against a tree, head bowed, staring down at his hands as though they could stop time. He felt her before he saw her.

She ran to him as if drawn by gravity, as if reaching him could change fate.

He straightened, his breath catching at the sight of her. Wild-eyed, desperate, and yet beautiful in her anguish.

But she stopped before she reached him, suddenly struck by the reality of what being here meant.

After witnessing Kaya's humiliation. After seeing the town's cruelty laid bare.

She shouldn't ever have come.

But there would be no other night.

He looked at her, waiting for her to come nearer. The ache in his chest threatened to split him open.

"I've been waiting for you," he said quietly, willing her to come closer, his eyes never leaving her face.

"I'm getting married tomorrow," she whispered, not moving.

"I know." His voice was steady, gentle, but the words fell between them like stones into still water, each ripple carrying the weight of everything they couldn't have. "And even then, I'll still be waiting for you."

And then she came closer, shaking with every step, and when she reached him, she pressed her palms flat against his chest as if she could anchor herself to him, as if she could stop time itself.

"After tomorrow, I can never—we can never—" Her voice broke on the words, a sound so raw it tore something in him. Her hands fell from his chest as she stepped back. "This is the last time I'll see you."

"It doesn't have to be." He held out his hand, palm up, an offering. A prayer.

Sahira shook her head violently. "It does. You know it does. I'm getting married tomorrow and—" the words died in her throat.

But her hand moved to meet his anyway, as if drawn by some force beyond her control.

Their fingers touched and the world contracted to that single point of contact. The forest's night sounds fell away; even the river's constant murmur paused, as if nature itself held its breath for this moment.

Skin against skin. A conversation more intimate than any kiss, more revealing than any unveiled body.

He looked down at her henna-painted hand in his, and then up at her face. "Tomorrow, you'll be bound to another man. Tomorrow, threads will tie you to him." And then his free hand came up to cup her face. "But it doesn't have to be this way," he said, his voice rough.

Sahira looked at him, willing herself not to cry.

"It doesn't, Sahira," Syfir insisted. "We can leave. Tonight."

"No, we can't." She pulled back to look at him, hope and desperation warring in her eyes. "Where would we go? How long before they found us? And when they did—"

"We could disappear. Go somewhere they'd never think to look."

"Running forever." The words hung between them, heavy with possibility and impossibility both. "Always looking over our shoulders."

"I'd rather run with you than live without you," he said simply.

The simple honesty of it broke something inside her. She reached up to touch his face, her fingers tracing the line of his jaw as if she could memorize the feel of him.

"And I'd rather know you're alive and far from me than risk them hurting you," she said. "I couldn't bear it, Syfir. If something happened to you because of me, I'd never forgive myself."

He shook his head, clenching his jaw. "Sahira, we can find a way. Maybe—"

Her breath hitched. "No," a sob tore from her throat, and suddenly she was clutching at his kurta with desperate hands, as if she could hold onto this moment, hold onto him. "Syfir," she gasped between tears. "We can't. And you can't try to stop it. Promise me, Syfir, you have to promise me—"

Her mind raced to her mother, who had also belonged to someone before marriage. To Mirza, who had tried to steal her away and paid with his life. To all the stories that ended in blood and tragedy.

"You can't do what Mirza tried to do, Syfir–you have to swear you'll stay away—" panic seized her. "They'll kill you. They'll—"

"Hey, hey—" His hands moved to cradle her face, forcing her to look at him. "Hey, breathe. Look at me."

But her eyes were wild now, seeing ghosts in the shadows.

"Syfir, I mean it—I can't—my mother stopped him from coming to the wedding, but it didn't matter. It didn't matter because he loved her and they still—Syfir, I can't lose you too. I have to marry him, I have to save my family's name—I can't—"

"I won't do anything, I won't," Syfir promised, eyes shining as he blinked back tears. "I won't do anything you don't ask me to."

"You won't." His forehead pressed against hers, his voice fierce and tender. "You won't lose me. I'm not going anywhere."

"Promise me." Her hands fisted in his shirt, knuckles white. "Swear to me you won't try to stop the wedding. Swear it on my life—on your life—on whatever matters most to you."

A pained sob escaped Sahira's throat.

The moonlight caught the tears in his eyes as he looked at her. And when he spoke, his voice was barely a whisper.

"I swear it," he said. "I would do anything for you. I would tear apart the Covenant stone by stone if you asked. But I won't do anything you don't want me to do."

Relief and grief tangled together on Sahira's face.

"I'll stay away," he continued, the words seeming to cost him everything. "If that's what you want."

"What I *want* is impossible," she said bitterly, desperately wanting what he offered. "Even if we could run—if you knew someplace we could hide forever—then what would happen to my family's name?"

They held each other in the silver silence, both trembling now, the weight of tomorrow settling between them like a stone.

"I wish it were all different," she said.

"What?"

"Jaraan. Our community. The Covenant," she spat the last word, and she laughed out loud, an edge of hysteria entering the sound.

Sahira pulled back, feeling steadier now.

"So that's it then," she said, her voice hollow. "Tomorrow I'm his wife."

Syfir shook his head. "Tell me what I can do to make this better."

Sahira stood up straighter then, pulling her hands back and smoothing her kameez. She swallowed. "Give me what we'll never have again. I want… to live my entire life in this one night with you."

He looked into her eyes, considering her words. "Is that really what you want?" he asked softly.

She swallowed, her throat suddenly dry, and then took a deep breath, gathering her courage. "Yes. I want… tonight."

The air between them changed, grew heavier, charged with something ancient and electric. Her pulse quickened as she watched something shift in his expression.

His restraint was like a physical presence, his desire held carefully in check, waiting, and it made her burn inside with a want she'd never known she could feel.

Syfir swallowed hard. His voice was rough with desire, and yet his body showed his restraint. "Sahira, if we cross this line—"

"We can't go back," she finished, nodding. "I know."

Syfir closed the small distance between them, their arms at their sides, their bodies almost touching. She could feel the warmth radiating from him, could feel his heartbeat.

He looked down into her eyes as their breath mingled between them, warm against the night's cool air. He brought his lips closer to hers, and she could feel the promise of contact in the space between them.

Her eyes fluttered closed for just a moment before opening again to find him watching her with an intensity that made her breath catch. Then he reached his hands around her, his fingers finding the base of her long, loose braid.

Her eyes stayed locked on his as his fingers slowly unraveled her hair, working their way up strand by strand. She could feel each gentle tug, each careful movement as he freed her hair from its binding. It was almost unbearably intimate.

When he reached the nape of her neck, unraveling the very last part of her braid, she shivered, feeling the touch of his fingers against her neck. He let his fingers slide up into her hair, the newly freed waves spilling over them like water.

"Sahira, are you certain?" he asked again, holding perfectly still.

She bit her lip, the gesture drawing his gaze to her mouth for a heated moment.

Her cheeks warmed under his intense stare. "Yes." Her gaze lowered under the intensity of his.

"No—look at me," he murmured, his voice barely above a whisper as he drew her gaze back to his. "You have to say it," he said, his thumb brushing over her lower lip, tracing it with such tenderness it made her shiver. "I want to hear you say—"

"I want this," she whispered, her voice gaining strength even as it trembled, no longer hiding from the hunger that had been building since their first encounter. The words released something inside her, a dam breaking after years of containment. "I want... you."

The confession hung between them for a breathless moment.

And then his lips were on hers, claiming her mouth with a fierce hunger that matched her own. His arm wrapped around her waist while his other hand remained tangled in her hair, and he drew her against him with deliberate slowness, as if savoring every inch of contact. She pressed herself to him, her body melting into his warmth. She wrapped herself around him, into him, her own fingers tangling in his hair, pulling him closer, wanting more, wanting everything.

He pulled back from the kiss, both of them breathing uneven now, their foreheads touching as they shared the same heated air. His fingers found the knot at her hip—the base of the dupatta she had thrown across her shoulder. The simple touch made her breath hitch.

She brought her hands down to his, not to stop him, but to help him untie it, their fingers intertwining in the intimate task.

And then the knot was undone, the fabric falling away like a discarded barrier.

Her fingers followed his as he pulled up the fabric of her kameez, his hands moving on her skin slowly, deliberately, leaving paths of fire in their wake. One hand moved down and grazed her hips as he loosened her salwar. The garment fell to the ground easily, pooling at her feet, and she stepped forward, out of it, into him, closing the last whisper of distance between their bodies.

And then he was pulling her kameez up, and she was letting him slide it over her head, raising her arms to help him. The cool night air kissed her heated skin.

His eyes darkened as he stopped only long enough to take her in, his gaze traveling over her with an intensity that made her feel beautiful, desired, precious. The way he looked at her—like she was something sacred—made her heart race even faster.

And then his lips found hers again, more urgent now, as his hands moved over her hips, her waist, and then her own fingers were reaching for his kurta, tugging at it with unexpected boldness. He drew back just long enough to help her, pulling it up and over his head in one fluid motion, tossing it aside without care.

The moonlight revealed the blue markings that traced patterns across his chest and arms, pulsing now with heightened luminescence.

And then his lips returned to her, no longer content with just her mouth. He brushed kisses along her neck, her jaw, finding the sensitive hollow beneath her ear that made her gasp softly. Each point of contact was a revelation, awakening nerves she hadn't known existed.

He helped her down to the ground then, guiding her onto their soft collection of clothes on the forest floor.

She lay back, her hair spilling around her like water, remembering fleetingly the last time she lay back beside a man. But she pushed the memory away, knowing in her bones this was something entirely different. This was not him taking. This was her giving, willingly, joyfully, completely.

Fingertips brushed—first her arms, then her shoulders, then the delicate curve of her throat. She gazed at him as he slid his hand down her body, slowly, reverently, over her undergarments —each touch a question, each moment of contact a potential answer.

His hands moved curiously as her body arched toward him, and he committed every shiver he drew to his memory, learning her like a sacred text written in a language only he could read.

And beneath her skin, barely visible blue patterns responded to his touch, glowing brighter where his fingers went.

Then his mouth followed where his hands had been—the hollow of her throat, the curve of her shoulder, mapping constellations of sensation, leaving behind a trail of fire.

He seemed to understand when she could barely keep still from want, and removed her undergarments with a patience that was almost torturous, stretching out every moment.

His hands moved over her body again, slowly, deliberately, as if they had a lifetime.

"I've been thinking about touching you like this since the moment I saw you in the marketplace," Syfir murmured, his breath hot against her ear.

And then when his touch grew more intentional, and she instinctively guided his hand to help him find the rhythm of her desire.

"Of having my hands on you this way," he breathed, and his fingers found the center of her pleasure.

She gasped and arched against him, and bit her lower lip to keep from crying out, the sensation almost too exquisite to bear. His eyes locked with hers, hungrily drinking in every slight change in her expression.

"Don't hide what you feel from me," he whispered, his voice dark velvet. "I want to hear how you feel—I want to memorize every sound you make. I want all of you."

The command in his voice sent a shiver down her spine, his hunger for her desire, pushed her somewhere unknown. The sensation began as a whisper, then grew. The intensity built, and then his fingers grew more insistent.

And then something inside her began to unfurl, a storm building in intensity, and her body arched—a movement of pure, unfiltered sensation—and she cried out.

Time stilled. The forest grew silent. Stars flickered like distant witnesses. And the river pulsed in response, powerful waves rising and falling in perfect synchronization with her pleasure.

Syfir watched her traverse this boundary, enraptured by her pleasure, and aching with the intensity of his own desire.

His hands remained present, but peripheral, as Sahira exhaled, her body relaxing back onto the forest floor. She felt like she had just discovered a new language.

Her gaze refocused on Syfir's face glowing in the silver moonlight, and she wrapped her arms around his neck, drawing him nearer.

His lips brushed hers softly, and then he adjusted his body over hers, the question in his movement clear. In answer, she slid her hands up into his curls, and arched her body toward his.

But he waited. "You have to say it," he said, his body hovering above hers, the heat of him so close she could barely think. It wasn't permission he was after. "I have to hear it. Tell me you want this," he said, his voice dropping to a register that vibrated through her bones.

He wanted her to be complicit in this choice, an active participant in what they would do. The realization filled her with a burning desire. "Yes," she whispered immediately, decisively, her eyes on his. "I want this." She clutched his face, drawing him even closer. "I want you."

A low sound escaped him, half groan, half her name. "Say it again," he whispered, positioning himself at her entrance but not moving forward. His control frayed at the edges. His hands gripped her, his body tensed with the effort of waiting for the words.

"Please," she breathed, a word she'd spent a lifetime saying from obligation now transformed into a desperate demand. She arched against him urgently. "I want you, Syfir."

Something broke in his expression then, a rawness that matched her own need. "I've wanted you since before I knew your name," he confessed.

And then he entered her, and it was more than a physical joining. It was revelation, and it rewrote what she knew about herself. She felt her body's profound wisdom: expanding, contracting, remaking itself.

They moved together, their bodies locked in that timeless language of surging and retreating, their dance mimicking the river's rhythm. It was a rhythm older than the Covenant. Older than the town's carefully drawn boundaries. Older even than the Old World. The forest leaned in, cradling them.

"Look at me." His voice was rough with intensity. When her eyes met his, she saw something primal and possessive flash in their depths.

They were no longer separate entities. The river, Syfir, Sahira—they were a single breathing organism. Desire. Power. Inevitability.

And at the moment of his release, he groaned her name against her throat, his entire body shuddering above her.

She watched in wonder as his carefully maintained control shattered, his face transformed by pleasure she had given him, before he collapsed against her, saying her name again and again, like it was the only word that mattered, like it was a prayer that could stop time itself.

As THEIR BREATHING slowed and their bodies cooled, Syfir remained draped over Sahira, his forehead pressed to her chest, their connection unbroken. She traced lazy patterns through his hair and on his neck, marveling at how right it felt to have her body intwined with his.

"I think I've wanted you since before I knew what want really was," she admitted. She looked down to see him peering up at her, his chin on her chest.

"I would drown worlds for you," he confessed in response, pressing the words into her skin. It was not a threat but a terrible, vulnerable truth.

The words, his honesty, his devotion, all made her heart ache. She reached for his face, cradling his jaw in her hands, and he lifted himself up, gazing down at her.

She was exposed under his gaze, but felt no shame. Not for her nakedness, or for her want. The very awareness of this made something stir inside of her, made her bite her lip. Her body had its own memory now.

He saw and felt her reaction, and then repositioned himself so their faces were close. "I would do anything for you," he said earnestly. "Destroy anything. Build anything. Give anything. If you asked."

Tears pricked her eyes, but there was a now-familiar desire building inside her body again. "I know you would," she breathed. "But I'm asking something worse. I'm asking you to stay alive. And to do that you have to stay away," she said, swallowing.

She hadn't meant to say it like that, but it was the truth.

"I've never wanted something less than what you're asking of me." His voice was rough with heartache, but also with desire. His hand traced a slow path down her ribs, her waist, making her breath hitch.

"I've never wanted to ask something less," Sahira managed, though her voice wavered as his fingers found the place that made thought impossible. She tried to hold onto the conversation, but her body was already responding. "How can I want you again so soon?" she whispered, incredulous at her own hunger.

"Because this is what we are," he said, his voice low with his own want. His fingers moved, making her gasp. "It's what we're made for."

Her hips moved against his hand, chasing sensation. "Syfir—"

"I know," he murmured, bringing his lips to her throat tenderly. "I feel it too. Like I could never have enough of you." His voice broke slightly on the last words. "Never enough time, never enough touch, never enough—"

She silenced him with her mouth, pulling him down to her, and he groaned into the kiss like a man drowning.

AFTERWARD, they lay entwined, spent, their heartbeats gradually slowing to match the river's gentle rhythm.

The quiet between them felt different now. It was the quiet of two people who had crossed a threshold together and were only beginning to understand what lay on the other side.

"Can I ask something?" Sahira asked softly, feeling foolish.

"Anything," he said, his fingers gently moving a loose strand of hair from her face.

"Have you—I mean before now," she began.

His eyes softened. "Yes. But it was nothing like this."

She nodded, his honesty a comfort, and yet she felt a pang in her heart at the thought of him with someone else. A pang that solidified into an ache when she realized he would again someday be with another.

She swallowed, shoring up her courage. "Syfir, I've—also—" she swallowed again, unable to form the words in the correct order. "With Tavin."

"I know."

"It wasn't like this. I didn't feel—I didn't want—" her eyes were wide.

"I know," he said again, gently.

Sahira took in a shuddering breath as reality began to set in. Here she was admitting to having a past with Tavin, when Tavin was about to become her future. It was this night here with Syfir that would be her past. The thought made something clench in her stomach and she shook her head, trying to banish the thought.

Syfir watched her intently, as if he knew what was on her mind, and then found her hand, interlacing their fingers. "This night is just for us, remember?" he said, gazing into her eyes.

"It's strange," Sahira said some time later, her fingers brushing through the river silt, "how the body opens. For love. For birth. For death. It stretches... and then closes again."

"Like a snake," Syfir nodded, a smile at the edges of his mouth. "They can unhinge their jaws and swallow something ten times their size. And then slip back into stillness. The body knows how to make space for something larger than itself. And then—remake itself again."

"They fear it, I think," Sahira said, turning to lay on her back, one hand still interlaced in Syfir's, holding the other in front of her face, looking closely at the faint blue lines that shimmered under the surface. "That kind of power. The kind that bends but doesn't break."

Syfir leaned closer, his eyes on her body as moonlight spilled across her skin, silver and luminous. "In every story—Naga, Mami Wata—it's the serpent who guards the threshold. Who chooses what passes through."

"And the serpent," Sahira responded, drawing her hands from Syfir's, and looking closely at both her hands in the moon-light, "is often a she."

"No wonder they taught you to be still."

She looked at him, and saw his smile.

They lay together like that for some time, breathing in unison by the river. The water lapped gently at the shore, a rhythm as old as memory. Sahira felt transformed. A door had opened inside her, that she feared would never close again.

"Look," Syfir sat up, pointing toward the water and motioning for her to look. Where the river met the bank, waves formed and broke in rhythmic patterns as if dancing. The surface rippled in perfect concentric circles behind each wave, though no wind disturbed the air.

"What's happening?" she asked.

"The water responds to you," Syfir said, looking at her thoughtfully. "But now it's stronger. Your emotions... the river feels them now."

A tendril of water rose like a curious finger. It pulled away from the river, forming a sphere that glistened in the moonlight, and for a breathless moment, it held its impossible shape, before falling back into the current.

"I'm not doing that," Sahira whispered. Yet she felt a resonance deep in her blood, as if the water's movement matched some internal rhythm.

"Not consciously," Syfir agreed. He touched Sahira's palm, where the faint blue markings were glowing slightly as they watched the water. "Your mother could do this. Speak to the water without words."

Sahira's brows furrowed as she extended her hand, her eyes full of wonder. A perfect droplet rose from the river to meet her fingertips before falling back to the forest floor.

"The river knows who you are," Syfir said in awe. "Even if you're only beginning to."

The display should have frightened her. Instead, she felt a deep sense of coming home to herself.

~

Some time later, they sat together, knees pulled to their chests, watching the earliest hint of dawn beginning in the distance, knowing these were their final moments.

"I have to go back," she said, her eyes stinging.

"I suppose you do," he said, not turning to look at her.

"There's nothing else I can do." Tears blurred her vision.

She wanted to stay. To follow him into the forest and disappear like a ghost. But she could still hear her aunt's voice, her father's expectations, the weight of generations of women who had chosen duty over desire.

"You decide what happens next," he shrugged.

"There's nothing to decide," she said, the tears threatening to spill over. "I'll be married today."

"And so you believe you have no choice," he said, the words carrying a challenge beneath their gentleness.

She laughed bitterly. "What choice would I have?"

He reached for her hand then, and looked at her mehndi, his free hand gently tracing the swirls. Then he looked at her face again, his eyes sad. "There is always a choice, Zarouni girl."

*Choice.* It echoed in her mind like a stone dropped in still water, sending ripples through everything she thought she knew about her life, her duty, her future.

"Trust the river," he said softly, his thumb brushing away a tear that clung to her lashes.

She almost asked him what he meant, but then he leaned forward and kissed her, long, and deep, holding her face in his hand.

And then the kiss was over.

And Syfir stood slowly, his hand lingering against her face for one heartbeat before he stepped back.

"Remember," he said simply, then turned and melted into the shadows between the trees. The water rippled beside Sahira, as if the river itself mourned his leaving.

She pressed her fingers to her lips, still tender from his kisses, trying to memorize the sensation before it faded into just another impossible dream. She had swallowed the sun. And tomorrow she would be expected to be a shadow again.

She remained by the water's edge long after Syfir had gone, her tears falling quietly into whatever dawn awaited.

~

THE SUN still was not up when Sahira slipped back into her bedroom, river water still clinging to her salwar. A shadow moved in the corner, making her jump.

"You scared me," Sahira hissed as Leela emerged from beside the wardrobe.

"Shh," Leela hissed back, sliding into her cousin's bed. "Sahira. What were you thinking?" she whispered, her face demanding answers.

"I was just—I was getting air."

"Don't you understand what you're risking?" Leela's voice was urgent in the predawn darkness of Sahira's bedroom. "If they find out—"

"They won't," Sahira insisted, though the certainty felt hollow. She peeled off her damp salwar, hanging it on the hook in her closet. "I was just at the river, that's all."

"Three girls were taken for purification last month just for humming near the well," Leela persisted. "Maya's sister was forced to drink bitter herbs for a week because they found river flowers in her pocket. Kira was exiled just for asking questions about the Old World. And you—" She gestured at Sahira's hands, where faint blue lines pulsed beneath the skin. "You're changing in ways they can't ignore."

Sahira said nothing.

"I know what you're really doing when you go to the river," Leela's voice trembled. "You're meeting him. The Mehr'an musician."

She paused, letting the words sink in. "I saw you go, once. I didn't follow. But I knew."

When spoken aloud, the transgression sounded enormous. Sahira sat heavily on her bed, the reality of her actions penetrating the haze of awakening that had surrounded her these past weeks.

"Leela!" Sahira hissed. "Leela, it's bad enough that I—you can't—"

"If they catch you, it won't just be purification," Leela continued, her voice dropping even lower. "After Kaya… It will be exile. Or worse."

The words hung between them, awful in their implication.

Leela looked down. "Elder Nefret already seems like she's always looking at you."

"What do you mean?"

Leela shook her head. "I don't know. It's just something I've noticed." Her lip trembled. "Didi, if they decide you're corrupted, they'll take you away. I don't think they'd let you marry Tavin. What if they lock you up somewhere? Or what if I never see you again?" Tears were spilling down her cheeks then.

Cold fear replaced the lingering warmth of Syfir's presence.

Defying the Covenant meant risking everything—her safety, her father's position, her family's security, her very life.

Sahira looked at her hands and her arms, where the evidence of her transformation grew more visible each day.

She thought of her father, who had protected her since her mother's disappearance. Of Leela, whose questioning mind might be silenced if suspicion fell on their family. Of the younger girls who watched her with secret hope, seeing in her something they recognized in themselves.

Sahira looked at her cousin, and suddenly the truth clawed its way up her throat. "Leela, it's over," she whispered, the words scraping her throat raw.

"I don't believe you," her cousin said through tears.

"It's the truth," Sahira rasped. "But my heart will belong to him forever."

Leela's eyes grew wide. "Didi, are you in love with the musician?"

"I—" Sahira stopped, her heart fracturing. How could she explain that the river and Syfir had become inseparable in her mind? That awakening to one meant awakening to both? "It's the river," she said. "But he's... part of it now. Part of me."

"Your wedding is hours away," Leela whispered, tears spilling over. "Please, Didi. Just... promise me. Just get through this day."

Sahira reached forward, wrapping her arms around her cousin, feeling the weight of a promise she wasn't sure she could keep.

"I will," she whispered back.

# PART TWO
# FLOW

CHAPTER 11
# MARRIAGE

Sahira was still holding her cousin in an embrace as the sky bled from pale grey to the clean brightness of morning. She hadn't slept since she came back to her room, and had instead lain with her arms wrapped around Leela, knowing it was the last time.

It was a day for many endings.

Today, she would become Tavin Daraio's bride.

Leela stirred beside her. And then her eyes opened. "I had another dream," she whispered, her face inches from Sahira's. "About the river. About your mother."

Sahira stiffened. "Leela—"

"No, listen." Leela reached up, her voice urgent. "In the dream, she said she had a message for you. She said, *the river won't allow it*. I don't know what it means, but—."

"Stop." Sahira gripped her cousin tighter. "You can't talk like this anymore. Your first blood will come soon," she said, her voice low and fierce. "And then they'll treat you like a woman. And punish you like one. And I'll be gone, so you have to promise me."

Leela nodded, and folded herself deeper into the hug. "I promise."

THE WOMEN of her family and Tavin's arrived before dawn. They moved around Sahira in hushed tones, hands practiced, motions efficient.

No one met her eyes.

Tharima braided Sahira's hair herself, weaving in the green silk ribbon gifted by the Daraios. She took great care to position its intricate gold patterns so they faced outward, tying the end into a perfect bow. Then she tucked jasmine into the braid as a final touch, kissing Sahira's head in a rare gesture of affection.

The scent made Sahira think of her mother.

And suddenly, she couldn't breathe.

She was smothered—by the scent, the fabric, the hands.

She tried to press the feeling down, willing it to leave.

It wasn't working.

Her heart began to race.

She closed her eyes.

She thought of the river. Of Syfir. Of water rising to meet her hands.

Then she thought of the marriage ceremony just hours away, and tried, earnestly, to believe in its potential goodness.

This marriage would honor her father's name.

This marriage would mean fulfilling her duty.

This marriage would mean distance.

And distance meant safety for Syfir.

This was the life she had always expected.

It would be as if… nothing had ever happened.

As if Syfir had never happened. As if she had never heard the river's call.

Everything would return to how it was meant to be.

It was working.

Her breathing slowed. She kept her eyes shut, focusing on each breath as it came in, as it went back out.

# CHAPTER II

The women finished dressing and adorning her, then brought her to a mirror.

The deep red of her bridal lehenga reminded her of blood.

Fitting, for what felt like a death.

∽

THE RAAZAAN and Daraio families arrived at the temple. The women gathered in one waiting room, the men in another. After a few minutes, Sahira was led to a small antechamber for the final preparations.

Tradition dictated she spend an hour in silent meditation before the ceremony, contemplating her wifely duties and praying for strength to uphold the Covenant in her soon-to-be new home. No one was to speak to her.

Left alone at last, she sank onto the prayer cushion, and closed her eyes, seeking the stillness that had once come easily.

Ten breaths in, ten breaths out.

In an hour, she would stand in the temple courtyard, before the elders, before her father and aunt, before Leela, before Tavin, and say goodbye to whatever had begun awakening inside her. She would close the doors in her mind that led her to want things she was never meant to want.

She would let go of the pull toward the water.

She tried to focus on the stillness she would need to step into this new life.

Ten breaths in, ten breaths out.

But it wouldn't come.

Instead, she found something else. A current of memory, of yearning, of rebellion. Behind her closed lids, images flashed: Syfir by the river, his eyes full of unknowable truths. The blue markings swirling at her wrists. The river, swollen with monsoon rains, breaking free of its banks…

She opened her eyes with a gasp.

The small basin of water before her was no longer still.

Ripples moved across its surface, though nothing had touched it. As she watched, transfixed, the motion deepened: concentric circles, then flowing lines, then shapes. The movement seemed to be communicating something to her… *"There is still time to run."*

The door opened abruptly. Elder Nefret entered, her purple ceremonial robes rustling with significance, her face a mask of ritual solemnity.

"It is time," she announced. "The families await."

Sahira rose, smoothing her lehenga with trembling hands.

But the elder's eyes were fixed on the water bowl, and her expression sharpened.

"Did you disturb the water, child?" she asked, her voice deceptively mild.

"No, Elder," Sahira said truthfully. "It moved on its own."

Elder Nefret's eyes narrowed. She said nothing, but reached down and emptied the bowl, wiping it dry with the edge of her robe. Then she refilled it from a different pitcher.

The elder's knowing look sent ice through Sahira's veins.

"Water reflects the state of the soul," she said. "Stillness in the vessel, stillness in the heart. Disturbance in one… corruption in the other."

The words were familiar Covenant teachings. But now, they were a warning.

"The marriage ritual is not merely symbolic," she continued. "It is a binding. Of families, yes. But more importantly, of your nature to proper constraints. The Daraio household will provide structure for your… tendencies."

"My tendencies, Elder?" Sahira kept her voice deferential, despite the shiver running down her spine.

"The complications of your Zaroun blood," the elder said flatly. "Your father was never strong enough to control your mother." She shook her head. "You need someone who can control you."

The elder frowned. "Zarouni women have particular… irregularities. Your marriage to Tavin Daraio was approved for this very purpose: to bind your blood to steadier blood."

At Sahira's look of confusion, she continued. "Dafar Daraio's mother was a Zaroun woman—your grandmother's cousin. Surely you knew that?" The elder didn't wait for a response. "But Dafar's father managed his wife's irregularities with admirable firmness," she said, almost approvingly. "Far better than your own father did. The Daraio men are experienced in controlling their women. We expect Tavin to be more like his grandfather. To keep you in control."

Sahira's stomach turned.

Before she could respond, a temple acolyte appeared at the door, signaling that all was ready.

Elder Nefret turned, expression once more composed. "Come," she said.

THE COURTYARD HAD BEEN TRANSFORMED. Mirrored lanterns hung from ancient trees, their light glinting off shallow pools of rainwater that had gathered on the cobblestones. White flowers and ribbons adorned every surface, standing out in sharp contrast against gray stone.

The families had separated into their groups. Raazaans to the left, Daraios to the right, the Samiti of Elders in a semi-circle at the front.

Behind the ceremonial screen, Sahira's hands trembled despite the cooling cloths her aunt pressed into her palms.

The jasmine in her hair was suddenly suffocating. The ribbon itched where it touched her skin. And her lehenga clung like a second skin she couldn't shed.

"Still yourself," Tharima whispered. "You are about to restore our name."

Sahira barely heard her.

Through the carved lattice, she watched the crowd. The Samiti elders. Girls from stillness practice.

Tavin, in ceremonial white, standing at the altar, waiting beside Sahira's father.

Ten steps forward, and her life would be sealed.

"Daughter of Raazaan," Elder Nefret called. "Present yourself for binding."

Sahira didn't move. Or rather, she couldn't move.

"Step forward," Tharima hissed.

Sahira willed her body with all of her might to move.

And it did.

She found herself walking forward, despite the resistance in her bones, guided along by Tharima.

But with every step closer to the altar, a strange tingling sensation was growing in her wrists, her palms.

When Sahira reached the center of the courtyard, her aunt placed her hand in her father's, and then her father placed her hand in Tavin's, transferring her protection and authority to him.

Tavin squeezed her hand gently, and then Elder Nefret stepped forward to begin the binding ritual, her voice carrying across the courtyard with practiced authority.

"We gather to witness the joining of two bloodlines, two households, two futures bound as one," she announced. "The Covenant teaches that woman finds her strength in surrender, her purpose in service, her virtue in stillness. Today, Sahira Raazaan enters the protection of the Daraio household, accepting their guidance and authority."

She unspooled the gold thread to bind their hands.

"With this cord, we bind your futures," Elder Nefret announced.

The elder began to wrap the thread around Sahira and Tavin's hands.

Once.

Twice.

And then as the third loop was almost completed, Sahira

opened her mouth. She didn't mean to speak. But the word came anyway, barely audible.

"*No.*"

The lantern flames flickered briefly, though there was no wind. The courtyard stilled. Even the birds went quiet.

And then, the golden thread darkened.

Dampened.

The wind started again, but it blew the wrong way.

And then, the golden thread began to dissolve entirely, becoming nothing but water that dripped from their joined hands onto the stone floor.

Gasps erupted from those gathered close enough to see what had happened.

Leela's words echoed in Sahira's mind. *"The river won't allow it."*

Tavin's grip tightened. "What have you done?" he hissed through clenched teeth.

But Sahira could think of nothing to say.

Elder Nefret stared at their bare hands, at the growing puddle between them, as the crowd's silence gave way to murmurs that swelled into shocked exclamations, as people began to understand they'd witnessed a miracle. Or perhaps a curse.

Elder Nefret's face had gone pale. She stared at the water as if it had struck her. And then, she looked up at Sahira, her eyes blazing with fury.

"Follow me," she commanded, her voice cutting through the rising chaos. "Now."

# CHAPTER 12
# UNBOUND

"Listen to me," the Elder said in a sharp voice. "You will not discuss anything about the marriage ceremony with anyone." She looked from Sahira to Tavin. "No one was close enough. No one knows exactly what happened to the thread—they only know what they think they saw. I will inform the community that the two of you are married in the traditional manner, but that we had to cut the evening short due to a headache."

And with that, the elder backed out of the room, her eyes now boring into just Sahira's. "Do you understand?"

Sahira nodded, her heart pounding. She dared not look at Tavin.

Just as the elder slipped out of one door, the Daraios burst in from another, Tavin's mother leading the group.

"What is the meaning of this?" she demanded.

"I—" Sahira stammered.

"No, don't you lie to me," Neelma said, making her way toward Sahira, "tell me what you did to that thread."

"It was a trick of the light, Mother," Tavin interrupted smoothly.

Neelma paused, looking at her son suspiciously.

"Elder Nefret told us that a temple acolyte thought—" he paused to laugh. "If you can believe it, she thought our thread was somehow becoming water!"

Neelma's brows knit together. "It did look that way from where we were sitting," she said slowly.

Tavin laughed again, his eyes crinkling. "Can you imagine?"

A moment later, Sahira's father, her aunt, and her cousin came into the room.

"We came as soon as we could! Guards stopped us in the hallway!" Leela said, bursting in and throwing her arms around her cousin.

Sahira slowly returned the hug, trying to look reassuring.

"What's…" Leela began. She looked down and saw that Sahira's feet, and the bottom of her lehenga, were soaking wet.

Leela looked back up, and saw the briefest flash of terror in Sahira's eyes, followed by an almost imperceptible shake of her head.

But Tavin's mother saw.

Neelma Daraio had followed Leela's gaze to the bottom of Sahira's lehenga.

And then her eyes went to Sahira's hands, where a faint blue swirl was fading into invisibility.

But not before Neelma saw it. "I want this witch gone from my sight," she said in a barely controlled whisper.

This apparently crossed a line for Tahir Raazaan, who now glared at his oldest friend.

Dafar ignored Tahir, and instead turned to Neelma. "My dear, let us leave the newly wedded pair a few minutes." He offered a smile to Tavin and Sahira—a smile that wavered only slightly.

But Neelma shook her head as she backed away from her husband. "Oh, no," she said, crossing her arms. "There is no wedded pair. My son is unmarried. This ceremony was incomplete, and I will not let this—this—"

"Dafar, control your woman!" Tahir's fury was barely

contained, in the first and perhaps only display of defense Sahira had ever witnessed from her father.

Dafar's eyes narrowed at his old friend now.

But he turned to his wife. "Let us leave now. I am certain they will sort this out, and we will have a better sense of things by evening," he said coolly.

He nodded to Tavin as he turned to leave. "Congratulations," he added before escorting a seething Neelma from the room.

Sahira couldn't speak. She glanced over to her father as he reached up and pinched the bridge of his nose, exhaling slowly. Tharima's face was turned away in a look of forced calm.

"I think it would be best if we took Sahira… to my home," Tahir managed. "Just for now, while we all rest up."

"I agree," Tavin said, too brightly. "Best to have a new bride rested. I'll come see her in the morning," he added.

At this, Tahir's face brightened. "Indeed," he said with a nod. "Come, Sahira," he added in a more brusque voice. "Let us get you—" he paused, as if weighing something. He settled on "—to your father's home."

Sahira nodded, and glanced over at Tavin.

And then she silently followed her father, aunt, and cousin out.

Tahir Raazaan locked Sahira in her room.

No one said anything to her. No one asked her anything.

By afternoon, a heavy downpour had begun and rain pounded against her window in great sheets of water that blocked everything from view.

She lay on her bed, and the memory of the golden thread dissolving played over and over in her mind.

She heard movement outside her bedroom door—Leela's footsteps—and then the muffled sound of Tharima's voice; Leela's insisting on something; the sound of footsteps retreating.

No one came to her room.

The entire evening went by with the downpour outside drowning out the world, leaving Sahira replaying the day over and over.

She stared at the water basin in the corner.

Extending her hand, she willed the water to rise. A thin, weak column wavered upward.

She could control it deliberately now.

OVER THE FOLLOWING DAYS, the Raazaan house fell into a strange rhythm. Tharima kept up the pretense, speaking of household duties as if Sahira were a new bride, simply resting, inexplicably, in her father's home.

Yet nothing was normal.

Leela was kept apart from her, forbidden to talk with her. Tahir Raazaan no longer acknowledged his daughter at all.

Tavin continued his visits, bringing gifts and maintaining a strange fiction that they were married, despite living apart.

And his eyes had grown watchful. Suspicious.

During those visits, Sahira drifted. Her hands moved through the expected motions, accepting gifts, offering polite responses.

But her mind wandered back to the river.

To Syfir. To the strange current that now pulsed beneath her skin.

Tavin noticed. Of course he noticed.

His questions grew more pointed. "You seem… different," he'd say, the word balanced carefully between observation and accusation.

And Sahira's body was changing faster.

Water now beaded on her skin without cause.

The swirls on her arms began to appear and disappear without warning, regardless of her moods or proximity to the river.

And every night, the river called to her with rising urgency.

~

ON THE EIGHTH DAY, when Tavin came to speak with her again, it was with an urgency he had not shown before.

"Sahira, you have to tell me what's happened to you," he now pleaded.

"I don't know what you mean," Sahira said flatly. "Nothing's happened."

"Sahira, I know what you've been doing. I've been watching you," he said, his voice cracking. "Once, before the marriage… I followed you. To the river."

Sahira looked at him sharply. "What do you—"

"I saw you looking at it," he said, desperation in his face. "Like it was alive. Like it could talk to you."

"I don't know what you're talking about," she said dully.

"If you'd just explain," Tavin continued. "If you'd just tell me what's happening, I could help you. But if you won't talk to me, how can I help you?"

"I don't know what you—" she began again.

"Sahira!" He grabbed her shoulders. "Just tell me what's happening! If you tell me, I'll understand. Maybe it's a phase, a confusion, I don't know. But we can fix it."

Sahira stared at him, suddenly struck by how little she wanted to do what he asked. How little she cared now to protect his feelings.

"I just want things to go back to how they're meant to be," he said, his eyes shining with something like grief. "I just want *you* to go back to who you're meant to be."

She studied his face. There was real concern there. And the quiet conviction that he was saving her from herself.

"This ends now," he said, gentle. Mournful. "Before it destroys everything. Please, Sahira. This is it."

She understood then. This was her final chance to return to the life she was supposed to want.

Or to say nothing, and keep walking the path already opening beneath her feet. A path that could not end somewhere good.

She said nothing.

And Tavin hung his head, and turned and walked away.

And as he left, Sahira knew she had just sealed both their fates.

WHILE SAHIRA SAT by her window that same evening, watching rain streak the glass, Tavin paced his family's courtyard.

He had tried reasoning. He had tried patience.

Now only one option remained. One that made his stomach clench with self-loathing, even as he convinced himself it was necessary.

That night, he made his way to the temple, every step heavier than the last.

Elder Nefret's private chambers were austere, befitting an elder who had dedicated their life to the Covenant.

He found her sitting alone, reviewing ancient texts by lamplight. Yellowed scrolls were spread across her desk.

"I need your help," Tavin said without greeting. His voice sounded strange to his own ears.

Elder Nefret looked up, eyes calculating. "What troubles the son of Dafar Daraio at this hour?" She sat up straighter. Tavin caught the words *Purification Archives* on the scroll she moved aside. "Is your wife still not living in your home?"

"Sahira…" The name felt wrong to speak aloud. "Before our marriage, she… she was speaking with the river."

"How certain are you?" Her tone was cool.

"Certain. I've been… following her." He swallowed hard. "I

saw her at the river's edge. The water." He hesitated. "It moved. Not naturally. It responded to her."

Elder Nefret leaned forward slightly, her interest sharpening. "I see. Anything more?"

"I... yes. Some time ago, I saw her with that Mehr'an musician." The humiliation burned his face. "They were... intimate."

Elder Nefret's eyes narrowed. "You say your betrothed has been corrupted not just by river sickness, but by a Mehr'an man?" she asked, each word precise and dangerous.

Tavin nodded, shame rising like bile in his throat. "She was supposed to be my wife. I tried to guide her, protect her. But she's gone too far."

"These are serious accusations, Tavin Daraio," Elder Nefret said, sitting back in her chair as she studied his face for any sign of uncertainty.

"I know what I saw," Tavin said flatly.

Elder Nefret was quiet. Her fingers tapped the wood of her desk. "This threatens everything we've built," she said finally. "You understand cleansing her will require significant measures?"

"Whatever it takes," Tavin said immediately.

"And afterward? A purified girl is not the same as an untainted one. Your family's reputation—"

The question caught him off-guard. He had expected judgment, even absolution—but not a negotiation.

"I want her back," he said, before he could think better of it. "Before she's lost completely." He faltered, then firmed his voice. "I want her cleansed. Purified. Whatever it takes."

"Even if it means ritual purification? Public correction?" Her voice dropped. "You understand what that entails?"

He didn't. Not fully. But he nodded.

"You'll take her back even after public shame?"

"If the shame is for river corruption, yes. Not... not anything about... the man." He cleared his throat. "Her mother's legacy isn't her fault. Once she's purified, it will be like nothing happened."

"Still," Elder Nefret mused, "the humiliation would be... difficult for your family to overcome. Your father's position in the Samiti—"

"The marriage contract—" Tavin swallowed hard. "My father will demand that you dissolve it. As soon as possible."

He looked away, pained. "But after the purification, once she's clean again..." He looked up, desperation naked in his eyes. "She could still be redeemed. We could still have a future."

Elder Nefret's expression remained unreadable. "You would take her back? Even after public shame?"

"The shame isn't her fault," he said fiercely. "It's the corruption. Once that's gone—"

"Once that's gone," Elder Nefret finished softly, "she'll thank you for saving her. Perhaps the town would as well."

Even as he spoke, doubt crept into his voice. *Would his father ever agree to such an arrangement? Would the community accept Sahira back, even if cleansed?*

Elder Nefret's lips curved into a tight smile. "It's a good plan," she said coolly. "And better than losing her to another man, to be certain."

At that, Tavin flinched. He thought of Sahira with the Mehr'an musician. Of their bodies entwined by the river's edge, and felt a new wave of humiliation run through his core.

"Never mind that now," Elder Nefret said, smoothing her robes as she rose. "We will purify her."

"And the Mehr'an man?" Tavin asked, unable to keep the edge from his voice.

"I will deal with him personally," Elder Nefret replied. "The town has ways of dealing with those who corrupt our daughters."

As Tavin left the temple, he told himself he had done the right thing—the only thing. That they could still have the future they had been promised since childhood. That his family would even accept her after some time. That Sahira would thank him one day, once she was cleansed of the river's corruption.

Sahira sat in the central room, absently folding fabric, her eyes fixed on some distant point. Across the room from her, still forbidden from speaking to her, Leela practiced her embroidery, occasionally glancing up at her cousin with worried eyes.

The commotion at their front door barely registered until Tharima appeared in the doorway, a crate trembling in her hands. "A servant from the Daraio household delivered this."

Sahira's father, who sat nearby but ignored Sahira's presence, looked up from his morning market report. "What is it?"

She set the crate down on the table and opened it, revealing a box of jewelry the Raazaans had gifted the Daraios before the marriage, and a long scroll.

Tahir set down his chai and extended his hand. "Give it here."

Tharima surrendered the scroll, and Tahir untied and unfurled the scroll, his eyes narrowing as he read. He glanced at his daughter, then his sister, before placing the scroll on the table.

The marriage contract with the Daraio family—painstakingly negotiated over years—lay unfurled like a dead thing, with one word stamped across the bottom:

*Annulled.*

"What—" Tharima moved closer to the table. "Oh." Her face contorted as she took in the scroll's contents.

Her father stood and moved to the window, his back to them all.

"What's happening?" Leela whispered, but Sahira could only shake her head slightly.

"Quiet, girl," Tharima snapped, silencing her daughter with a sharp glance.

Tahir did not turn around as he spoke, his voice dangerously quiet. "How could you bring this shame upon us?"

Sahira remained silent, unable to find words. Leela moved closer to her, a small act of defiance that didn't go unnoticed by her mother, who frowned deeply.

"Nearly twenty years I've protected you. Provided for you." He turned, his eyes meeting hers. "Secured you a husband from the finest family."

"I can't marry him," Sahira whispered.

Tahir closed his eyes. "Take her to her room," he said quietly to his sister. "I don't want to look at her anymore."

Tharima nodded and stood.

And then Tahir spoke again. "She is dead to me."

Leela started to protest, but her mother gripped her shoulder firmly, pulling her away from Sahira.

"Leela, you go to your room as well," Tharima ordered.

"But—"

"Now!"

With a last anguished look at Sahira, Leela reluctantly obeyed. Tharima then led Sahira away.

FROM HER ROOM, Sahira could hear raised voices. She crept to her door, cracking it open just wide enough to slip into the hallway, where she nearly collided with Leela, who had also emerged to eavesdrop.

Her cousin wrapped her arms around her in the tightest hug she could. Sahira held her in the embrace as long as she could before releasing her to move closer to the door of the central room.

"Returned gifts!" her father seethed. "As if we are beggars to be pitied!"

Something crashed against a wall.

The girls pressed themselves against the corridor wall.

Through the shadows, they glimpsed Tahir pacing, his usually composed face flushed with humiliation and rage.

"The bangle," he froze. "Where is it? That gold bangle Tavin put on her. I want it returned immediately."

Sahira's fingers moved instinctively to her wrist, still sore where the metal circled tightly. Leela's eyes widened, noticing the angry red marks where the gold had bitten into her cousin's skin.

"I'll fetch her," Tharima sighed.

Before Sahira and Leela could slip back into their rooms, Tharima was already in the hall.

"Leela. Back to your room. Now." Her voice was sharp.

Then, in a surprisingly gentle tone: "Sahira. Come. Your father wishes to speak with you."

Leela squeezed Sahira's arm before retreating into her room with one last glance.

Sahira followed her aunt slowly into the central room, where she kept her gaze lowered, unable to meet her father's eyes.

"The bangle," he said, his voice tight with controlled rage. "Remove it."

"I—I can't, Baba," Sahira said, extending her arm. "It was loose during the ceremony, but now..." She tugged at it, wincing. "It's like it's grown smaller."

"More strangeness," he muttered, releasing her wrist in disgust. "Keep the cursed thing, then. What's one more shame heaped on this house?"

"Tahir," Tharima began, her voice unusually soft. "Perhaps—"

"Enough." He cut her off with a raised hand. Then, to Sahira, without looking at her: "Go to your room. Stay there until I decide what's to be done with you."

Her father did not speak to her again.

As Sahira turned, Leela was already in the hallway. She pulled Sahira into her room before she could return to her own.

They sat on Leela's bed in silence, listening to Tahir's final bitter words echo down the corridor.

"My humiliation is complete. My daughter rejected by the Daraios. Corrupted by the river. And still wearing their gold." His voice cracked. "How much more can one man bear before he breaks?"

Sahira didn't meet her cousin's eyes, and instead examined the bangle.

Whatever the reason, it remained, fixed to her wrist. A physical reminder of the life she was leaving behind, and the path that now waited ahead.

"I don't think the bangle shrunk," Leela whispered, touching it cautiously. "I think… the river doesn't want you to take it off yet."

Sahira turned to her cousin in surprise. For a breathless moment, something passed between them. A recognition.

And though she should have seen it sooner, Sahira began to understand only now that Leela, too, might hear the river.

AT THE SAME time the Raazaans received the annulment scroll from the Daraios, Elder Nefret was announcing new protocols in a closed Samiti meeting: household inspections would begin immediately, conducted without warning, with a focus on homes with unmarried daughters.

Other girls were changing.

"The corruption spreads quickly," Elder Nefret declared. "Those showing signs must be identified—and corrected— before they infect others."

By that same night, the Samiti had begun house-to-house searches. Word of the failed wedding had spread, emboldening the elders to act.

Three girls were taken from the eastern quarter before dawn, their mothers silenced with threats against younger siblings.

And then they came for Kaya Muktan.

Kaya who had already faced public humiliation, and who now bore faint blue patterns blooming across her palms, awoke to strange rustling at the front door before the guards entered.

No one shouted or resisted. There was only the quiet efficiency of power long unchallenged.

When the guards emerged from the Muktan home, Kaya was between them, her nightdress clinging to her body, soaked through with rain, or sweat, or both. Blue markings shimmered on her trembling hands.

Her mother stood in the doorway, tears sliding silently down her cheeks, one arm wrapped tightly around Kaya's younger sister, who struggled and screamed.

Her father didn't watch. He turned and went back into his room.

Kaya was dragged into the street.

And then she was beaten.

# CHAPTER 13
# PURIFICATION

Three days after the annulled marriage contract arrived, the summons came.

Sahira answered the door.

The folded parchment was delivered by one of the temple acolytes, a woman barely older than Sahira herself.

As Sahira unfolded it, it felt unnaturally heavy in her hands.

*"Sahira Raazaan is commanded to present herself at the temple courtyard by midday for a ceremony of purification."*

PURIFICATION.

No explanation was given. They didn't need to name a crime; there were too many now to choose from.

She felt no fear. She felt no panic. She felt no anger.

The scroll was steady in her hand as she stepped into the main room and handed it to her father.

He looked at it, and for a moment said nothing. Then he stood, suddenly unsteady, and walked out of the room without a word.

Sahira watched him go.

And still, she felt nothing.

~

A FEW HOURS LATER, Sahira fastened the simplest white kameez she owned.

No color or adornment, except the bridal mehndi, still vivid on her hands.

She combed her hair, and then began weaving it into a braid, and then paused.

Water was forming on her skin.

Tiny droplets, rising from nowhere, beading along her arms. They traced delicate, shifting patterns from her wrists to her shoulders, before vanishing.

And in their place, faint blue marks lingered, pulsing once before fading.

~

SAHIRA and her family made their way to the temple courtyard in silence. It was already packed when they arrived.

Elder Nefret stood at the center, flanked by the Samiti matriarchs and Elder Varden, all of their faces carved into masks of judgment.

Instead of only women and girls, there were men present—Samiti members, family patriarchs, even young men. Their presence was unprecedented, sending murmurs of fear through the crowd.

So Sahira would be stripped, berated, and branded, before the women, and also before the eyes of every man in Jaraan.

Their gaze was to be part of her punishment.

"The corruption of one woman threatens all families," Elder Nefret announced as Sahira was escorted into the center. "And today, fathers and future husbands must bear witness the consequences of failed guardianship."

Elder Nefret turned to her. "Arms out, please."

Sahira complied. The elder's fingers moved with slow deliberation over her shoulders, arms, and wrists, as if cataloging her body for disassembly.

"Name," the elder demanded, though everyone already knew.

"Sahira Raazaan," she replied, voice flat but steady as she tried to guess what crime they would name for her presence on this stage.

Would they name the binding marriage thread that became water? Did they know about Syfir? Would they name him? Did they know of what happened in the shed? Would they name Tavin?

Would they name the river?

"Sahira Raazaan stands today in need of Purification from river corruption."

So just the river then.

Whispers surged through the crowd—"like her mother," "the river's taken her," "Ameera's daughter"—until Elder Nefret silenced them with a raised hand.

She motioned to two acolytes, who rushed forward with heads bowed. "Remove her outer garments."

They stripped her methodically, each layer removed a stripping away of identity. Her dupatta. Her salwar. Her kameez. Each piece was folded and taken away.

They left her in only her undergarments, the bridal mehndi still visible on her hands, and the gold bangle that refused to leave her wrist.

She looked out at the gathered crowd and resisted the urge to wrap her arms around herself, the urge to hide.

Faces Sahira had known her entire life stared back, their expressions flickering between pity, revulsion, and morbid fascination. She saw them all, and then fixed her gaze beyond the courtyard. Beyond the temple gates.

Eastward, toward the river.

The Purification began.

Elder Nefret approached Sahira with a vial of cloudy liquid.

"We must purge the river corruption from this daughter," she announced, holding it high. "This blessed water comes from deep within the temple. It is infused with the venom of snakes, whose poison is stronger than the poison of the river. With this tincture, we will cleanse her."

Elder Nefret paused before her. "Repeat after me: I will embrace stillness."

Sahira repeated it, meeting the elder's eyes defiantly.

"The modest woman keeps her eyes lowered," the elder whispered.

Sahira's eyes did not waver.

The elder raised a brow, and tilted Sahira's chin up. "Open your mouth, child."

Sahira did as she was told, and tried not to choke as the liquid was poured down her throat.

The liquid burned so badly that Sahira had to fight the urge to scream.

It tasted like death.

It also tasted like power.

As it burned its way down her throat and down into her belly, she felt something uncoiling inside of her. As though something in her blood recognized the venom, not as a threat.

As kin.

And then as if called forward by the venom, water began to rise on her skin.

Sahira shuddered as the water beaded at her collarbone and began streaking down her arms. The thin white fabric of her undergarments clung to her like a second skin now.

Sahira barely noticed as several men in the crowd leaned forward, their eyes fixed on her form as the fabric turned increasingly transparent with each drop of water that emerged from her skin.

And then, as quickly as it had started, the shuddering subsided. The water stopped coming, and her eyes were able to refocus.

"Good," Elder Nefret announced approvingly. "It appears that the venom has begun to destroy the corruption already."

Sahira's eyes swept the crowd.

Her father stood with his sister, his gaze locked on a point on the ground. Her aunt's face was unreadable. Leela stood between them both, visibly shaking.

Near the front, stood the Daraio family. Tavin stood pale-faced and rigid, his jaw clenched, his eyes averted, unwilling to bear witness. His father elbowed him sharply and Tavin nodded, but did not look up.

Beside them, Sahira noticed with distant confusion, stood a girl she recognized—the same girl who had shifted during stillness practice, who had been corrected for clumsiness: Malsi Sharma. Flanked by her parents, wide-eyed.

Understanding hit like cold water. They were already preparing Tavin's next match, to twelve-year-old Malsi.

Before Sahira could think about it further, Elder Nefret's commanding voice drove all other thoughts away.

"Now, it is time to exorcize the corruption that has taken hold of this Covenant daughter." She nodded to the acolytes, who came forward again, with a brazier of glowing coals, the second with the branding iron.

The iron gleamed, indifferent and institutional.

Elder Nefret placed it into the fire, the hiss of metal meeting heat sharp in the silence.

And just then, a distant rumble echoed from the east.

From the direction of the river.

Several members of the Samiti shifted uneasily, glancing toward the sound.

Elder Nefret retrieved the iron from the brazier, glowing red, and raised her voice over the murmurs. "We will not be deterred by natural disturbances."

The smell of heated metal stung Sahira's nose.

"Let us rid this daughter of her corruption. Let this be a reminder of what it means to be a Covenant daughter," Elder Nefret proclaimed.

Acolytes seized Sahira's arms as she fixed her eyes on a rooftop in the distance and clenched her teeth.

And then the rumbling grew louder.

Someone pointed east, across the town square, and murmuring broke out in the crowd.

"The river," someone cried, "look at the river!"

"Silence!" Elder Nefret shouted over the rising commotion. "Let this be a lesson to all!"

Then, Sahira felt the heat of the iron close to her shoulder, and tasted metallic fear in her mouth.

She heard a scream—Leela—and clenched her eyes shut, as if to shut out her voice, and the coming pain, as Elder Nefret pressed the branding iron to Sahira's shoulder with a sickening sizzle.

But no pain came.

Sahira's eyes opened, and she turned to see Elder Nefret standing frozen, her eyes were wide and full of horror.

The iron hovered inches from Sahira's skin.

And water—warm, clear—welled from Sahira's shoulder.

Where there should have been seared flesh, only steam and moisture rose.

And then, chaos erupted.

A shout erupted from the market, from just outside the court-yard. "The stalls! The river's taking the stalls!"

Through the courtyard gates, vendors were seen scrambling as muddy water surged into the lower square. Baskets, crates, and cloth were carried away in the current.

In the distance, the Bakki had turned from its usual blue-green to a roiling, churning brown, and had swollen beyond its banks.

The branding iron fell from Nefret's hand, clattering to the stone.

Sahira looked down. Water streamed from her wrists, pooling into the courtyard dust.

The acolytes released Sahira's arms and backed away, their faces mirroring Elder Nefret's horror.

"What have we awakened?" Elder Nefret whispered.

Sahira felt the words rising within her, surging from a place beyond reason, beyond thought, beyond self.

"The river flows in my blood," she said, her voice coming from a place deep inside herself. "You cannot burn away the river."

Elder Nefret stared at her in horror.

"Get to higher ground!" someone yelled.

Half the congregation scattered, sprinting toward shops and homes as water crept up the courtyard steps. Muddy water lapped at the temple stones. Families ran through the square, knee-deep in flood.

"Guards!" Elder Nefret shrieked, backing away. "Take her!"

Two guards surged forward and seized Sahira—too late to undo everything that had been seen. As they dragged her toward the temple's inner chambers, the river surged behind her.

The river had risen for her. And even those who refused to listen could no longer deny what they had witnessed.

# CHAPTER 14
# ESCAPE

The inner sanctum of the temple, a cluster of rooms usually used for administrative records, became Sahira's temporary holding cell as the emergency Samiti convened.

Half the elders called for execution. The rest, shaken by the flood, by the failed branding, and whispers of Old magic protecting Sahira, urged caution.

It was Tavin Daraio who broke the stalemate. "She was purified," he reminded Elder Nefret quietly. "The ritual was performed. After some time passes, I still intend to accept her as my wife."

Elder Nefret's eyes narrowed. But the solution was politically convenient, and it made the Samiti look deliberate, not divided. She changed her vote.

By nightfall, the decision was sealed: Sahira would return to her father's home under strict confinement. The temple guards would install iron bars on her windows. She was not to leave her room.

The doors to the sanctum were opened.

It was release, but not freedom. Home, but under guard.

Temple guards escorted Sahira and her family through the

aftermath of the flood: collapsed stalls, vendors picking through waterlogged goods, the stench of rot in the air.

Her father's voice was flat as he turned the key in her bedroom lock. "Try not to cause any further problems while we await what is to be done with you."

By night, locked in her room, Sahira pulled open her window and pressed her forehead to the iron bars that caged her.

The air smelled of river silt.

"Tell me what to do," she whispered into the wind.

And the answer came. Not in words, but it came, passing from river to air to blood, filling her with a certainty that settled in her bones.

She had to leave.

She packed quickly: spare cloth, a flask of water, the blue river token from Syfir, her mother's letter.

At the window, her fingers grazed the iron bars, and they began to weep rust. By dawn, they would crumble.

She lay down fully clothed, satchel tucked to her chest, eyes fixed on the bars as rust flaked quietly to the sill.

And by first light, when she slipped from her bed to touch them, they gave way.

By the time Tahir checked her room, Sahira would be gone.

She slipped from her father's house into the early gray light, pulling a dupatta over her head, cloaking herself in its shadow.

She paused to look back one final time. The courtyard where Tharima had taught her to embroider. Her room, where she and Leela whispered stories late into the night.

All of it belonged to a girl who no longer existed.

She pulled the door closed with careful silence and stepped into a world that held no place for her yet.

But before she could reach the far side of the hedges, a voice stopped her.

"Didi?"

She turned. Leela stood barefoot in the dew-wet grass, clutching a small bundle wrapped in red-checked cloth.

"You weren't even going to say goodbye?"

Sahira rushed forward and pulled her into a fierce embrace.

They held each other tightly, the weight of everything they couldn't say pressing between them.

When they parted, Leela pressed the bundle into Sahira's hands. "Biscuits and dried fruit. I told Maru I wanted some. I think he knew they weren't for me." Leela sniffled, making Sahira's heart lurch.

Sahira looked down at the red-checked cloth and pressed the bundle to her chest, and then looked back at her cousin.

"My first blood came," Leela said softly. "Stillness practice starts tomorrow."

The words struck Sahira like thunder. She pulled Leela back into her arms.

Then she pulled back just enough to look her in the eye. "Listen to the elders," she said, voice breaking. "Don't make noise. They'll treat you like a woman now."

Leela nodded, tears running freely down her face.

Sahira tucked a strand of hair behind her ear. "Don't look for me," she whispered.

Leela wiped her cheeks and stood up straighter. "Please be safe."

Sahira studied her face one last time, memorizing every freckle, every loose strand around her cousin's face, even the look of her tears on her cheeks.

Then she turned.

She slipped through the hedge and out through the loose fencepost. She did not look back.

THE MARKET SQUARE LAY QUIET, stalls still shuttered against the early morning chill. One merchant scrubbed the outside of his booth, muttering about how the Covenant had failed to hold back the flood.

Sahira pulled her dupatta lower and kept walking.

The morning market would not begin for hours, but Sahira went to the fabric merchant's stall, where Tavin had bought her ribbon—and she hoped against hope that the fabric merchant's allegiance would be to coin before Covenant.

The gold bangle from Tavin still squeezed her wrist. She had tried for days to remove it, twisting and pulling this way and that, but the bangle had remained stubbornly in place, as if determined to maintain Tavin's claim upon her.

Leela's words from weeks ago echoed in her mind: *"I think the river doesn't want you to take it off yet."*

The river had been saving this resource, for when she truly needed it.

Now it was time.

The stall's front counter was still shrouded in darkness, the protective curtains drawn, but Sahira detected movement inside. She rapped softly at the side door, her knuckles barely grazing the wood.

"Who disturbs Karam so early? Come back after sunrise," came the fabric merchant's voice through the slats.

Sahira knocked again, more insistently this time. She couldn't afford to wait.

"I have gold," Sahira said quietly.

The door cracked open and the woman's eyes widened. "The shamed daughter of Tahir Raazaan? What could you possibly—" She stopped. Sahira had already extended her arm.

The bangle caught the weak morning light, emeralds flashing like trapped stars against the gold band. Sahira's skin beneath was chafed, raw, crusted with dried blood.

Karam drew in a sharp breath. "That piece is recognizable," she said carefully, glancing around. "Your… the Daraio family may want it back."

"What is the bangle worth?" Sahira asked bluntly.

Karam's weathered fingers reached out, tilting Sahira's wrist to better examine the bangle in the weak light. "Fifty coin for the gold. Seventy-five for the stones alone. But Karam cannot sell this anywhere. Such a distinctive piece would be recognized anywhere in the valley. "

"I don't want coin," Sahira said. "I need supplies. And silence."

Understanding flashed across Karam's features, and she held out her hand for the bangle.

Sahira hesitated. "I can't remove it." She showed the bloodied skin from her failed efforts. "I've tried."

Karam studied her for a long moment, something softening in her face. Then she nodded. "Wait here."

She disappeared into the stall and returned with a bolt cropper, its dull metal jaws already open. "Hold still. This may pinch."

The cold metal slid between the bangle and skin. Sahira braced.

And then came the snap, like a bone breaking.

For a moment, nothing happened.

And then, as if moving through honey, the bangle dropped to the dirt, landing with a dull thud.

Sahira stared down at it. Just broken metal in the dirt.

Karam stooped to retrieve the gold and tucked it into her pocket. "Follow me."

Inside, she handed Sahira a canvas bundle. "Water-skin, food." Then thick-soled boots. "Better than those slippers." She disappeared again, then returned with a blue-and-brown shawl embroidered in silver.

"It can be used on either side," she explained. "Green on one side, brown on the other. Useful for being unseen, if that is your need."

Sahira's throat tightened. It was more than she'd hoped for. "Why help me so well?"

The woman's expression hardened. "Karam's sister heard the river's call, three decades past. Karam tried to help her escape. They caught us at the eastern boundary." She held out her arm and revealed an old, angry scar on her forearm.

She didn't finish the story.

"Your gold might buy Karam passage to another place. Sometimes, coin and salvation walk the same road."

Sahira swallowed. Nodded.

"You were never here," Karam added. "But they may know. Gold leaves a trail."

"Melt it down," Sahira said softly. "Make something new from what was meant to bind me."

The fabric merchant's weathered face creased into a grin. "Perhaps I will."

Sahira made her way straight to the river's edge, and found… nothing. No trace that anyone had ever been there.

She waited until her legs stiffened from crouching in the reeds and the sun began to sink. Still, he didn't come.

So she followed the river south, toward the place of pale stones where the current ran thin.

She pulled off her shoes without thinking, crossed where the water barely kissed her calves, and didn't stop.

She walked until the light was gone, until the moon tracked across the sky, until her heart pounded with worry.

At least, she came to a clearing—and froze.

An abandoned Mehr'an settlement.

Trampled cooking fires. Scattered belongings. Bootprints in the soft earth from temple guards.

Only an elderly woman remained, collapsed beside an overturned basket, her sari streaked with blood.

Sahira rushed forward. "Are you alright?" The question came out before she could stop it. The woman was dying.

The woman stirred, barely lifting her head. "I know you," she whispered.

"Shhh," Sahira said, offering water from her satchel. The woman took a sip, then closed her eyes.

"What happened?" Sahira whispered. "Where is everyone?"

"The guards…" the woman wheezed weakly, "they came… said one of ours was… corrupting a Covenant daughter by the river…"

Sahira's heart stopped. "Where's Syfir?"

The woman's gaze sharpened briefly as it landed on Sahira. "Covenant daughter… they meant you, didn't they?"

Sahira nodded, shame burning her throat.

The woman's eyes blinked shut. "They beat him… and his mother. She's alright. But the boy…" Her voice faded. "Beat him… badly… Our people carried him… south… to heal. If the river wills it…"

Panic twisted in Sahira's stomach and rose in her throat. She forced it down. "Why are you still here?" Sahira asked, trying to focus on the woman and not her rising fear.

"Gave us till sundown to scatter," the woman rasped. "Beat me… I was too slow."

Sahira tried to offer the woman more water, but the woman turned away. She knelt beside her, helpless.

The woman's hand shot out and gripped Sahira's wrist. "Listen… to me," she gasped. "Go south… find the Mehr'an."

Sahira felt sick. For this old woman, who was dying before her. Sick for Syfir's mother. Sick for Syfir.

She saw him in her mind—collapsed by the water's edge, his smirk gone, blood in the reeds.

She held the woman's hand until her breath slowed. Then stopped.

A sob escaped her.

She had tried to let him go to keep him safe.

And still they came. They came for him, and for his people, and for this woman.

She tugged a blanket from the overturned basket and pulled it carefully over the woman's body, tucking it around her shoulders.

"May the river carry you," she whispered. She didn't know where the words came from. Only that they felt like the right way to say goodbye.

She stood up. And as she did, a glint in the mud caught her eye. Syfir's river-stone pendant. She picked it up, and squeezed until the stone bit into her palm.

Then she slipped its leather cord around her neck, letting the river token now rest against her heart.

Then she turned south—to find the Mehr'an. To find Syfir.

FOR THREE DAYS, Sahira hid in caves and hollow trees as she made her way south.

Each day brought endless walking and sweat and exhaustion.

And despair, as she replayed every wayward thought, every stolen moment by the river, the failed marriage ceremony.

All of it had led here.

All of it had led to the destruction of the camp. To that woman's death. To Syfir's suffering.

Each night brought dreams that weren't her own. Girls awakening with blue marks, girls cast from their homes.

And yet, for all the grief and fear, Sahira felt more alive than she ever had. There was no stillness now.

No expectations, no watching eyes, no silence. Only the forest. Only the path ahead.

And her first breaths of freedom.

# CHAPTER 14

ON THE FOURTH MORNING, she woke covered in dew, the droplets curling into spirals that echoed the blue markings beneath her skin.

That afternoon, she sat beside a stream and tried to move the flowing water. But nothing happened. She willed it to rise, but it only flowed on, indifferent.

That night, she dozed fitfully in a shallow cave.

Torchlight flickered at the entrance.

Sahira jerked awake, heart pounding, and pressed herself deeper into the cave, but it was too late.

A gruff voice called out. "Movement in here."

Three Samiti guards stepped into view. Their torchlight found her face, and recognition flared.

"The river-corrupted," one whispered, raising a staff.

Primal terror shot through Sahira's body.

And as if in response, the cave walls began to weep.

And then flow with water.

"Come quietly," the lead guard ordered, stepping forward. "Elder Nefret wants to—" The words died.

An impossible rain began to fall.

Inside the cave.

It began to pour from the ceiling in sheets, forming a wall between her and the guards that shimmered like a mirror, reflecting their torchlight and pressing them back away from her.

Terror, it seemed, was a kind of prayer water understood.

The guards stumbled backward, and their confusion gave time enough for Sahira to flee into the darkness.

The water bent around her, parting before her as she fled into the dark.

SHE RAN until her legs gave out, collapsing beside a small stream.

She was farther from Jaraan than she'd ever been.

The guards were gone. Only the trees, the wind, the sound of running water remained.

Heat prickled her chest, pulsing down to her fingertips in waves that made her skin tingle.

She looked down.

Blue markings had spread up her wrists, coiled around her forearms, and now wound around her elbows.

SHE KEPT MOVING, as if drawn by something older than memory.

The forest around her had changed. She didn't recognize the trees. The scent of woodsmoke and unfamiliar spices drifted through the air, drawing her deeper into unknown forest.

After days of cold and hiding, the promise of warmth pulled her onward despite the thrum of caution in her chest.

Not long after, she heard women's voices.

Then, through a clearing, she saw it: a hidden encampment nestled among ancient trees. Temporary dwellings of woven branches and hides that blended with the forest. Laughter, movement, and music filled the air.

A child spotted her first, and within moments, the camp's attention had turned toward the tree-line where Sahira crouched.

An elderly woman emerged from the largest dwelling, silver hair unbound, clouded eyes somehow finding Sahira despite the distance.

Sahira felt an ache. A homesickness for something she'd never known but might once have belonged to.

It felt, inexplicably, like wanting her mother.

"Come forward, river daughter," the woman called in a voice that reminded her at once of the river's rise and fall.

She stepped into the clearing. Tears pricked her eyes.

"Mehr'an," she breathed.

# CHAPTER 15
## MEHR'AN

Sahira recognized their distinctive clothing and the way they moved: fluid, unhurried, like the water itself.

An elderly woman emerged from the largest dwelling, her silver-streaked hair unbound, her eyes milky with old age, fixing immediately on Sahira despite the distance.

"The river has returned another daughter to us," the woman announced, her voice carrying an authority that made the others stop and turn.

"Fateh Bibi," one of the younger women whispered, approaching Sahira. "This is her. The one Syfir spoke of. The Covenant daughter who heard the river's call."

The name sent a jolt through Sahira's body. "Syfir? He's here?"

Fateh Bibi stepped closer, studying Sahira's face. "He was brought to us three nights ago. More dead than alive. The Samiti guards were… thorough in their questioning."

"Please, take me to him."

"He is with my daughter, Chatti. I will take you."

~

THEY LED her to a small dwelling set apart from the others, where healing herbs hung from the ceiling and a small fire burned with blue-tinged flames.

On a pallet of soft furs lay Syfir, his face bruised almost beyond recognition, his chest rising and falling with labored breaths.

She rushed to his side and fell to her knees. "What did they do to you?" she breathed, hands trembling as they reached for his.

"They discovered him returning to town, looking for you," an older Mehr'an woman, who must have been Chatti, said quietly, dipping a cloth in water and placing it on Syfir's forehead. "Elder Nefret herself, and her guards, questioned him about your whereabouts."

Chatti's eyes flickered with recognition as she noted the fading bridal mehndi on Sahira's hands.

And the river token around her neck.

Sahira held his hands, trembling. She glanced up at Chatti, and recognized her as the woman from the stall. "Are you Syfir's mother?"

"In every way that matters," she responded, gazing at Syfir. "His parents were taken from us when he was young. I have raised him as my own, yes."

"I'm so sorry," she whispered, her hands touching his, her voice breaking.

"This is not your burden to carry, child," Chatti said, though she wore a sad smile. "The settlement's guards watch only the boundaries they can see. He escaped because we Mehr'an know other ways through stone and shadow."

"He has suffered because they know I love him," Sahira admitted in a shaky voice, her hands still holding his.

"He has suffered because the people of Jaraan have lost their way," Chatti responded gently. "You were meant to be married, but instead you were punished. Tell me what happened."

So Sahira told her everything: the marriage, the dissolving

threads, the storm, the humiliation, the branding, the river's response.

"The river responded," Chatti said quietly. "It recognized what they were trying to destroy. Was there much damage?"

"Enough that they'll remember," Sahira replied. "The marketplace, some homes near the riverbank. But no one was hurt..."

"But they won't ignore what happened."

Sahira nodded.

"And now you are here. You have left everything behind," she observed, voice gentle with understanding. "Your family. Your betrothed. Your place in the Covenant."

"They were never mine," Sahira said, the truth of it settling deep in her bones. "They were paths drawn by others. This—" she touched his hand, gently "—only this is mine."

Chatti nodded, understanding without need for further explanation.

FATEH BIBI LAY on a cot nearby. Sahira sat beside Syfir's bed, studying the blue patterns that had crept further up her arms overnight.

"I don't understand what's happening to me," Sahira whispered.

Chatti sat beside her, stoking the fire. "Few do, in the beginning."

"I'm... changing," Sahira whispered.

"Becoming," Chatti corrected. "Remembering what your blood has always known." She frowned. "But the transition is dangerous. Without guidance, you could lose yourself entirely."

Sahira silently considered this for some time, watching the fire.

Then she looked at Syfir's battered face, feeling helplessness transform into rage. "I want them to pay. For what they did to him. For what they tried to do to me."

Fateh Bibi groaned as she turned over on her cot, apparently not yet asleep. "That hunger... for vengeance, for violence... it's the most dangerous current of all." The old woman's voice sounded exhausted. "Follow it, and you'll become worse than the Covenant itself. It's what got my son killed."

She turned away, the conversation finished.

Sahira turned to Chatti, eyes wide. "Her... son?"

"She will grieve him forever." Chatti glanced toward where Fateh Bibi sat by the fire. "She has carried that loss for nearly twenty years."

"Fateh Bibi is..." The words dissolved on her tongue. Realization struck her like physical pain.

"Mirza's mother."

Sahira stared at Chatti. "But Fateh Bibi is your... then that means you're..."

Chatti nodded. "I am the sister of Mirza of the Water."

THE NEXT MORNING, Sahira watched rainwater trace shallow, stone-lined channels.

"Clever design," she murmured.

"Syfir's work," Chatti said with pride. "He is our water shaper."

Understanding dawned. "It's his work that gives the Mehr'an the right to trade in Jaraan?"

Chatti nodded.

"Why didn't he tell me?"

Chatti's smile was wry. "Men often think women only want to hear their songs." She sighed. "They never seem to understand we love a good man for what he does, not just how he sounds."

Sahira turned to her, eyebrows raised.

"There was a drought three seasons ago. In the south. Their irrigation system failed, and the soil drank everything before it could reach the roots. Syfir studied the river's memory, and built them a new system that required less water, yet more moisture to roots."

Sahira stared with new eyes at the filtering stones placed with mathematical precision. She shook her head. "I've never seen anything like this."

She smiled. "Growing food keeps a community alive. Water must be both revered and understood." Chatti's voice held a mother's pride. "It's what moves him most."

Sahira nodded slowly, feeling a strange glow of admiration.

"Sounds as though the two of you have missed some important conversations," Chatti admonished gently. But her smile took any sting out of the words.

SAHIRA STOOD at the settlement's edge, watching the morning unfold in ways impossible in Jaraan. Unlike the rigid hierarchies she'd known, where each person had their designated place and role, the Mehr'an moved like water itself.

Children ran freely between dwellings, carrying messages and sharing meals wherever they found them. Elders sat weaving with teenagers, their conversation flowing seamlessly from technique to gossip to the nature of earth itself.

The dwellings told their own story: tents of thick canvas arranged in loose clusters, with channels that carried water to each door.

"How do you maintain order?" Sahira asked Chatti, looking around.

"We participate," Chatti replied, her hands never pausing in their herb-gathering. "Order without participation isn't order. It's control." She glanced up. "Nothing is perfect. But we value change. We value flow."

In Jaraan, rules were rigid, fixed into place. Here, boundaries existed, but bent with season and need.

As Chatti had admitted, it wasn't perfect harmony. During an evening meal, two older men argued heatedly about whether certain families should settle closer to the river, their voices rising until a circle formed around them.

Unlike in Jaraan, no single authority silenced the disagreement; instead, the community witnessed it, voices adding perspective until balance emerged.

"Not everyone agrees with how open we've become to outsiders," Chatti explained later, nodding toward a small group who kept apart from the main gathering. "Some believe we should remain hidden, preserving our ways rather than sharing them. They fear diluting our practices or drawing the Covenant's attention."

"What do you believe?"

Chatti's expression grew thoughtful. "I believe isolation ultimately leads to stagnation. But I understand their fear. We've lost many to violence. Many have been injured." She looked toward where Syfir lay healing.

Sahira followed her gaze.

"Every time we reach out," Chatti said, voice low, "we risk losing someone. And still, some of us keep reaching. Because the cost of change is high. But the cost of stillness is extinction."

She looked Sahira in the eye. "The question becomes: is the possibility of transformation worth that risk?"

SIX DAYS PASSED before Syfir's fever broke. Sahira spent them learning the rhythms of Mehr'an life, absorbing their understanding of water and memory, their fluid approach to community itself.

And every night, she was still haunted by dreams. She saw Kaya hiding blue marks as her mother approached. A baker's daughter staring at water rippling without wind, and her father watching, horror rising in his eyes. More girls, more families, more desperate attempts to hide what could not be hidden.

Every morning, she would wake with water beading on her skin—and the certainty these weren't dreams at all.

In her second week with the Mehr'an, Sahira began training. At dawn, she would wade into the shallows with Navya, who had been teaching water-listening for over a decade.

"Bring intention," Navya said, guiding the water with her palms, "but not force. You're not commanding water. You're reminding it what it already knows."

Sahira's first attempts produced only ripples but eventually she could create wavering columns that collapsed the moment her concentration faltered. Her frustration mounted until Chatti suggested a different approach.

"What makes you want to connect to the river? Why build this bond?"

"I don't—" Sahira began, then stopped, thinking hard. And then she took a deep breath, as the answer made itself clear. "They told me to sit still, to be quiet, to be nothing." Her face hardened. "But that isn't what I'm meant for—what *we're* meant for. The river won't let me forget who I am."

Chatti nodded. "Then stop trying to make the water obey. Just remember the river. Remember who you are."

That evening, instead of trying to conjure shapes, Sahira closed her eyes and listened. Beneath the surface patterns of current and reflection, she felt something respond. Something like intention itself.

When she opened her hands, the water rose.

It spiraled upward in shapes that echoed the markings on her skin.

By week's end, she could sense rain before it formed, raise water in tendrils, and feel its presence inside every living thing.

"You listen to the water," Fateh Bibi observed, watching from the shore. "The river speaks through you."

BY THE SEVENTH EVENING, her mehndi had faded completely. In its place, blue markings curled across her shoulders and collarbone.

That night, Syfir began to stir and speak in whispers, and Sahira sat upright and immediately moved to his side.

"Sahira." His voice was thin.

"I'm here," she said, reaching for his hand.

"River," he rasped. "She's not a drop…"

"Syfir, I'm here," she whispered, "I'm here."

"Not a drop in the river," he murmured unevenly.

"What do you need?" she asked, scanning his face, his bruised chest, searching for any sign of pain. She held his hand tightly in both of hers.

His hand shifted in hers. "Sahira's… the river," he breathed, his eyes unfocused.

Sahira froze, looking down into his face.

His eyes focused on hers then.

"You're the entire river in one drop," he said softly, squeezing her hand, then closing his eyes, exhaustion overtaking him.

SOME HOURS LATER, Chatti drew Sahira aside. "There are things you must know about your mother. Things that will help you understand your path."

Sahira looked up. "What about my mother?"

"All the Mehr'an knew your mother." Something flickered across Chatti's face—an old grief. "Your mother carried wounds no one could see. The river gave her what the Covenant never would: a place to speak truths men refused to hear."

"Your mother always heard the call of the river. Perhaps that's why she and Mirza first fell in love. But it was after he was gone that her awakening began." Her eyes grew distant. "By the time you were born, the markings had begun. They were subtle. They started on the soles of her feet, as if the river knew she had to hide."

"What happened to her?" Sahira asked, the question that had haunted her entire life. "The night she disappeared."

Chatti grew somber. "Your mother knew her time in the settlement was ending. The markings had spread too far to hide. The water responded too visibly to her presence."

"So she left me? Came here?" Sahira whispered.

"No." Chatti said sharply. "She would never leave you. She wanted to run away with you. She wanted to wait until she knew whether you'd hear the river, too."

Tears blurred Sahira's vision.

"That final night, your mother brought three young girls to me. Daughters who showed early signs of transformation. She believed she could create a bridge for them. A connection to the water that would remain even after she was gone."

Fateh Bibi approached from where she had been listening silently. "She was creating a legacy," the elder woman said, her milky eyes reflecting moonlight like water. "For all the daughters of the river to come."

"We found her shawl on the bank the next morning," Fateh Bibi continued. "The river told us what happened. We saw in the water's memory how she tried to create a barrier between herself and those who came for her."

"But instead?" Sahira whispered.

"Someone held her under."

The words struck Sahira like lightning.

"Someone—" The word caught in her throat. "Someone murdered her?"

"They tried to. They didn't understand that water won't turn on its own." Fateh Bibi's ancient eyes held infinite sadness. "Your mother was already too connected to the river. Her consciousness transferred into the current. But… they killed her body, yes. "

Sahira stood so abruptly she nearly fell.

Ten years believing her mother had abandoned her. Ten years fearing the madness that might lurk in her own blood. Ten years carrying shame that was never hers to bear.

She paced in a tight circle, then sank back down. "They killed her." The words came out raw, broken.

The water basin beside Syfir's bed began to tremble, then overflow, responding to her anguish.

She pressed her hands against her face, but couldn't stop the storm rising in her chest. "How am I supposed to go back there?" she whispered through her fingers. "How am I meant to face them without—" She couldn't finish.

She didn't know yet what she would do when the time came. Only that it was coming.

"This is why your path matters," Chatti said softly. "You could destroy them. But you have the chance to become what your mother tried to be. A bridge between worlds."

The room seemed to tilt around Sahira. Her chest tightened until she could barely breathe, white-hot rage building beneath her breastbone where the blue markings converged.

Sahira sat, breathing deeply to calm herself. "What happened to the three girls—the ones my mother tried to help?" she finally asked.

Chatti smiled. "They came to our settlement. Married Mehr'an men. Became part of our community."

Sahira was quiet for a time. "Do you know who held her under the water?" she asked, her voice hardly more than a whisper.

The two Mehr'an women exchanged a glance.

"The water remembers," Fateh Bibi said. "But some truths must be discovered rather than told. When you face the one responsible, you will know."

# CHAPTER 16
# DIVERGENCE

On the night before the full moon, Sahira sat beside the river.

Fateh Bibi joined her, lowering herself carefully to the ground.

Sahira looked over as the older woman settled beside her, her gaze drawn to the patterns that flowed and swirled along Fateh Bibi's forearms.

"Your markings are different from everyone else's," she observed.

"So they are." Fateh Bibi traced the now-wrinkled lines on her skin. "These are a chief's markings, as my son Mirza bore before the river took him."

"You're the chief?" Sahira stared at her, stunned.

"I am."

Sahira looked away, absorbing the revelation.

"Do you know," Fateh Bibi asked, motioning to Sahira's hands, "that each set of markings tells its own story?"

Sahira shook her head.

"Yours speak of convergence. Of a coming together."

Sahira looked down at her hands, her arms, a question forming behind her eyes.

"Maybe of you and Syfir," Fateh Bibi said, answering what Sahira did not ask. "But patterns are rarely about just two people."

She studied Sahira for a long moment. "Your markings mean there is a current inside you that gives you life. I want you to try to listen for it."

Sahira glanced at her. "How?"

"Not with your ears. With your body. The river speaks in rhythms. In subtle shifts beneath the surface."

Sahira closed her eyes.

At first, she heard only the ordinary rush of water. But slowly, as her mind stilled, other sensations rose. Voices too faint to be called sound. Images forming and dissolving like ripples across still water. Memories that passed through her, rather than surfacing.

"I can feel…" she began, struggling to name the strange awareness. "It's like the water remembers everything it's touched. Everyone who's ever entered it." She opened her eyes.

Fateh Bibi nodded, solemn. "The water carries history. Silenced voices. Old magic. It's all preserved in the current."

Her gaze moved to Sahira's chest. "And now, your markings have reached your heart."

Sahira looked down. Blue lines curved across her collarbone, spiraling inward. She placed a hand over her chest, where the pattern pulsed in rhythm with her heartbeat. "What does it mean?"

"That you're ready for the final test," Fateh Bibi said solemnly. "When you return to town, you'll need to change many minds. Are you ready to do that without hurting them? Without turning the river against them?"

Sahira's eyes grew distant. "They told me to sit still. To be quiet. To be nothing," she whispered. "They killed my mother. They almost killed Syfir."

Fateh Bibi shook her head. "They have lost their way. You

have found yours." She took Sahira's hand and turned it over. "Only this is true."

Sahira looked down. The blue pattern on her palm glowed softly.

"The danger," Fateh Bibi said, "is not in what they might build to contain you, but in what you might unleash upon them. In the temptation to become the destroyer rather than the bridge."

Sahira swallowed.

"You have the power to drown their voices," Fateh Bibi said. "To wash away their structures, and raise something older, wilder, in their place. But you'll resist."

"How?" Sahira breathed.

"Because you'll remember your purpose." Fateh Bibi nodded toward her hand.

Sahira looked at her palm.

"Convergence," Fateh Bibi said, eyes lifting to Sahira's face.

Sahira met her gaze.

"You weren't awakened to destroy the old world, child. It may be that you were awakened to help birth the new one."

THE NEXT MORNING, Chatti gestured for Sahira to follow her to a small clearing just beyond the Mehr'an encampment.

The older woman moved with surprising grace as she pushed aside hanging vines. "Sit," she said, indicating a smooth stone beside a thin stream.

Sahira settled onto the stone, grateful for its solid presence beneath her, and looked around the wide clearing. They were surrounded by walls of green, and somewhere in the vastness above them, clouds were forming, gathering moisture that would someday fall back to earth. Back to the river.

"I want to tell you about how I became Syfir's mother."

"Many years ago, we were far from here. The town we were

near was… harsh. Harsher even than Jaraan." Chatti's eyes grew distant. "That town's Samiti discovered we were helping awakening women escape." Her voice dropped to barely a whisper. "Syfir's parents bought time for three women to flee upriver. They held the guards at the main crossing, and they… were killed."

Sahira felt her chest tighten. "The women they saved?"

"One is a teacher now in our community. Navya, who taught you water-listening." Chatti smiled through her grief. "And then we had to tell Syfir his parents were dead. He was seven."

Sahira blinked back tears.

"When he learned of what happened to his parents, it… began to storm. It stormed for days. We feared it would never stop. The river broke its banks. It washed away half our encampment. While others fled to higher ground, Syfir walked directly into the flood." She closed her eyes. "When we found him the next day, he was sitting on a rock in the middle of the raging water, completely dry, crying."

Sahira stared at Chatti, horrified.

"Since then, his connection to water has been unique. Even now, it will storm if…" she stopped. "If… his body is in great distress." Chatti winced. "You'll have felt it. The day of your marriage ceremony. When he was… with the guards. In the afternoon there was a great storm."

Sahira gasped, remembering the way the rain had fallen in torrents, blinding her view from her bedroom window.

"The river carries memory through time." Chatti's eyes lifted to the night sky. "And rain travels between worlds."

Sahira stared at Chatti, grasping to understand. "And that's why he found me? Because he's… rain?"

Chatti's laugh was unexpected, warm and genuine. "Oh, child. He found you because some waters are destined to meet, no matter what mountains stand between them." Her expression grew more serious. "It also means your paths are entwined. Though they may sometimes diverge."

"Diverge?" Sahira asked softly.

Chatti reached forward and squeezed her hands, but said nothing.

"He's going to leave?" Sahira whispered. Her throat tightened.

"*You* will," Chatti said softly, her gaze steady. "You'll return to the town, and save your people." She fell quiet, then reached out and touched Sahira's cheek. Softly, like a mother would.

Sahira's eyes filled with tears. "And Syfir?"

Chatti's gaze was steady but kind. "He will travel with us. The channels of water he created use half the water of traditional irrigation but yield twice the harvest. Our people need his skill."

Sahira remained quiet.

"There are other settlements beyond our valley, other children of the river beginning to remember," Chatti continued. "We must find them and guide them, before their towns silence them, as they tried to silence you."

"When?" Sahira breathed.

"Soon."

"When your work in Jaraan is done, I hope you'll join Syfir," Chatti said. "Join us."

As if summoned by their conversation, a soft rain began to fall. Yet the space where they sat stayed dry, as if protected by something unseen.

"He's listening," Chatti said, her gaze tilted toward the camp, toward him.

Sahira closed her eyes, feeling the rain's music all around her.

THE DAYS that followed blurred together. Sahira spent mornings continuing to train with the Mehr'an women, afternoons gathering herbs with Chatti, and evenings keeping vigil beside Syfir's bed as his strength slowly returned.

Nearly three weeks after she arrived at the camp, Syfir finally began to sit up for longer periods, though he still tired easily.

Sahira awoke to find Syfir watching her with eyes that held both relief and concern.

"You're here," he said, his voice rough from disuse.

"Where else would I be?" She moved to his side, warmth rising in her chest as she took his hand.

His fingers found hers, weak but deliberate. "I dreamed you'd gone back. To face them."

"Not yet," she said. "But soon." She squeezed his hand gently. "First, you need to heal."

A ghost of his familiar smile crossed his bruised face. "I will. You're here."

"Syfir… at the marriage ceremony, the binding threads dissolved. They turned to water. In front of everyone." She shook her head. "I don't understand it."

"Mm." He closed his eyes, smiling faintly. "The river listened."

Sahira frowned. "Listened to what?"

His eyes opened again, meeting hers with an intensity that made her breath catch. "When they took me that morning…" he began, smile fading. "I asked the river for something." Then a flicker of mischief creased his bruised face. "Even bound or beaten, I can still talk to the water."

Sahira stared at him, her heart pounding. "What did you ask?" she breathed, her hand unconsciously tightening around his.

"I asked it to protect its daughter," he whispered, reaching up weakly to touch a strand of her hair. "To deliver you to your true destiny."

"What destiny is that?" she asked, holding her breath and hoping with every fiber of her being that Syfir didn't ask for something she wouldn't have herself asked.

"Not mine to say," he said, and Sahira exhaled.

His gaze carried the weight of ancient knowledge. "The river makes its own choices, Sahira. It couldn't create something that wasn't already there."

A shadow passed over Sahira's face. "The river took Mirza."

"No." Syfir's hand moved to cup her cheek, his thumb brushing away a tear she hadn't realized was falling. "The river doesn't take. It transforms. Your mother asked Bakki to hide Mirza... keep him safe for her. But rivers don't understand halfway. They flow to completion."

"She wanted to save him," Sahira whispered.

"But Bakki kept Mirza in its current... until your mother could come too." His voice held wonder rather than grief. "Think about it. The river carries them both now. Forever."

The revelation hung between them, charged like the air before lightning strikes.

Sahira blinked back tears.

Syfir's eyes fell on the river token hanging from her neck. "She wears my pendant," he murmured to himself, his lips curving into a smile.

And then the smile disappeared as he took in the blue markings now visible on her collarbone. "You're changing fast."

"I don't have time for a slow awakening," she said. "The women in town... some of them are beginning to change. I can feel them, Syfir. Their confusion, their fear. And the Samiti's response..." She shuddered. "They're taking girls for purification now. Even those who've shown no signs but ask too many questions. I can feel their fear in my blood."

Syfir's face hardened.

"I have to go back," she said. "To show them awakening isn't corruption. That another way is possible."

"If they try to hurt you—"

"Then I might end up like my mother," she finished for him.

"You've already come so far," he said, his fingers threading through hers. "They might never follow now. We could be free. We could be together. Stay with my people."

He squeezed her hand.

And then his voice dropped to barely a whisper, that somehow carried the weight of every river that had ever flowed toward the sea.

"Marry me."

The words hung in the air between them, carrying the weight of everything they'd found and everything they might lose.

Syfir reached up to touch her cheek. "I mean it. Marry me."

"Your mother would like that," Sahira said, smiling despite the weight in her chest.

He smiled back, his eyes holding both humor and heartache. "Of course she would. How could anyone not want you as a daughter?"

Tears filled Sahira's eyes at the words.

"I have to return to the town, Syfir. I can't hide here while no one speaks for them. I have to finish this."

*Or die trying*, she didn't say.

"Finish it, and then return. And then marry me," he said.

*Don't die*, he didn't add.

"I'll finish it, and then I'll come back to you," she echoed.

"Is that a promise?" he asked.

She nodded, her face streaked with tears now, her hand squeezing his tightly. "It's a vow."

The words hung between them, a bridge across whatever distance might come. She leaned forward and kissed his lips.

He yelped in pain, and they both laughed.

Dawn broke over the Mehr'an camp with unusual activity.

Word had arrived in the night: rumors of unrest in Jaraan were spreading. Covenant patrols were expanding into nearby regions, and merchants were rerouting.

The river's surface, usually calm at dawn, carried a strange undercurrent.

"What's going on?" Sahira asked, moving past a mother

packing up her belongings as her children made the process more difficult.

"Trade's been disrupted since the flooding," a scout explained. "I just returned from watching the main routes. Merchants are nervous about the river's behavior, and some are taking the long route through the eastern pass to avoid Jaraan entirely."

An older man with a weather-beaten face frowned. "We already moved once. No one is near yet. We can move the camp later."

Others disagreed, citing traditions about seasonal movements. The debate grew heated until Chatti gestured for quiet.

"We should hear from Syfir," she said.

Despite his obvious weakness, Syfir's presence immediately shifted the group's attention. His recent ordeal had only enhanced his standing. Here was someone who had suffered for their community.

"What does the water tell you?" the first man asked, deferring to Syfir without hesitation.

"The river will rise," Syfir confirmed, "but not beyond the boundary stones. Still, this is no time for large gatherings. The Samiti is watching. We risk drawing their eyes. Our tribe should move."

Fateh Bibi had been listening from the edge of the group, her milky eyes reflecting some inner sight.

Now she moved to the center, and the Mehr'an instinctively formed a circle around her.

"The water speaks of journeys taken in stages," she announced.

The Mehr'an men and women gathered around her, their faces solemn as she began.

"Some will depart at dawn," Fateh Bibi said, "to warn our sister communities. To prepare what may come. But we do not abandon this place."

A Mehr'an man with intricate blue markings layered under

hand-made markings of ink stepped forward. "Who remains and who travels, Bibi?"

She paused, her gaze sweeping the circle. "Seven families will remain. Small enough to stay hidden. Close enough to watch the river's edge. Syfir will be among them. If the Samiti draws too near, they can scatter quickly."

Murmurs rippled through the gathered people.

"And when will they follow?" the man asked. "Syfir is our water-shaper. We need him as we travel."

"When the river's daughter returns to claim her place among us," Fateh Bibi replied, her clouded gaze finding Sahira in the crowd. "She will return, and when she does, we must be here."

THAT NIGHT, Sahira sat with Chatti, looking across the clearing to where Syfir sat with the elders, his hands moving through the air as he described water patterns. Though still weak from his injuries, his eyes were alive with purpose.

He glanced up, catching her watching him. Instead of the knowing smirk she expected, his expression softened into something more vulnerable.

"He's different when he speaks of water," Sahira observed.

Chatti nodded. "The river gives him certainty that nothing else in this world can. Except perhaps you." She studied Sahira thoughtfully. "He's never looked at anyone the way he looks at you."

"How is that?"

"Like he's finally found the current he's been searching for," Chatti said.

Sahira said nothing.

"We will wait here for you," Chatti said simply. "However long it takes."

Sahira's hands stilled. "You believe I will return? To go south with you?"

Chatti stopped sorting, and looked up at Sahira's face. "Where else would the river's daughter belong but with her people? Once you've shown your town what they need to see, you'll come home."

~

As dusk settled over the camp, Syfir made his way to the central fire despite his lingering injuries, settling beside Sahira. Their shoulders almost touched as they watched preparations continue around them.

Sahira had finished packing—food, water, some herbs, Chatti's cloak.

The blue markings on her skin had stabilized overnight, no longer spreading but pulsing with quiet certainty, like water finding its level.

"You're leaving now," he said. Not a question, but an acknowledgment.

"The longer I wait, the more women will suffer." She wrapped the cloak tighter around her shoulders, checking that the water-resistant weave was properly sealed against the coming weather.

He nodded.

The air thickened with unspoken words, with promises, both made and implied.

"I don't know how long this will take," she admitted finally. "Changing an entire community's understanding…"

"Time moves differently for water." His thumb traced the blue markings on her hand, and their fingers wove together naturally. "We will be here when you return."

"And if they try to stop me from coming back?" The question emerged unbidden, giving voice to the fear she'd tried to contain.

Syfir's eyes met hers. "How long can they hold the river?"

He leaned forward then, his forehead touching hers in a

gesture that reminded her of her mother. "When this is finished," she whispered.

"Then we will go south," he finished, his voice low and certain. "To the great seas."

His lips found hers then. A seal more binding than any golden thread.

When they finally broke apart, Sahira felt the truth of their connection settle into her bones. Whatever happened in Jaraan, whatever choices lay ahead, this connection was true.

This connection would endure.

Sahira took a deep breath, and then released his hand.

She stood up, and Syfir caught her hand one last time.

He brought his other hand to his chest, and then drew his fingers away in a flowing motion that mimicked water.

*This means remember what flows in your blood.*

Sahira blinked back tears, and began walking, every step carrying her back toward the town that had tried to break her— no longer the girl who had left.

Behind her, she knew, Syfir watched until she disappeared among the trees.

THE FIRST HOUR passed in solitude, only her footsteps marking her path. But as the trees thickened, a different rhythm began to echo her pace.

Always just distant enough to dismiss as imagination, yet persistent enough to prickle at her awareness.

She paused by a creek to drink, listening carefully. The sound stopped when she stopped. Resumed when she moved.

Someone—or something—was tracking her.

On the second day, she glimpsed movement through the trees behind her—a flash of dark fabric that vanished the moment she turned.

When she called out, only silence answered.

By the third day, she had circled back toward Jaraan, staying hidden in the forest paths that ran parallel to the Bakki. The sense of being watched never left—whatever followed was keeping its distance, never revealing itself fully.

That evening, rain poured in dense sheets, swallowing the forest whole and turning paths into rivers. She pulled her Mehr'an shawl over her head and wrapped it tightly to shield herself from the downpour. The fabric kept her both hidden and dry.

Shivering, cold, and starting to feel herself weakening, Sahira sat under the canopy of an ancient tree.

Through the rain, she spotted something that made her heart lift with relief: the stone walls of an old way station. Her father had once described these traveler shelters from his merchant days, before the Covenant had restricted movement between settlements.

She approached the abandoned structure cautiously. Its walls were still standing, but much of the roof had surrendered to time and weather.

The entrance was partially blocked by fallen stone, but Sahira found a narrow gap and slipped through.

Inside, the single room was surprisingly dry, despite parts of the roof being gone. In one corner, a stone hearth remained intact, its chimney still reaching skyward.

And there in the center of the room, a perfect circle of dry earth. River stones, arranged in a swirling pattern. The arrangement was clearly deliberate, too precise to be accidental. Someone had been here before her.

Recently.

She knelt, still damp from the rain, and examined the stones more closely. Carved into each were delicate spirals.

Patterns that echoed the ones that swirled from her wrists to her palms.

"I wondered when you would find this place!" a tinkling voice sang from the doorway.

# CHAPTER 17
# DASHA

An elderly woman stood in the doorway, her arms clinking with bangles threaded with river stones.

She wasn't Mehr'an. She was from town.

Dasha.

The woman who had stopped Sahira in the market. Who had told her she had her mother's face, remembered the jasmine, and called her the river's daughter.

"I'm glad you've come, daughter of the river," she said, her face lighting up. She carried a bundle of dried herbs and a small pot.

"I—I'm sorry, it was raining, and—"

Dasha laughed. "Thank the river for the rain, then! The river for the rain, the rain for the river," she rambled.

"You know, your mother thought this was a good shelter too, so many moons ago. She found this place just as you did, yes, she did."

The old woman set her things down near the hearth and began arranging kindling with practiced hands. From her pocket, she produced flint and steel, striking them expertly. The kindling caught immediately, flames dancing higher than such small sticks should have allowed. "I've been waiting for you to arrive. There is bedding you can sleep on tonight. You'll stay until tomorrow."

Sahira sank to the floor beside the fire, its warmth reaching into her chilled body. "How did you know I would come here?"

"Your mother told me!" Dasha's matter-of-fact tone made the extraordinary statement sound mundane.

Sahira stared at the woman.

"She speaks to me in dreams," Dasha said, serious now. "When the moon is high, and the river is loud. Not all who vanish are lost."

And then her eyes suddenly looked fearful. "She tried to return for you once. I found her by your window one night—not as a woman but as mist rising from the ground. The effort nearly dissolved her completely." Dasha's eyes brimmed with tears. "She asked me to watch over you from a distance—until you were ready."

Sahira couldn't think of anything to say.

"She asked me to help you prepare, prepare for what's next." Dasha added, the strange musical quality returning to her voice.

"What's next?" Sahira asked through tears that she now quickly brushed away.

Dasha's face lit up with a broad smile. "You complete your transformation."

Then, the old woman fell silent for a time, adding herbs to the pot and hanging it over the fire. The scent of rosemary and something sharper filled the small space.

"So... did anyone tell you about your mother?" she asked, tilting her head to the side.

"What do you mean?" Sahira asked.

Dasha looked at Sahira with a suggestive brow raise.

"You mean... about the love she had to give up?" Sahira guessed slowly.

Dasha clapped, her face the picture of joy. "Good, good! So you know about your father!"

Sahira looked at her, confused. "I—yes, I know that she was in love with someone else before she married my father."

"You're confused!" The old woman threw her head back, laughing. "You think I'm talking about Tahir Raazaan." She laughed so hard she was holding her stomach now. "The man did raise you well," she said, catching her breath.

Sahira shook her head, perplexed.

The old woman reached for a small clay pot, opening it to reveal blue paste that smelled of river silt and night-blooming flowers. "What I meant was: do you know who your father is?"

Sahira stared at her.

"The Zaroun brothers would never let their sister love a river man, of course," she said, dipping her finger in the paste. "Within days of the Mehr'an river chief's disappearance," she giggled.

Sahira's heart thundered in her chest as what Dasha was implying began to settle in.

"You were born seven months later! So strong," she continued, rubbing the paste into her fingertips. "A child of the river!"

Sahira's chest tightened. "You're saying—"

"Oh, yes! Rain fell. Breath began. And two hearts became one." Dasha giggled. "You are Mirza's daughter. The river chief's child."

The revelation burned through Sahira like flame through paper.

She was not Tahir Raazaan's daughter. She was the child of Ameera and of Mirza, the Mehr'an river chief. The very man her mother had loved and lost. The truth had been hiding in her blood all along, flowing through her veins, whispering to her in dreams.

Everything she'd believed: every story, every assumption, every foundation of her identity. Her mother's death. Her father's identity. All of it was... a lie.

It explained why she was drawn to the Bakki since childhood, why the blue markings had appeared so readily beneath her skin, why water had always seemed to recognize her.

But it also raised questions too painful to contemplate. Had her mother known she carried Mirza's child when she married Tahir? Had Tahir known he was raising another man's daughter? Was her entire life with him a carefully constructed fiction designed to hide a forbidden love?

She thought of Syfir then. Who had called her "Zarouni girl" rather than "Raazaani girl." He knew, she realized with sudden clarity. Or at least suspected.

She reached for her satchel, drawing out her mother's letter, folded carefully inside. She unfolded it, and carefully reread the first lines.

*There are truths the Covenant cannot teach, powers they will not name. The river's call is one. Love that defies their rules is another. You are the product of both.*

*When they tell you your awakening is corruption, remember: Some things are inexplicable to those who have never felt them. You are exactly as you were meant to be.*

*I love you forever.*

And then, a slow, strange calm began to settle into Sahira's stomach. A strange sense of homecoming. The pieces of herself that had never fit into the Covenant's expectations suddenly made sense.

"Time is short, Daughter of the River." Dasha's voice was suddenly lucid, and she straightened her spine. "It will be time to confront the Samiti soon."

Sahira shook her head, trying to clear it.

"I'm ready," Sahira said, sitting up straighter.

"Oh! You're not, not yet!" Dasha said, laughing. "First, you must understand what you are—completely!"

The old woman rose, moving to the stone circle at the room's center. She gestured for Sahira to join her there.

"Look inside!" Dasha said.

And there, inside the stone circle, was a small puddle of water, in a perfect circle. It shimmered with something reflective and alive.

And then… images.

Sahira looked up at Dasha, shocked.

"Ah, good, good! You see it!" Dasha said, clapping.

Sahira looked back inside the water, and saw new images: *Girls throughout town, waking from dreams with water on their pillows. Women humming melodies they'd never been taught while washing clothes by the river. Girls being dragged from their homes by temple guards.*

"It's already begun," Dasha whispered. "Your awakening has triggered others. The river is remembering, and through it, so are they."

She scrambled to retrieve a scroll of paper. "For generations, the river has carried memory from women's power from the Old World. It's been whispering, whispering, waiting for those with the right bloodlines to hear. But no one wanted to hear all the memory. No one could carry it all." Then, she unrolled the scroll, spreading a crude map of the town across the way station floor.

"And… I can carry it all?" Sahira asked.

"Almost. You can almost carry it all," Dasha smiled. "First, you must go to the Mouth of the Serpent. You must complete a circle broken generations ago," Dasha explained, her voice dropping to a reverent whisper. "When your transformation is complete, you'll make the river's truth heard."

Dasha's finger moved across the map, drawing a line from a housing complex to the temple. "Girls are humming melodies no one taught them, dreaming of water. And the Samiti is taking them." Her eyes looked panicked even as she laughed.

Sahira watched her in horror. "It's my fault," she said slowly.

Dasha shook her head. "No, no, no. You didn't teach the girls the melodies or give them dreams."

Sahira shook her head. "But it all started after my markings appeared. As if my awakening somehow triggered theirs."

"Not triggered," Dasha corrected, her voice taking on the sing-song quality again as she wagged a finger. "Remembered! The door was always there, just hidden, forgotten in their blood."

Sahira shook her head.

"You're not their source, river daughter. You're the amplifier!" She traced the air above Sahira's blue-marked skin in a spiraling pattern that grew wider, her bangles chiming with each movement. "And each newly awakened girl makes more awaken. Like pebbles dropped in still water... circles growing wider and wider."

"So it's not just about me," Sahira murmured.

"Not unless you lined up the stars!" Dasha replied, her eyes catching the firelight like twin moons. "When water and blood and stars align, what was forgotten returns with the tide! You're not the cause, you're remembering revived!" she sang, her expression expectant, as though she were awaiting applause.

"But... the Samiti—they're taking girls who show signs?"

"Because of what this all represents. Because of the power they've tried to bury for generations. Things are changing, changing, changing!" Dasha was singing now.

The surface of the shallow water trembled, then went still.

"I have to go back," Sahira said, rising. "I have to stop them—"

Dasha leaned forward, cupping Sahira's face. "Eat," she said. "Rest. At dawn, we meet the one who remembers what even I've forgotten."

"Who?"

Her eyes glinted. "Naga."

Sahira thought of Leela. Of the serpent mother story.

But before Sahira could ask Dasha anything more, the old woman had slipped through the gap in the stones and disappeared into the rain.

SAHIRA SLEPT on a makeshift pallet near the hearth, her dreams blazing with vivid memories and images.

*The scent of river silt filled her nostrils. Cold water lapped at her calves. Her mother's hands, weaving patterns in the air that the water followed. Women with serpent tattoos on their wrists, dancing beneath a moon three times larger than any Sahira had ever seen.*

*And then the dream changed. Syfir was being dragged by temple guards, his face bloodied.*

*The dream changed again. Elder Nefret stood triumphant in a circular chamber, arms crossed, the bodies of the entire Mehr'an tribe laying dead at her feet.*

SAHIRA WOKE AT DAWN, her skin glistening with sweat. The rain had stopped overnight, but the air in the way station was thick with moisture.

Dasha returned carrying a large basket, just as Sahira was getting up from the pallet.

Sahira watched Dasha wincing as she moved about the way station, clutching her left shoulder. "Are you in pain?"

"The rain, the rain," Dasha replied with a dismissive gesture. "Old bones remember old hurts when water falls from the sky!" She lowered herself onto a worn cushion near Sahira.

"What happened to your shoulder?"

Dasha's eyes grew distant. "Temple guards," she said, her usual singsong cadence flattening. "Many years, so many years. I spoke of the river's voice too loudly. They tried to break me." She made an exaggerated expression of sorrow. "Almost succeeded, too! But didn't break my body, no. Left only my mind a broken pot."

She smiled, tapping her temple. "But even broken pots can still carry water."

Understanding bloomed in Sahira's heart. Dasha's scattered manner, her strange speech patterns. It wasn't madness. It was a way to survive. "May I?" she asked, gesturing to Dasha's shoulder.

The old woman studied her face, then nodded, pulling aside her shawl to reveal a shoulder mottled with old scars. Sahira knelt beside her, gently placing her hands on the old woman's shoulder and massaging gently.

"Same hands as your mother—just the same."

Then, unexpectedly, Dasha grasped Sahira's wrist. "But you are stronger than she was. More complete." She released it.

Sahira continued working silently, considering how Dasha had known her mother in ways Sahira never could. "There," she said finally, her hands growing still. "Any better?"

Dasha rotated her shoulder, surprise spreading across her features. "Better! Better! The river heals. And you, you heal too." She reached down into her basket and pulled out a long swath of undyed cloth. "It's hot where we're going—too hot for your Covenant clothes. Do you know how to tie this?"

Sahira looked down at the cloth and thought of the fabric draped on the bodies of the Mehr'an women, the ones she had seen at the river. Sahira shook her head.

"Stand, then."

Dasha wrapped the fabric around Sahira, winding it through her legs to form loose pants, then around her waist, across her chest, and over her shoulders.

Sahira shook her head in amazement.

Dasha laughed, then beckoned. "It's time. The mouth is open."

# CHAPTER 18
# SYFIR

Three days after Sahira's departure and farther down the Bakki, Syfir stood at the river's edge, sensing her progress through the water's memory. His ribs still ached, but enough strength had returned for him to move freely through the camp, and to help prepare the remaining Mehr'an for whatever might come.

Chatti approached, her face shadowed with worry. "Scouts report Samiti guards searching the eastern forest. They're moving in patterns. Systematic, thorough. They're hunting."

"For Sahira?" Alarm sharpened his voice.

"For all of us," she replied grimly. "But especially for those with blue markings." She touched his wrist, at the faint patterns there. "And for you, in particular."

Syfir looked toward the town, where Sahira had gone to face her people alone. He had felt her determination, her clarity of purpose. Now he felt something else: a growing tension, like storm clouds gathering.

"If they find our camp," he began.

"The others will be at risk," Chatti finished. "The other families who stayed." She didn't need to elaborate.

They both remembered well what had happened the last time Samiti guards had descended.

Syfir's expression hardened into a grim line.

"You and I can move farther into the forest in the morning," Chatti said firmly. "We'll give them something to follow."

And as he nodded, he made his own decision.

THAT NIGHT, as Syfir knelt by the river, the water rippled in response to his touch, carrying his intention outward. "Forgive me, Ma," he whispered to the current.

He dressed in distinctive, indigo-hued Mehr'an robes and packed lightly.

Still weak from his injuries, he began moving, taking care to leave no trace of his movements yet.

Then, when he was half a day from camp, he deliberately crossed west, away from the Mehr'an encampment. He began snapping branches underfoot, brushing against trees, rustling leaves—creating a false trail—in a path leading far from the camp.

When the guards found him later that day, he offered no resistance.

Their rough hands seized him with undisguised contempt, binding his wrists with ropes soaked in salt water, a trick that weakened those with river connections.

"The Mehr'an witch-man," one guard spat.

"Where are the others?" Another demanded, shaking him, and aggravating his existing injuries.

Syfir kept his head bowed, his face neutral. "Gone. I travel alone."

"Liar," the first guard snarled, landing a blow to his barely-healed ribs that sent pain exploding through his body. "Your kind always move in packs."

As they dragged him toward town, Syfir focused on the

distant sensation of water in his blood, sending one final message outward, willing it to reach Sahira: *"Not captured. Choice. Stay hidden. Stay safe."*

He tried to shut out the pain he felt, and focus solely on his purpose.

The river had shown him this path in dreams.

He was protecting the camp, and positioning himself exactly where he needed to be—in plain sight, when Sahira faced the Samiti.

They would meet again. But not as either of them had expected.

# CHAPTER 19
# VISION

Dasha led Sahira north from the way station. "Naga is not like anyone else," she said, her voice losing its usual melody the deeper they went into the forest. "She was never bound by Covenant laws. She is older than the Covenant itself."

"How old is she?" Sahira asked, ducking beneath a low branch.

"Old enough that she witnessed the Old World's collapse. She has lived through cycles of remembering and forgetting that span centuries."

Just days ago, Sahira would have dismissed such claims. Now, everything seemed possible.

They walked for hours. The forest grew denser, the trees older and more gnarled.

Few from town ever ventured this far—the elders warned of wild animals, treacherous terrain, and lingering corruption from the Old World.

But Sahira felt no fear.

By midday, they reached a clearing where the forest suddenly opened into a wide circle.

"You need more than knowledge and strategy," Dasha said.

"You need to cross." She pointed to the patterns circling Sahira's chest. "You're ready for the next threshold."

"What threshold?" Sahira asked, a slight tremor in her voice.

Dasha gestured to the blue patterns glowing faintly beneath Sahira's skin. "These aren't just decorations. They're channels—pathways for ancient memory to return."

She reached into her satchel and pulled out a small leather pouch, pressing it into Sahira's hands.

"Eat the roots," she instructed as Sahira unfastened it, revealing two long roots still crusted with river silt. "Chew them quickly. Their essence will open your eyes to what was… and what might be again."

Sahira hesitated, then shoved the roots into her mouth, chewing and fighting the instinct to spit them out. They tasted of rot and earth, and burned as they slid down her throat.

A moment later, the world tilted.

Sound stretched and compressed. Sahira stumbled, reaching blindly for balance.

"Easy," Dasha said, steadying her and guiding her to her knees. "Let it come. Don't fight what the roots show you."

Time melted.

Expanding, contracting, folding in on itself.

When Sahira blinked, the clearing was gone.

The forest floor dissolved into smooth stone pathways that gleamed beneath the sun.

*She watched women move with confidence—hair unbound, voices raised without shame.*

*Men walked beside them as equals, carrying children, offering open affection.*

*Women and children shaped the elements with their hands: water, air, earth rising and swirling at their touch.*

*It wasn't chaos or corruption. They all moved with no fear.*

"What… what is…" Sahira tried to speak, but her voice echoed strangely inside her head, confusing her.

And then—a flash of light.

Sahira collapsed, retching into the undergrowth as her body expelled the roots.

Tremors wracked her limbs as she vomited, her mind struggling to make sense of what she had seen.

"The veil thinned for you," Dasha said gently, wiping her mouth with a cloth that smelled of mint and river water. "As it did for your mother. As it has for all true daughters of the river." The woman's eyes held a knowledge far too vast for her frail frame. "What you saw was memory. The world as it was…"

Sahira stared at her, still trying to steady her breath.

"Now you are ready for the Mouth of the Serpent," Dasha said, her voice low. "The place where transformation either completes… or consumes. Few are invited. Fewer survive."

She leaned closer.

"Naga guards the entrance. She's been waiting for you."

Sahira's heart pounded.

Dasha watched her. "We're almost there. Come. It's time."

# CHAPTER 20
# TRANSFORMATION

The ancient tree stood alone in the moonlight, on a ridge overlooking the valley. Its roots spread like serpents across stone and earth. Beneath it lay the entrance to the Mouth of the Serpent—a buried place of transformation.

As Sahira approached, a new sound emerged: the soft rasp of scales over stone.

A woman slid from the shadows—tall, serpentine, glistening with otherworldly iridescence.

One of her eyes was clouded with age, the other dark and sharp.

Sahira took a sharp breath.

*Naga.*

"The river's daughter returns to the source," Naga said, her voice low and layered, as though she spoke with many voices at once.

A chill rushed over Sahira's skin as she bowed instinctively.

Dasha, too, inclined her head. "Time grows short, Naga. The elders have begun seizing girls who show signs. Three since yesterday."

"So it begins again," Naga said, deep sorrow in her voice.

She turned to Sahira. "Are you ready to enter the Mouth?"

Sahira glanced at Dasha, who nodded at her.

"Yes," Sahira said quietly.

"Good," Naga said. "Your town's elders preserve a version of the past. But they buried the truth in fear. Before you face them, you must remember what they tried to erase."

She stepped aside, revealing a stone passage hidden among the roots. "You stand now where your mother never had the chance to. To become what she could not, you must pass through the Mouth."

"This is where I leave you," Dasha said, stepping back.

Sahira opened her mouth to protest, but Dasha raised a hand.

"The old ways require old prices," she said cryptically. "But some debts are paid willingly."

Sahira started to ask what she meant, but Naga interrupted.

"Remember: The Mouth reflects what you carry: fear or courage, resistance or surrender. It devours or transforms. What you bring determines what emerges."

She reached for one of the snakes coiled at her wrist as it raised its head to taste the air with a flickering tongue.

Sahira nodded, swallowing down her fear. She glanced over to Dasha for reassurance, but her friend was gone.

Naga pressed a serpent tooth into Sahira's palm. "Go now, Daughter of the River. I cannot guide you in this form."

And she melted into the darkness.

Sahira accepted the tooth and stepped toward the tree. A keyhole waited in its roots, and when she pressed the tooth into place, it clicked softly.

The ground rumbled, and then parted, revealing stone steps that disappeared into the darkness below.

She took a breath and began her descent.

Luminescent moss lined the walls, providing just enough light to guide her down the spiraling stairs. They led her into a space that was impossibly vast and filled somehow with moonlight, despite being buried underground.

At its center stood a curved structure like an open mouth, large enough for a person to step inside. Water spilled endlessly over its stone lips.

The Mouth of the Serpent.

Above its opening, words were etched.

*What flows remembers*
*Awakened may enter,*
*the sleeping may not*
*The mouth exacts its price*
*In death, reborn*

As she moved deeper into the chamber, her body began to respond.

The patterns beneath her skin glowed softly, and her breathing synchronized with the gentle drip of water from the ceiling overhead. Her heartbeat slowed, deepening, as if her blood were aligning with the rhythm of the place itself.

And then she heard them.

Voices, not physical but remembered, carried in the water that flowed through the temple's channels. Women's voices, overlapping, separated by years, generations, and yet speaking to her directly:

*"Daughter of the river, we've been waiting. Remember us."*

Sahira closed her eyes, letting the voices wash over her, through her. The voices grew stronger, more distinct:

*"They called us corrupt. Said our magic destroyed the world. But it was never destruction they feared. It was our power. It was our return."*

Sahira opened her eyes.

She stood now at the edge of the great carved mouth, where water poured over stone lips in a ceaseless, whispering flow.

From the shadows, a new voice emerged. "The temple does not contain transformation," it said. "It *is* transformation."

The figure the voice belonged to stepped into view.

She was young and ancient at once, and so beautiful that Sahira gasped.

Tall, and serpentine, she glowed with a warm light, and water rose to meet her fingertips as she trailed them along the carved channels of the chamber, moving closer to Sahira with every step.

Naga. The river goddess and the serpent mother.

"This place has changed over time, as all living things must. As must you." Her eyes held Sahira's. "The Mouth cannot create what doesn't already live in your blood. But it can awaken what sleeps. And it will ask a price."

Sahira turned toward the chamber beyond.

A curtain of falling water veiled the entrance like skin. Behind it, glistening scale-like carvings shimmered.

A low sound emanated from within, resonating in her blood rather than her ears. A pulse through her bones.

She thought of the women who had come before, some who emerged transformed, and some who never returned.

"Will I die?" she asked, unable to keep the tremor from her voice.

"The girl you have been will," Naga said. Her voice echoed across the chamber. "What comes forth will be your truest form."

The mouth seemed to widen slightly.

She turned to Naga. "Are you the river goddess? From the legend?"

The young-old Naga bowed her head slowly. "The river and the serpent mother," she said as if in introduction. "I live in your blood."

Sahira stepped forward, and the blue marks on her skin blazed brighter.

She drew in a deep breath.

And the water parted to receive her.

And then closed behind her like a living curtain.

THE WATER SHOULD HAVE DROWNED her. Instead, the current cradled her, womb-like, lifting her from the earth.

Time unraveled.

Sahira felt her body dissolving and reforming, cells reshaping themselves according to patterns written in her blood before birth.

The pain was extraordinary. Yet her consciousness floated both within and beyond her changing form, experiencing transformation from every angle, as if her mind, body, and soul were mirrors facing one another, reflecting into infinity.

And then, a choice:

She could surrender completely to the water. Become river, formless, free of self.

Or she could refuse. Force herself back into the body of the girl she had been, and leave the river, the serpent, this destiny behind.

There was a third choice, hidden, just out of reach.

But deep in her blood, she wanted, yearned, desperately needed, to become something new: Both water and woman. Memory and presence.

She willed it into reality with every fiber of her being, her intention rippling through the water like a vow:

"I choose the third path. Water and woman. I choose both."

TIME DISTORTED.

Sahira looked down at her hands, where the blue markings

no longer flickered with proximity to water, but glowed steadily. A living signature of her dual nature.

The memory of every woman who had come here lived now in her blood. She saw her mother clearly then: standing in this same current, facing her own awakening. She saw generations of women who had chosen change over safety, growth over stillness.

And then a vision:

*A rainstorm that split open the sky. Her mother as a newborn, gasping her first breath. A ripple in the river, deeper than the rain that broke the surface. A small boy in a Mehr'an camp turning his face to the rain, a smile on his round face.*

The vision changed, flashes coming quickly.

*Ameera, barefoot at the river's edge. Her hair unbound, her arms marked with blue patterns that glowed as she neared the water.*

*A glance north, toward the ancient tree that guarded the Mouth. Then a look down at her belly, glowing with new life.*

*Her face tear-streaked but determined.*

*Ameera cradling a baby in the dark, whispering stories in secret. Blue marks flickering faintly beneath sleeves, hands passing bread to quiet girls with frightened eyes.*

*The river called. But her child called louder.*

Then the vision turned darker:

*"I won't leave her," her voice trembling but resolute. "I've found a way I can be both. River and mother, awakened and present. We won't have to choose between worlds."*

*"There is no middle path," came a cold voice.*

*The guards moved at a signal from the source of the voice. Her mother fought, the water around her ankles rising in her defense.*

*And then the guards seized her and forced her head underwater.*

"No!" Sahira cried, but the vision moved on, unchangeable.

*They forced her down. She thrashed, fought back.*

*Until she couldn't fight back anymore.*

*And from the shore, a figure in elder's robes watched, face hidden in hood and darkness.*

Sahira sobbed, her entire body shaking with the truth.

Chatti and Fateh Bibi had already told her, but seeing it with her own mind's eye, seeing that moment of terrible clarity, made Sahira's grief crystallize into purpose.

"I will be what you tried to become," she whispered into the water that held her mother's memory. "I will walk the third path you never got to. Water and flesh. Both."

And then, another vision flooded Sahira's awareness.

*As Ameera's body began to still, the water around her began to glow with an intense blue light. The river, recognizing she had been forced under, made a final offer.*

*"Will you accept this half-life?" it seemed to ask, just as Ameera's consciousness was slipping away.*

*"Yes," came her mother's answer.*

*And Sahira saw it happen. Her mother's consciousness surrendered to the river before death could fully take her.*

*She became river.*

Sahira's vision began to fade, but then she heard a voice through the growing darkness.

*"I couldn't come back to you in body,"* her mother's memory whispered through the water. *"But in this way, I could call to you. I could wait until you were ready to hear."*

And then another voice, deeper, vaster. The river itself.

*"You are transformed."* Naga.

And then, blackness.

THE PALE OF early morning cast the world in an ethereal glow as Sahira stepped from the Mouth of the Serpent, water dripping from her transformed body.

The morning air caressed her body, and the leaves above rustled gently as if greeting her.

She drew a deep breath and took her first steps away from

the mouth. Then stopped. There was a strange emptiness in the air. As if something vital had been drawn away.

And then she saw her.

Dasha, collapsed just paces from the tree's roots.

"Dasha!" Sahira cried, rushing to her side. The old woman's skin was pale, her vibrant energy diminished to a flickering ember. "Dasha, what happened?" Sahira fell to her knees beside her.

"You're ready now," Dasha whispered, reaching weakly for Sahira's hands, "To speak to those... who've forgotten... what the river remembers."

"What happened to you," Sahira pleaded, tears streaming from her eyes as she gripped the older woman's hands.

"The serpent's threshold," Dasha whispered. "It demands... balance. A life freely offered... for one transformed."

Sahira gripped her hands tightly. "You knew... this would happen?"

Dasha's eyes suddenly cleared, the scattered fragments of her mind collecting itself whole for a final moment.

"The Mouth doesn't need blood... but it requires completion. Balance." She smiled faintly. "I gave... the river... what remained... so you could awaken. Don't mourn..." Her eyelids fluttered. "I gave it freely."

Tears fell freely from Sahira's eyes, and she reached for Dasha's wrinkled face. "Don't," she begged.

"I was... a broken pot," Dasha murmured, her voice beginning to slur. "But sometimes only broken pots..."

A tremor passed through her, and her eyes closed one last time.

The leaves above shimmered as the first rays of morning sun filtered through the canopy, lighting Dasha's still form.

Sahira knelt beside her, head bowed. *I can't leave her here,* she said silently to the river she now knew would hear her.

A narrow stream rose from the soil beside them, tracing a path downhill.

Back to the river.

It gathered around Dasha's feet, then her arms, weaving around her in a gentle embrace.

And then, slowly, reverently, the water began to carry her toward the riverbank.

She watched as it took her friend. The woman who had given her life so Sahira could awaken. So others who heard the river's call could follow.

And somewhere in Jaraan, the one who had killed her mother was free.

# PART THREE
## BALANCE

CHAPTER 21

# RETURN

By late morning, Sahira had crossed the river again, and Jaraan loomed ahead.

The sun was high by the time she reached the edge of the marketplace.

But she was not the same girl who had left.

The midday light illuminated the changes that made her nearly unrecognizable: The blue patterns that had once shimmered faintly beneath her skin now glowed across her arms and throat, pulsing with their own inner fire. Her body was wrapped in the draped cloth of the Mehr'an. Her hair, once carefully braided in the Covenant style, hung loose and wild.

The first to see her, a young man carrying a tray of clay bowls, dropped them in shock, shards clattering across the cobblestones. He stared. Another boy rushed forward and yanked him away, glancing back with a look of fear.

Sahira walked openly through town, head unbowed. People stared, fear plain on their faces.

They feared her because she no longer feared herself.

A child pointed, only to have her hand quickly pulled down by her mother.

"River-witch," hissed a voice. "Look how she's changed," came another, quieter voice.

A few, mostly young girls, followed her with their eyes, recognition flickering in their expressions.

One broke free from her mother and ran forward. "Are you the river's daughter?" she asked. Her mother snatched her back, eyes darting between terror and fascination.

"It's alright," Sahira said, her voice now carrying the depths of the river. "Curiosity is no sin."

Whispers rippled through the gathered crowd.

Sahira could feel the change in the air. Women moving through their morning routines, who found themselves humming an ancient melody with no memory of learning it. Girls braiding their hair who suddenly stopped and questioned why they always bound it. Mothers preparing breakfast, who froze in their motions, momentarily lost in thoughts that didn't feel quite their own.

The awakening was spreading.

She considered this, gazing out at the people, when a hand touched her arm, pulling her attention sharply back to the moment.

VAREENA, the town midwife, stood blocking Sahira's path. Her silver hair was impeccably arranged, but her eyes were wild with desperation. She grabbed Sahira's arm and jerked her chin toward the door of her storefront apothecary.

"Come with me."

Sahira followed.

Inside, Vareena unfastened the tie at her neck, then yanked back a curtain.

A young woman lay curled on a cot, arms wrapped around her stomach. Blue swirls pulsed faintly beneath the sleeves of her robe.

"Look," Vareena demanded, lifting the hem of the woman's robe to reveal a swollen belly streaked with glowing marks.

Sahira stepped back.

"My grandmother delivered babies during the Great Correction, when the northern settlements collapsed into lawlessness," Vareena said. "She told me what happened to women when the old protections failed." Her voice cracked. "I've spent my whole life helping new life into this world. I know what women need to be safe. And it's not this."

Sahira's eyes softened. "How far along?"

The woman flinched. "Don't come near me," she gasped. "You'll make it worse."

Her eyes darted down, toward her belly. "What if it's not… human anymore? What if it's… something else?"

Sahira took another step back.

Vareena turned. "This is what's happening to our daughters."

Sahira looked at the girl more closely. The same hard set of jaw, the same pained eyes—this was Vareena's daughter.

"I can only tell you what I know," Sahira said gently. "You won't be alone. The river's daughters—"

"The river's daughters *nothing*," Vareena cut in. "You're corrupted. Deluded. I won't lose my family to this madness."

Sahira's voice stayed calm. "She's still your daughter. She's not corrupted. She knows the river now, but she's still yours."

But Vareena had already turned away. "I just needed you to see what you've done. What you've cost me." Her voice dropped, cold. "Stay away from my daughters."

Sahira turned to go. And then paused.

There, at the edge of Vareena's collar, just visible above the seam, was a faint blue mark.

Small and faded. But unmistakable.

TAVIN EMERGED from his father's shop, drawn by the unusual quiet.

He spotted Sahira and froze.

She met his gaze directly now. "Tavin."

He staggered back. "Sahira," he whispered, swallowing.

"You're back. Sahira, I—I was only trying to protect you," he said, the words tumbling out, unsteady. "When I told her, I never imagined..." he froze as if realizing what he had said.

Sahira closed her eyes briefly, taking a deep breath as her mind processed his admission.

She opened her eyes. "Never imagined what?" She squinted at him, seeing him as if for the first time.

"Never imagined they'd strip me bare in front of the town? In front of your father? In front of *my* own family?" She laughed bitterly. "Never imagined they would try to brand me?"

He glanced around as she spoke. "I thought they would... show you mercy."

"They don't show us women mercy."

Tavin swallowed. "The river was... taking you. Like your mother."

"No. It was calling me. But it didn't take me. I chose it."

"But—the ceremony. Our threads—the water. You were becoming something else. The river was turning you into something else."

She shook her head. "This is always who I was."

"Please, let me help you," he insisted. "I can still—we can still heal you—the Samiti will listen to me."

She met his gaze steady. "I don't want your help."

As she turned away, he caught her arm. "You don't understand what this means for me. My father arranged for me to take Elder Varden's position next spring. Everything I've worked for—"

"Power," she said flatly. "That's what this is about."

"No. It's about us." He straightened his back. "Sahira, I'll forgive your... indiscretion," he said, ownership creeping back into his voice. "Most men wouldn't be so understanding. You should appreciate the generosity I'm showing."

"Stop," she said, pulling free. "I should have used my voice to tell you no once before. I am saying *no*."

Something cracked in his expression—the confident mask slipping. "Sahira," he whispered. "If I don't marry you, they've already chosen someone else for me. Malsi Sharma. She's barely thirteen."

Sahira's blood chilled. Malsi. The girl who had been corrected for moving during stillness practice. Who had stood beside Tavin's family during Sahira's humiliation. A child.

Sahira looked at Tavin more carefully. "Then don't marry her," she said quietly.

"I can't—my father, the Samiti, everything—"

"You can. There is always a choice," she said quietly. "Even when it costs everything."

"You think I'm free? That this path was my choice?" He laughed bitterly. "Why did you even come back?" he whispered.

She looked at him, seeing suddenly a man who seemed like a boy. "To try to do what's right."

GUARDS PUSHED THROUGH THE CROWD, their expressions grim. At their center walked Elder Nefret, her deep red robes immaculate, her face a study in controlled rage.

"Daughter of corruption," her voice rang out across the square. "You dare return to contaminate what remains pure?"

Sahira turned to face the elder, but said nothing.

"Your very presence is poison," Elder Nefret went on, her gaze fixed not on Sahira's face but on the glowing blue patterns across her skin. "Look at what you've become. Neither woman nor human. Ever since you started going to your precious river, you've been infecting Jaraan."

"I only want to help," Sahira said.

"You've done quite enough," Elder Nefret continued, her voice rising. "Girls disappearing into the forest; women abandoning their families; betrothals broken—all because of your corruption."

"I came because the river remembers what you've tried to forget," Sahira said calmly.

"Your very existence is a cautionary tale," the elder spat. "Guards! Apprehend her."

They stepped forward. Elder Nefret followed, drawing close enough to speak only to Sahira.

"I will still the river in you," she hissed. "I will silence what you've awakened."

One guard faltered, just for a moment, before snapping back to duty. The others seized Sahira's marked arms, their grip like iron shackles.

As they dragged her toward the temple, Sahira caught sight of the crowd: some horrified, some relieved.

But some—young women, mostly—watched with eyes that shimmered with recognition, as if they, too, had heard the river's call.

And in their faces, Sahira saw the spark of awakening.

She smiled as they pulled her away.

Her return had not been in vain.

# CHAPTER 22
## SEVERING

The guards dragged Sahira through the temple's side entrance and down into the inner sanctum below.

The heavy door slammed shut behind her. Instantly, the river's presence thinned—like a voice calling from across a long distance.

The walls here were lined with strange metal that seemed to dampen her abilities. Still, she could feel water somewhere nearby, faint but persistent.

The first night, her dreams were not of the river but of Syfir. He stood at the place where river meets sea, his back to her. When he turned, his eyes were vacant, unseeing.

*"The journey ended differently than we planned."* His voice was like an echo across water. *"Remember me, Zarouni girl."*

Sahira woke with tears already on her face.

OVER THE THREE days that Sahira was held in the inner sanctum, girls throughout Jaraan were changing.

Across town, her cousin Leela stirred from dreams of a woman with her own mother's face but her cousin's eyes, standing waist-deep in the river, arms outstretched in welcome. She woke with her braid undone, hair spilling across her pillow like dark water, her blanket beneath her inexplicably wet.

When Tharima entered to wake her, the woman stopped short, taking in her daughter's unbraided hair, the wet sheets. "What happened…" she began.

"Nothing," Leela insisted, quickly gathering her loose hair. "It must have come undone while I slept."

But her mother was already backing toward the door. "I'll fetch the bitter herbs. We still have time to stop this before anyone notices."

"Stop what?" Leela asked, though something inside her already knew. Had always known.

"The river-sickness," Tharima's voice trembled.

Across the settlement, similar scenes unfolded as the awakening spread from woman to woman, girl to girl. Some families responded with fear, others with violence, still others with a terrible, knowing silence.

Kaya dreamed of standing unashamed, her body marked with flowing lines. Her father found her hands moving on their own, fingers tracing patterns in the air, motions her body remembered though her mind had never learned them.

He struck her across the face, breaking the trance. "You will not bring any more shame on this family," he hissed, grabbing her wrists. "I won't allow this corruption to continue."

Seventy-year-old Nisha dreamed of dancing to forbidden music. She woke with arthritic hands curved in gestures from her girlhood. "So it begins again," she whispered to her empty room, a lifetime of enforced stillness lifting from her shoulders like mist from the river at dawn. "We remember what they tried to make us forget."

By midday, reports flooded the Samiti: unbound hair, women laughing too loudly at wells, water rising against gravity in impossible patterns.

"It's spreading," Elder Nefret announced, panic cracking her voice. "The corruption has taken root."

The town was cracking along invisible fault lines that had always existed beneath the Covenant's carefully maintained surface. Woman from woman. Mother from daughter. Sister from sister. Those who remembered and those who chose to forget.

Elder Nefret ordered purifications, corrections, doubled guards. But for each woman punished, three more awakened in secret, the river calling them through dreams.

Sahira endured three days of starvation, bitter herbs, and private sermons from Elder Nefret, about women who had surrendered their dangerous natures for the community's salvation.

By the third night, her blue markings had faded.

She sat huddled in the corner she was chained to, her connection to water tenuous and distant.

Elder Nefret entered the chamber alone, carrying a red lehenga folded into a dense square. Sahira's marriage clothes.

"You can still be saved," Elder Nefret said, unusually gentle. "The Samiti has found a way back."

Sahira said nothing, her face unreadable.

"What do you expect to achieve?" Elder Nefret said, her face revealing frustration. "You have no place in your father's home. None in Tavin's home. There is no place in town that belongs to you if you go on like this."

Sahira continued to remain quiet.

"It can still be as it was meant to be." Something like pleading crossed the Elder's face. "The Samiti has consulted the ancient texts. There is still a path back."

"What way?" she asked, her voice cracked from thirst.

"Severing. Drink from the Still Waters, take seven vows of

silence." She unfolded and laid the red lehenga across Sahira's lap.

"I have just spoken with Tavin. He will still honor the original betrothal. Says he will still take you as his wife. He is important to the Samiti. We would help him establish his own home separate from his father. You'd be protected."

Sahira looked down at her lap, staring at the red garments.

"The severing would not be easy," Elder Nefret continued, "but you would survive it. Many have. I did."

Sahira looked up sharply. "You?"

The elder's hand moved to her high collar. A strange look crossed the elder's face. Something almost like grief.

"We are not so different, Sahira Raazaan," the elder said, her voice suddenly brittle. "I too heard the river once." She drew in a deep breath, and then her voice regained its authority. "But I chose order. I chose the community's needs over selfish desire."

"You made a choice out of fear," Sahira said quietly.

"I chose correctly," Elder Nefret snapped. "I saw what the river offered. Chaos. Pain." Her voice caught on the last word, a brief flash of ancient grief quickly suppressed. She stood up straighter, wiping a piece of invisible dust from her shawl. "But there are worse prisons than stillness."

The blue patterns beneath Sahira's skin had faded to almost nothing. The constant whisper of water in her mind had quieted to barely a murmur. Her limbs felt heavy. Ordinary.

She let her fingers brush the fabric and imagined the life that was still on offer. Mornings where she would drink tea with Tavin. Days where she would teach their children to be dutiful members of the Covenant—children who would never question why their mother stared longingly at water. Nights where Tavin would take what he wanted, as he had in the shed. A life contained within Jaraan's boundaries, protected by walls she would herself maintain. The kind of life her mother had agreed to, leaving her true love behind.

That other life—unknown, dangerous, difficult. She thought

of the river. She thought of Syfir. She thought of her mother's unbound hair flowing like the current itself.

"I need water," Sahira said quietly. "Before I decide. Real water, not the bitter tea you've been giving me."

Elder Nefret hesitated, then nodded. "A small mercy. I will allow it."

When the acolyte brought a clay cup of clean water, Sahira took it with shaking hands.

But water wasn't just water.

The first sip exploded like lightning. Memory, connection, truth flooded the hollow spaces of her being.

Her mother's voice, singing by the riverbank. Syfir's hands teaching hers to shape the current. The ancient knowledge of women who walked between worlds before the Covenant ever existed.

And beneath it all, something more.

The river recognized her now not just as its daughter, not just as her mother's daughter or the daughter of the chief.

But as a daughter of Naga.

The transformation that had been completed at the Mouth of the Serpent, now made her an extension of the river itself.

The faded blue patterns beneath her skin blazed back to vibrant life, stronger than before.

Sahira looked up at Elder Nefret, whose eyes widened as she recognized, too late, that the water was restoring what the bitter herbs had smothered.

"There are worse prisons than stillness," Sahira agreed, rising to her feet as water strength flooded back into her limbs. "But there is no prison worse than giving away choice." The red clothing fell to the floor.

Sahira met Elder Nefret's gaze, head held high. "I will not shrink. I will not renounce the river."

Elder Nefret's face contorted with rage, fear, and beneath it all, recognition. Then composure snapped back into place like armor.

"No, I won't allow this," she hissed, straightening her spine. She turned to the acolyte. "Call the guards. You fool, go now!"

The acolyte rushed away, and Elder Nefret edged closer to Sahira. "I will not let you get away with this."

A moment later, a guard appeared, and the elder turned to him. "Bring the basin, and call Elder Varden—and tell him to hurry."

Elder Nefret gave Sahira a sickly sweet smile.

Minutes later, Elder Varden entered with two guards carrying a ceremonial basin.

They set it down in front of Elder Nefret. The guards moved toward Sahira, whose restored power had begun straining against her chains—metal links groaning under the strain of her returning strength.

"The river's hold on her is too strong," Elder Nefret hissed. "We must sever her now, before it fully reestablishes."

Elder Varden nodded once. Together, the elders raised their hands over the basin, and began to chant words pulled from the oldest Covenant texts.

"With this ritual," Elder Varden intoned, "we sever not just this corrupted woman, but the river itself. The connection between water and those who would corrupt it will be broken forever."

With each word of the ancient chant, Sahira felt the threads snapping between her and the handful of women who had awakened in recent days.

And also between the river and everything it touched.

In homes across the settlement, girls cried out as faint blue markings just beginning to emerge now burned with sudden cold. Sahira felt their terror, their confusion.

She felt Leela's scream, Kaya's convulsions, elderly Nisha's collapse. Felt the water itself recoil from the river's edge.

And understood.

The current now flowed through her. And their ritual was severing the very connection that the water had just restored.

They weren't severing just her.

They were severing the river itself.

And the river was fighting back.

The ground trembled as a pressure began to build beneath it.

"Stop!" Sahira screamed, her voice raw. "You don't understand—"

The basin skittered across the stone. Cracks snaked along the floor. The chains at Sahira's wrists began to hiss with heat. Sahira gasped and strained against them, her legs nearly giving out from under her.

"I *am* the river now! You sever me, you sever the rain, the crops, the soil, everything!" She gasped. "You'll kill everything!"

The temple moaned—a deep, guttural sound as if the earth itself were wounded. Blood streamed from its walls.

Elder Nefret's hands shook. Elder Varden's chanting faltered. And for the first time, real terror crossed their faces.

Beyond the walls, the sky darkened unnaturally, clouds spiraling inward as the world responded to the river's agony. In the distance, they could hear screaming from the very earth itself as the natural order began to fracture.

"You have to stop!" Sahira pleaded, as blood seeped from the stone walls. As if the temple itself were weeping.

Elder Nefret froze, eyes wild. "This isn't over," she whispered, but her hands trembled violently as she and Elder Varden backed toward the door. "The trial will finish what this ritual couldn't. You'll beg for the severing before we're done."

And then the Elders were gone.

And Sahira collapsed in the dark. Weakened. Drained. And shaking with fury.

# CHAPTER 23
# TRIAL

S ahira's feet dragged as the guards led her into the great hall.

The chamber reeked of incense and too many bodies crammed too close. She barely registered the carved wooden doors, the gathered Samiti, or the crowd pressed shoulder to shoulder.

Her hair hung limp. Her skin felt cold. The draped cloth from Dasha now hung in tatters on her frame. Her blue markings had faded to the faintest shadow, diminished by the ritual that had nearly severed her.

The trial had been convened in haste, but the intent was clear: display her broken. A symbol of the river, tamed.

At the center of the circular chamber, Elder Nefret stood, with the full Samiti, their long white ceremonial robes stark against the morning sky.

Elder Nefret's voice rang out. "We face the greatest threat to our way of life since the Flooding Years. What began as one woman's corruption has become a contagion, threatening to unravel our way of life. Indeed…"

Sahira barely heard the rest. Her heart pounded in her ears.

Her limbs were leaden. The pain in her wrists from the over-heated chains still throbbed.

Sahira's gaze lifted slowly.

She saw Elder Nefret pointing at her, calling her a contagion, a force of evil.

"This carrier of evil, this… abomination before the Covenant, who wants to destroy everything good about our community."

Sahira's voice was gravelly and low, but audible to everyone. "I carry only the truth. The Covenant is not the only way to live."

Murmurs in the crowd.

Elder Nefret froze, and turned to Sahira, a look of incredulity on her face. "You dare interrupt these proceedings?"

The chamber fell silent.

"I am here to speak the truth."

"You will speak when spoken to," Elder Nefret hissed, nearly running over to Sahira, rage barely contained.

"I've either been banished, or I'm on trial. If it's the latter, I have the right to speak. Which is it, Elder Nefret?"

A faint warmth stirred in her chest—like the river was waking up.

Elder Nefret slapped Sahira across the face, and the sound rang out, echoing through the chamber.

There was complete silence.

She turned to Sahira, her voice dropping to a hiss that only those nearest could hear. "You are your mother's daughter after all. She too thought she could defy the natural order."

"Enough, Nefret," thundered Elder Murat, the eldest presiding member of the Samiti. Her voice radiated unmistakable authority.

"The penalty for corrupting our community has always been death," Elder Nefret said, her voice carrying across the chamber. "That is what the law demands."

A chill ran through the crowd. Several women unconsciously touched their throats.

"That is not for you alone to decide. Let her speak," said Elder Murat, her voice low. "We must all witness the full extent of what we face before judgment is passed." She turned to look at Sahira. "Speak now, child. Let us hear what you have to say before we decide your fate."

Sahira felt a strange constriction in her chest, and then a flicker. The water in her blood stirred, hesitant but responsive. As if listening.

She took a deep breath. "You've been told that stillness is salvation," she began. "That women's voices brought ruin. That our questions led to the collapse."

"But I've seen what the river knows."

She raised her hands, allowing water to gather between her palms. A few gasps came from the crowd as the droplets formed patterns in the air, shimmering with the same blue light that now coursed beneath her skin.

Several people in the crowd gasped.

The water shimmered, forming fleeting images: women leading assemblies; fathers cradling children; magic wielded in joy and healing.

As Sahira spoke, the faint blue of her markings deepened, each word tracing itself across her skin like ink returning to a page.

"The collapse didn't come from women's freedom," Sahira said, her voice carrying to every corner of the chamber. "It came from disconnection. From power without wisdom."

A few people shifted in their seats—those who stood looked around, avoiding her gaze.

And then she saw her father in the crowd. And he was looking directly at her.

She took a deep breath. "But we cannot thrive on a foundation of fear. On a foundation that does not allow half of our people the right to make choices. To have freedom. To live."

She looked around the room. "We must build it on mutual recognition, on balance freely chosen."

The water trembled, then fell to the ground.

"This isn't a trial anymore," Sahira said. "Things have already changed. I'm not here to destroy what the Covenant built. I'm here to name what you've tried not to see: that community doesn't require silence."

She turned to address the men in the assembly directly. "How has the suppression of women's voices created the harmony the Covenant promised?" Several men looked away. One coughed.

Silence followed, but it didn't feel like agreement.

Sahira lowered her hands, letting the water return to the earth. "The river teaches a different way. Flow. Abundance. Connection. This is what we have always known, beneath our fear."

A murmur moved through the crowd.

"I have not come to lead anyone away from the life they choose. The river calls to those who can hear." She looked around the room. "Each of you deserves the right to choose."

And then, a girl stepped forward from the crowd.

"I hear the river in my dreams," Leela said, voice trembling. "Does that make me corrupt too?"

Sahira's heart clenched. Brave, defiant Leela.

"Silence!" Elder Nefret shouted, but the word carried less power now.

Tharima grabbed her daughter and pulled her back as a ripple of whispers spread through the crowd.

A woman nodded from the crowd. "I do too," she said.

"Me too," said another, and the chamber erupted in murmurs and questions.

Elder Nefret began calling again for the guards when a familiar voice stopped her.

"Let the girl speak."

The voice, frail but commanding, cut through the noise in the chamber.

Elder Malik.

The old man hobbled down the aisle, stopping beside Sahira. He gave her a conspiratorial wink, then leaned heavily on his curved walking stick. "Go ahead, child," he nodded to Sahira.

Sahira nodded gratefully, and then turned back to the crowd. "We are your daughters. Your sisters. Your wives. Your mothers. We belong here… as we are," she said in a loud, clear voice. "We can keep fighting what's already unfolding… or find a way to coexist."

"Impossible!" Elder Nefret scoffed.

"That is not your decision to make, Nefret," Elder Murat warned.

"No, of course not," Nefret said coldly. "But this farce must end now." She turned to the guards. "Bring in the consequence of her defiance."

Sahira blinked. She glanced at the Samiti, but no one moved.

A strange stillness fell over the chamber.

Then, a side door creaked open and a guard stepped through, dragging someone behind him.

Horror rose in Sahira's throat like bile.

The figure's face was battered. His mouth was taped shut.

But his robes, loose and indigo-hued, were unmistakably Mehr'an.

# CHAPTER 24
# CONFESSION

Syfir sagged in the guards' grip, blood dripping from his brow.

"Let him go!" Sahira screamed, pulling against the guards' grip. The blue markings on her arms flared, sudden and sharp, like a scream beneath her skin. The water inside her surged in protest.

At the sound of her voice, Syfir's eyes snapped open, immediately finding hers across the chamber.

"Tahir Raazaan," Elder Nefret called out, her eyes scanning the gathered crowd.

Tahir stepped forward. He now looked nothing like the proud Samiti official who had once commanded respect throughout Jaraan. His formal robes hung loose over a gaunt frame, his face hollowed by weeks of grief.

Elder Nefret laughed. "Not so innocent, this daughter of yours, eh, Raazaan?" She turned to Tahir with theatrical delight. "Turns out she's just like her mother."

Confusion flickered across Tahir Raazaan's face as he looked from Elder Nefret to the bloodied man, and then to Sahira, who wept with an agony he hadn't seen since Ameera's death.

Recognition flared in his eyes and he began to move toward her.

Elder Nefret gestured and two guards seized Tahir's arms.

Then she nodded to the guards who held Syfir, and they dragged him closer to the altar, his blood leaving a trail on the stone floor.

"The penalty for corrupting our community has always been death. I'm giving this young woman an opportunity," Elder Nefret crooned, her voice dripping false sweetness as she turned back to Sahira. "Sahira Raazaan, you may accept that punishment, or pass it to this foreign filth you've been spreading your legs for."

"Nefret, this is unconscionable—" Elder Murat began.

"This is justice," Elder Nefret said calmly, not taking her eyes off Sahira. "Let them see what tolerance has wrought: corruption, adultery, foreign contamination." She smiled at Sahira. "Choose," she demanded. "Renounce the river and submit, willingly, to permanent severing, and your lover lives. Refuse—and watch him die."

Sahira's vision was blurred with fury.

She looked up into Elder Nefret's face. "You can't do this." She spoke to the gathered crowd. "I love him. And they beat him senseless for it. And not just today—they did it before, on the very day I was supposed to marry another man. Because love terrifies them—even more than the river does."

"You weren't 'supposed' to be married, you *got* married, you ungrateful whore!" Elder Nefret spat, fury on her face.

"The binding cords dissolved," Sahira shot back, angry tears falling to her cheeks. "Even the Covenant's bindings rejected the marriage. I belong to no one but myself."

Her voice rang out to every corner of the room. "You think you're safe because your mother shows no markings, because your daughter speaks in whispers. You're wrong."

"Enough!" Elder Nefret seethed. "You can end this now—

sacrifice yourself for the community's good, or watch your lover die slowly."

"It could happen to any of you," Sahira continued as if she hadn't heard the elder. "Any of you could love. Any of you could wake one morning and find you can hear the river." Her voice rang with certainty. "And if it happens to you, they will destroy you for it."

As she spoke, her eyes found Elder Nefret's, and something inside Sahira began to untangle. "They will stop at nothing," she said slowly. "To stop you from hearing the call. They will do whatever they deem necessary. They'll kill your sisters, your wives, your mothers."

*When you face the one responsible, you will know.*

"You were there," Sahira whispered. The pieces fell into place. "The night my mother disappeared."

Elder Nefret went very still. "You know nothing of that night. We *saved* your mother from the same fate you seem to want for yourself. She was a danger—"

"She was creating a bridge," Sahira said carefully. "She was helping three girls understand their own awakening. And she was trying to find a balance—to be both river and woman."

"She was going to destroy them! Young girls, practically children!" Desperation broke through Elder Nefret's voice. "She had to be stopped. She was infecting others with her river madness, just as you are now."

"And when the water rose to protect her?" Sahira asked. "What did you do then, Elder?"

A crack of thunder split the sky and the chamber trembled.

"I did what was necessary," Elder Nefret's voice hardened. "I held her under the water to cleanse her, not kill her!" Elder Nefret erupted, the words tearing from her throat.

And then she froze, horror on her face.

The confession hung in the air, impossible to retract.

For one breathless moment, there was silence. The guards

holding Sahira's arms exchanged uncertain glances, stunned by the elder's confession, though their grip remained firm.

Sahira's breath caught in her throat. The truth, laid bare.

*You could destroy them,* Chatti had told her, *but you have the chance to become what your mother tried to be.*

The river surged within her. The current inside had found its prison walls and was waiting to be unleashed.

She could end it here. Call the river down on her mother's killer.

Her hands began to tingle.

"Don't look at me like that." Elder Nefret's eyes darted around fearfully as she sank to her knees. Her body folded inward as if something essential had been extracted from her spine.

"The danger isn't gone," Elder Nefret whimpered desperately. "The river takes everything in the end. Please."

Fateh Bibi's words flooded Sahira's awareness. *You were not awakened to destroy the old world. You were awakened to help birth the new one.*

"You're wrong," Sahira said, seeing the elder as if for the first time. "The river doesn't take. It transforms. You killed my mother's body. But she lives on in the current. In me."

Just then Elder Murat rose from her seat, larger than life in both height and in her voice that cracked like thunder. She fixed her gaze on the guards who stood beside Elder Nefret, a look of uncertainty beginning to cross their faces.

"Guards. Take Elder Nefret to the inner chambers," Elder Murat commanded. "She will remain there until the full Samiti determines her fate."

They hesitated.

"Now."

One of the guards stepped forward. "Yes, Elder," he said, moving toward Elder Nefret with new resolve.

The other guards followed slowly and surrounded her. She

didn't resist as they took her arms. "This changes nothing," she said as they took her away. But her voice was hollow now.

Elder Murat ignored her, turning instead to address the gathered crowd. "The danger was the fear of what we might become if we remembered who we were." She took a deep breath. "And now, we deal with the danger of continuing down the wrong path."

Elder Nefret was led away, and Elder Murat took her place at the center of the chamber. The other Samiti members, still visibly shaken, rearranged themselves around her—a silent acknowledgment of the new order forming before their eyes.

As the chamber reorganized itself around this new reality, the guard standing beside Syfir hesitated, looking toward Elder Murat for direction.

Elder Murat nodded once. The guard knelt and cut Syfir's wrist bindings with a small knife. When he removed the tape from Syfir's mouth, he did so with unexpected gentleness—as if the truth revealed had transformed the balance of power along with something fundamental in how the Mehr'an man was perceived.

Syfir tried to stand, but managed only to kneel. Blood darkened the corners of his mouth. His eyes found Sahira's across the chamber.

The guards released her.

She ran to him. In full view of the elders, her father, her aunt, the entire town—the world that would have kept them apart. And then she fell to her knees before him and threw her arms around him, tears flowing from her eyes.

He groaned, and she drew back. "I keep getting beat up for you," he murmured. She laughed through her tears and held him as they knelt together.

Sahira stood, and tried to help Syfir to his feet, but found she couldn't do it alone.

And then Tahir Raazaan came to their side. For a moment, his eyes met Sahira's. Without a word, he helped her lift Syfir to his feet, and then helped her ease him onto a bench.

He squeezed Sahira's shoulder once before slipping back into the crowd.

Sahira watched him walk away, her mind still reeling—a mixture of grief, gratitude, worry, fear, all roiling inside her at once as she struggled to process all that had happened.

And then she heard a voice that pulled her attention: Elder Malik, who had been leaning against his walking stick, suddenly straightened as if waking from a dream. "Ah," he said, blinking owlishly at the crowd. "You know," he continued conversationally, as if discussing the weather, "Two currents can flow in the same river."

Elder Murat turned to him, and the rest of the room followed her gaze with visible unease. "Malik," Elder Murat said carefully, "what are you suggesting?"

"Balance!" he exclaimed, then immediately looked confused by his own enthusiasm. He looked around, as if surprised to find himself speaking to a crowd. "What do you think, Murat? Might it be time to try being a river instead of a dam?"

Elder Murat considered his words, her sharp eyes distant with thought. After a moment, she turned to the gathered community.

"On the matter of what to do with the river-touched girls… The Samiti will deliberate." she announced, her voice low. "Until we decide, there will be no more purifications. But this does not mean that we will condone what we do not yet understand."

Several elders exchanged uncertain glances. The solution pleased no one completely—which perhaps made it the only solution possible.

"And to Sahira Raazaan, we will offer this: You will not be executed nor banished. But this arrangement is temporary. We will see if… coexistence proves possible."

"Wonderful!" Elder Malik exclaimed, looking at Sahira.

As the assembly dispersed, Sahira found herself surrounded by girls and women looking at her. Kaya. Leela. Malsi.

Syfir's leg was badly injured. Sahira and Kaya helped him through the doors, away from the Samiti Hall, and down onto a bench.

"What happens now?" Kaya asked, her voice low and uncertain.

"Now we learn to build a bridge between two worlds," Sahira said quietly. "And we keep going."

# CHAPTER 25
# SAHIBA

Sahira went to her father's house and knocked at the door. Nobody came—no Maru, no servants, not even Tharima. But the door was unlocked.

She stepped inside and looked around.

She made her way to a room she hadn't been allowed to visit since childhood, then turned the knob. Tahir's study was unchanged—scrolls arranged, old pre-Covenant maps on the wall. Jaraan looked tiny, a fleck on the parchment beside the Covenant's sprawl.

The room looked somehow diminished, as if the certainties it represented had contracted.

She found him standing at the window of his study, gazing toward the east, in the direction of the river that had claimed his wife and transformed his daughter.

He turned his head at the sound of her footsteps.

"Baba," she said, stepping into the room.

Tahir Raazaan looked at Sahira, his expression unreadable.

A silence, long and empty, stretched between them.

"I thought you'd left us entirely," he said finally, his voice rough with emotions he'd spent a lifetime containing. "Like your mother."

"I'm still here," Sahira replied, though she understood what he meant. The blue markings that now traced patterns up her arms and across her collarbone marked her as something entirely other than the dutiful daughter he'd raised.

"I tried to protect you," he said, turning back to the window. "Everything I did—the betrothal, the restrictions, the prayers— this life. It was all to keep you from her fate."

Sahira moved to stand beside him, close enough to share his view but not touching. "And what happened to her?"

The silence stretched so long she thought he wouldn't answer. Then:

"She loved another man before me," he said, voice thick with emotion. "Her family married her to me. That man was wrong for her. Wrong in every way." He shook his head. "My father told me I was crazy. To marry a woman who had loved another." His lip curled at the memory. "Because she could be—" He glanced at Sahira. "Impure."

Sahira said nothing, listening.

"But I didn't even care. She was so beautiful, Sahira." His eyes closed. "The most beautiful woman in this world."

"I didn't listen when Elder Nefret told me she was corrupted by the river. That it spoke to her, changed her." His eyes opened now, and narrowed as they looked into the distance. "I didn't believe any of them—not at first. Your mother was... unconventional, but never unstable." His hands gripped the windowsill.

"Until the markings appeared," Sahira said quietly.

He shook his head, eyes fixed on the distant water. "She had them as long as I knew her. Blue markings, just like yours, beneath her skin. She had always been able to hide them, but as time went on... they got worse. I should have—" He stopped, swallowing hard. "The elders said there was only one way to save her. Purification. Separation from the river."

"But she refused."

He nodded. "She said they would destroy who she truly was.

That she had already given up too much, her past life, her name—"

"Her name?" Sahira asked, turning.

His gaze unfocused, remembering a long-forgotten past. "The world knew her as Ameera. But as a child, her family... they called her Sahiba."

"Sahiba?"

The name stirred the memory of the old woman in the market who had looked at her like she'd seen a ghost.

He nodded. "The elders insisted she leave behind childhood. Leave the old name behind."

*Sahiba.*

"We named you Sahira, after her old name," Tahir said, a smile almost touching his lips.

His face darkened again. "The day she..." he took a deep breath. "That day, we argued. I don't even remember what it was about. She left the house afterward, said she needed air. I thought she just needed time. I waited, but she didn't return right away. And I had to leave. I was due in another settlement by sundown. For a trade negotiation." His voice faltered.

For a moment, he seemed to struggle with whether to continue. Then, he stood up straighter. He walked to his bookcase, withdrawing a key wedged under the spine of a book.

He returned to his desk, and unlocked the top drawer. His hands trembled as he pulled out a small weathered box and placed it on his desk.

"I thought she'd be home before nightfall. For your sake, if not for mine." He looked up at Sahira, his expression pained.

"But when I came back, the elders were already waiting at the door." His eyes looked from the box to Sahira's face. "They found her shawl on the bank. Said she walked into the river. That the river claimed her in her madness."

He removed the lid. Inside the box was a torn piece of fabric, a silver pin, a folded paper, yellow with age.

He unfolded the paper—a fragment of an official report, its edges frayed.

"But she wasn't mad. She never had been."

And then he handed Sahira the paper. Her mother's name, a date, and two words: *Presumed Dead.* At the bottom of the page, a single name was signed: *Nefret Sutekh.*

"Nefret and the guards were at the river that night. I should have known." His voice broke. "How could I not have known?" He sobbed. "I let myself believe them. I helped them silence her. And then I silenced you."

Sahira didn't contradict him or offer easy absolution. But she stepped closer to him.

"Your mother would never have abandoned you," he said, finally looking at her directly. "How could I have not known?" he asked again, his eyes searching hers.

"You miss her," Sahira realized.

"Foolish, after so many years." His attempt at a smile failed. "And now… I'm losing you to the same river. And I don't know how to stop it."

"You're not losing me, Baba," Sahira said gently.

"No—you were never even—" he stopped. "I married her knowing…" he shook his head.

Sahira held her breath.

"I knew she loved someone before me. I always knew. But you are my daughter in every way that matters." His voice was gruff with holding back a deep sorrow.

"I don't know how to be your father anymore," he said. "Everything I taught you… it all feels wrong now."

"You're not losing me. I'm becoming who I was always meant to be. Just as Mama did."

"And where does that leave me?" The question held no self-pity, only genuine bewilderment.

Sahira reached for his hand, expecting him to pull away from her marked skin. Instead, his fingers closed around hers with surprising strength.

"Between worlds," she answered honestly. "As all of us are now. The old ways are breaking. But some things endure."

He studied their joined hands—her skin with its luminescent blue patterns, his weathered and unmarked.

"I don't understand what you've become," he admitted. "I probably never will."

"You don't need to understand to accept," Sahira said softly.

There was quiet between them.

Her father's expression cracked. "I think your mother would be proud," he said finally. "She saw something in you I couldn't recognize."

"The river," Sahira said.

He nodded slowly. "Perhaps."

He released her hand and straightened his shoulders, some of his old authority returning. "I don't know if the people of Jaraan are ready to accept all of this."

"And you?"

"I think..." he paused, the admission clearly difficult. He took a deep breath. "I think perhaps we've been afraid of the wrong things."

It was no acceptance.

But it was the beginning of a bridge between them.

A HEAVILY BANDAGED SYFIR, a crutch tucked under his left arm, waited for Sahira outside the Raazaan house.

"How did it go?" he asked as Sahira emerged.

Sahira gave a small, weary smile.

Syfir smiled, and held out his free hand. She moved closer and slid her fingers into his, careful not to squeeze.

They made their way toward the Government Colony gates. East. Toward the Bakki.

# CHAPTER 26
# PATH

O ver the next hour, Sahira and Syfir made their way slowly back to the riverbank, Syfir still favoring his good leg.

The sun was setting as they crossed the shallowest part of the Bakki. Sahira helped lower him onto a soft blanket and unpacked a satchel of food from Leela.

They ate in silence, watching the sun drown in the river.

Then, women began to arrive. Some came with lamps, others with food or blankets.

"You go to them," Syfir whispered. "I'll rest here. Can't go anywhere, so I'll be here when you're done."

Sahira gave him a grateful look and touched her hand to his before she got up to welcome the coming women.

~

By nightfall, the circle of women at the river had grown to twelve. A tiny fraction of the town's women, but it was still significant.

The last to speak was Malsi, the youngest girl present.

"I don't have markings," the girl said. "But I dream of being underwater. And in the dreams, I can breathe. Does that mean the river will call me too?"

As if in answer, a single drop rose from the river's surface, hovered in the air, and split into tiny droplets that caught the moonlight like suspended stars—then fell back into the current.

Sahira smiled at the girl, who looked like she got her answer.

"I don't know what comes next," Sahira said, her voice barely above a whisper. "The Samiti gave us breathing room, not acceptance. Tomorrow…" She shook her head. "Tomorrow we survive. We find ways to live apart from a world that may never fully accept us."

She knelt and pressed her palm to the damp earth. "Some of you may decide this is too hard. That the old life was easier. I would understand that choice."

As the small gathering dispersed, most slipped back toward town. Heads down, shoulders hunched against watching eyes.

Only Kaya and Leela remained by the water.

"Will they come back?" Leela asked.

Sahira looked around. "I think so. Some. Others…" She shrugged. "Safety is precious. Not everyone can afford the luxury of transformation."

Leela's face fell.

"We have the river on our side," Sahira said softly. "But remembering and acting are different things."

She looked back toward Jaraan, where most families slept, unchanged. Not knowing that tonight, some of their daughters had sat by forbidden water, dreaming impossible futures.

LATER THAT NIGHT, Sahira turned to Syfir, a thought striking her. "I need to ask you something."

"Ask," he said, reaching for her hands.

"Did you know?" Her voice was low but intent. "About my parents."

Syfir's expression shifted subtly.

"That Tahir Raazaan isn't my true father."

He gave her a crooked smile.

"So you knew," Sahira said, drawing back.

Syfir shrugged. "Not exactly."

"You knew, and you didn't tell me."

"I suspected," he corrected. "No one said anything. But… the way Fateh Bibi looked at you, I… suspected." He brought his hand up to her cheek. "Don't be upset. It wasn't my truth to tell."

Sahira gaped at him, torn between disbelief and under-standing.

He let his hand slide into her hair that fell in loose waves around her shoulders. "I suppose that makes us cousins?"

His smirk widened and she swatted his arm gently.

"What? Distant cousins."

"Stop it," she laughed, despite herself. "Your mother said she raised you as her own. But that you're not of Mirza's blood."

He made a face of exaggerated shock. "She's not my real mother? My entire life has been a lie."

They laughed, the sound light and relieving.

But as it faded, a weight settled between them.

Sahira turned serious. "Syfir, are you going to leave with the Mehr'an?"

His gaze dropped, then lifted. For a moment, something flickered behind his eyes. A hint of uncertainty, of paths not yet chosen flashed in his eyes.

"You are my life now," he said softly.

But it wasn't quite an answer to what she had asked.

He drew her into his arms carefully, wincing as he shifted.

And they both quietly, independently chose to save the conversation for another time.

THE NEXT MORNING brought an unexpected visitor.

Chatti's face was lined with worry that melted into relief at the sight of Syfir. "You foolish man," she scolded in greeting as she rushed toward him, her hands moving immediately over his injuries with practiced skill.

"Three broken ribs, a gash that should have been stitched immediately, and this leg..." She probed gently at his knee, causing him to hiss in pain. "You'll limp for months, maybe longer." She exhaled hard. "I should've kept my mouth shut about the guards. You could've been killed."

"But I wasn't," Syfir replied, wincing as she probed a particularly tender spot.

Chatti's glare softened, but only slightly. "The scouts lost your trail," she said, glancing at Sahira. "We thought the worst. Then word reached us… about the trial."

"I'm fine," Sahira assured her.

Chatti shook her head. "Nothing about anything that has happened in this town is fine. What they did to my brother wasn't fine. What they did to your mother. What they tried to do to you and to my boy—none of it is fine." Chatti was gritting her teeth. "I'll be glad once we're south. Far from this cursed place."

Sahira and Syfir exchanged a brief look.

Chatti caught it, and her eyes narrowed.

"You *are* meant to lead our people south," she said bluntly, looking at Syfir. "To be the water-shaper for our people."

"Ma," Syfir began.

"No, don't 'Ma' me," she cut in.

He kept his voice calm. "Sahira is building something here. Something new. And this place needs a water-shaper too."

"There are children dying in other settlements, Syfir. Wells failing. Women imprisoned in sheds while their elders burn their skin. And you want to stay here?" She turned to glare at Sahira then. "You should be coming with him—not giving him reasons to stay."

"She's not the reason," Syfir said, taking Sahira's hand. His voice didn't rise, but the act said everything.

Chatti blinked at their joined hands.

"Besides, our people have another shaper now," he added. "You'll guide him. He's ready, or he will be soon."

"Sarvan?" Chatti scoffed. "Sarvan is a boy, not a leader. He doesn't have your strength. Or your vision."

"But he has you," he said gently. "He will be ready soon enough. And you can guide him. Ma, the people here need me for the same reasons our people need me. I have a duty here, too. To help build what comes next."

"You want to build here," she whispered, betrayal flickering in her eyes.

"I want to build with her," Syfir said.

"Syfir, you bring her with you. I will not stand by while you abandon your own people."

"I have a duty to this community too," Syfir said quietly.

Chatti's chin quivered, and she jutted it out as if stopping the emotions from spilling over. "Your place is with us," she said, but it was a plea now, not a command.

Chatti stared at her son as if daring him to speak. And when he didn't, she turned, storming off.

Sahira started after her, but Syfir stopped her with a hand on her arm. "Let her go," he said quietly. "She needs time."

A week passed.

The river circle had grown. Fifteen women now gathered nightly by the river.

Chatti remained in their small camp, but kept her distance, watching quietly as Sahira tended to the delicate balance forming in Jaraan, her eyes constantly drifting back to her son.

As Syfir had predicted, Chatti was eventually ready to talk.

She approached Sahira under moonlight, arms crossed. "I owe you an apology," she said, not meeting her eyes. "You belong with Syfir. And with us. But I still don't want him to stay here."

"I know," Sahira said quietly. "But you have to know, I'm not making him stay."

Chatti let out a sound that was somewhere between a laugh and a sigh. "I know. That boy's never needed anyone's permission to make up his mind."

A silence stretched between them, filled only by the flowing of the river.

Then Chatti said, almost to herself, "The Mehr'an will need a new chief someday."

Sahira turned. "You mean Syfir?"

"It's meant to be you."

Sahira froze. "What?"

"You're Mirza's blood," Chatti said. "Fateh Bibi's granddaughter. The daughter of the last chief's line. And yes, I've always known."

Sahira shook her head. "But—no one expects that. No one sees me that way."

"They will," Chatti said. "The line matters. And the river has chosen you—that matters too."

Sahira stared at her. "I'm not meant to lead the Mehr'an."

"If you refuse, the people will understand. But... Syfir can lead," she said.

Understanding dawned on Sahira. "You want me to ask him to go," she said slowly.

"I'm not asking you to give him up," Chatti said. "But I hoped you'd help him see what's at stake. Sahira, you are kin. I accept you not only as my niece, but as Syfir's woman. But I won't accept Syfir abandoning our people. Not now."

"I don't want him to abandon them either," Sahira said. She

glanced in the direction of Jaraan. "But I also can't leave here. Not now. Not when the work is just beginning."

Chatti nodded slowly. "That's what a true chief would do. Stay where you're most needed."

Sahira's voice was quiet. "Then why won't you let him do the same?"

Chatti flinched, but said nothing.

"You said Syfir makes his own choices," Sahira said. "Let him."

Chatti's jaw clenched. "I'm just asking you to remind him who he is."

Sahira was quiet for a long moment, watching the river flow around the stones Syfir had arranged. "What if he's someone who refuses to choose between here and there?"

Chatti's brows furrowed. "A man cannot be in two places, child."

"No," Sahira said slowly, and then crouched, dragging her finger through the wet sand in a slow, widening spiral. "But rivers connect places. Not divide them."

Chatti frowned, and then bent down to examine the spiral.

"Rivers connects all settlements. Syfir could travel—to the failing wells, along the coast," her finger circled back to where it began. "Teaching and building bridges between communities. Returning here between after each cycle."

"Months away at a time," Chatti said skeptically.

"But not goodbye." Sahira looked up. "A new rhythm. A new kind of life."

Syfir appeared behind them, clearing his throat as he approached toward the two women.

He cocked his head. "Making plans for my future without me?"

"Writing a new destiny," Sahira murmured, still looking at the spiral.

He looked at the spiral in the sand. "A traveling water-shaper?"

"You'd travel with the Mehr'an," Sahira said. "And be here when you can. Train our people to live self-reliantly when you are here."

"I could train Sarvan while traveling," he nodded. "And one day, when he's ready to take over… I could return for good."

"Eventually," Chatti cut in. "That's a long time away, you understand… and it's not exactly what I asked for."

"But it might serve more people," Sahira said.

"A traveling water-shaper," Chatti studied her son, and then looked more closely at Sahira. "And you'll live with the uncertainty of his return?"

"There's no uncertainty," Syfir interjected, eyes fixed on Sahira. "I'll always come home to you."

SOME DAYS LATER, they lay together by the river's edge, Sahira's head resting on Syfir's chest, listening to his heartbeat and the rhythm of the river.

"Your mother's right," she murmured. "Those people do need you more than we do."

"Those people need what I can teach them. But this place…" He let his fingers tangle in her hair. "This place needs what we can build together. There's a difference."

"Is there?" she asked quietly. "Or are you choosing me over duty?"

"My duty is always to the future. And you are my future."

Sahira looked up into his face, and watched him carefully. "So then, is it time to go?"

Syfir's hand stilled in her hair. "What do you mean?"

"I see the way you watch the horizon. The restlessness in your hands." Her voice held no accusation. Only recognition.

His eyes searched hers.

"You get to have both," she said softly. She pulled herself off of him, and sat up, her eyes still on his. "The future with me, and the one where you help others. So we can live in a world where communities like the one we're building aren't miracles. They can just be normal."

He sighed, the sound merging with the water's gentle rhythm as he sat up beside her.

"The southern settlements have brackish wells. They won't survive the dry season without clean water." He began to trace a pattern in the sand. "I've been testing filtration systems using river stones, arranged like this," he said, gesturing to the pattern.

"And there's a water-shaper by the coast purifying saltwater."

Sahira watched the way Syfir's eyes lit up as he spoke, and realized she was smiling.

"But no one is sharing knowledge. All the communities are isolated. I want to build something more than irrigation," he said. "We need to build a network. Of understanding. Not just between water-shapers." He shook his head. "There are places where awakening and tradition have found balance. They should share their wisdom."

"This could help entire communities." A flutter of excitement rose in her chest as she looked at him. "You're talking about changing more than just Jaraan."

"I'm talking about us changing everything," he confirmed. "One connection at a time."

He wiped the sand clean and sat up, motioning toward the riverbank.

A thin stream near his hand flowed through a neat arrangement of stones. He adjusted one, and the current shifted instantly.

"Other settlements are already changing," he said. "I can help them—and train Sarvan along the way. Once he's ready, I'll stay here. Only travel when truly needed."

"When will you leave?"

"The southern settlements can't wait much longer," Syfir said as they lay by the river that night. "I need to leave within the week."

Sahira had been expecting this. "How long for the full circuit?"

"Some months in the south. A few more during planting season. Nine, maybe ten. Depends how quickly Sarvan learns." His fingers reached for her face, and slid into her hair.

"Teach him fast," Sahira whispered.

His eyes met hers. "I intend to," he said earnestly.

"How soon do you leave?" she asked.

"I've already delayed too long, because of my injuries. And because I couldn't bear to leave you."

He kissed her gently then. "What will you do when I'm gone?" he murmured against her lips.

"I've never had trouble keeping busy," she laughed.

And then her fingers traced the faint scars along his jaw, mapping the evidence of what he'd endured for her. "Are you well enough to travel?"

"Thanks to you," he said, catching her hand and pressing it flat against his chest, where his heart beat steady and strong beneath her palm.

She held his gaze. "Then it's time."

The simplicity of her acceptance nearly undid him. But then his eyes lit with sudden mischief. "Marry me first."

"What, right now?" She laughed. "Here by the river with no witnesses but the fish?"

He raised an eyebrow. "The river married us the first night I kissed you. Everything else is just ceremony."

Her breath caught at the truth of it.

"We'll have ceremony when you come back," she said, leaning closer until their foreheads touched. "To make sure you don't get distracted by any pretty girls in distant settlements."

"Impossible," he whispered. "There's only you. I'll always come back to you."

"Swear it," she whispered.

"I swear it," he said. "No matter what waters I must cross. No matter how far the current takes me. You are my home."

"I know," she said. "Rain always returns to the river."

She took his hand and pressed three fingers gently to his chest, over his heart.

"What does that mean?" he asked softly.

"Something my mother used to do," Sahira said softly. "It means I love you. It means come home to me."

# CHAPTER 27
# CONVERGENCE

In the weeks that followed, a fragile coexistence began to take shape.

Some families tentatively opened their doors—mothers who quietly supported their daughters' awakenings, fathers visiting the river's edge under cover of dusk, siblings inventing their own secret languages of care.

But others fractured. Kaya's father struck her name from the family record, distributing her dowry among cousins. Tharima disowned Leela and retreated into silence, refusing to speak even to her brother when he visited the river circle.

Some husbands left. Fathers dragged daughters home from the river by force. Sisters who had once shared everything became strangers.

"This isn't what I wanted," Sahira told Leela one day as they watched a young girl being forcibly led away from the river's edge by her father.

Leela's voice was flat. "The Covenant took generations to build. Did you think it would collapse in one season?"

Cᴜᴛ ᴏғғ ғʀᴏᴍ ғᴀᴍɪʟʏ ʜᴏᴍᴇs, awakened women were granted the right to rent market stalls, but only on the outermost ring, where foot traffic was lightest and the ground turned to mud with every rain.

Rules were strict: no river symbols, no displays of power, no gatherings of three or more.

Despite Elder Murat's promises to allow the river-touched women to coexist with the Covenant, the women were merely tolerated, not welcomed.

Timber and stone requests went unanswered. Merchants raised prices at the sight of river-marked women. Guards turned their backs during disputes.

The river circle's improvised shelters, adequate for autumn's mild weather, proved woefully insufficient against the valley's harsh winter. As the cold deepened and their situation remained precarious, the awakened women realized they needed a different approach entirely.

"It's not enough," Leela said, appearing beside Sahira, voice quiet but resolute.

Sahira didn't answer. But she felt it too.

As ᴛʜᴇ ᴄᴏʟᴅ finally gave way to the first bearable mornings, Sahira called a gathering of the newly awakened.

"We can't keep going like this," she said simply. The winter had been brutal. Their earnings were meager, their shelters insufficient. "We need more than defiance to survive."

"We do," Kaya agreed, her jaw tight. "But I won't crawl back to the Covenant."

The debate lasted days. Some argued for reintegration, for returning to traditional households. Others proposed retreating deeper into the wilderness.

It was Leela who offered a different kind of vision.

Her blue markings had spread further up her arms over the

past few months, and despite her age, when she spoke, her voice carried unexpected weight.

"We're thinking about this all wrong," she said. "We keep trying to fit into their system. But what if we didn't need their system at all?"

Kaya leaned forward. "Go on."

"If Jaraan won't treat us fairly in the market," Leela said, "then maybe we start our own. Make our own trading networks with other settlements. Make our own rules."

The idea took root slowly.

First, it was just Leela accompanying Kaya to gather herbs in the high meadows, carrying larger bundles than any one healer could use.

Then came the visits from women in other settlements—travelers who had heard whispers of the river healers and were willing to journey considerable distances to find remedies that traditional healers couldn't or wouldn't.

By spring, the transformation was unmistakable. The river circle was no longer a camp of exiles. It had become a destination.

Traders came not out of pity or curiosity, but because they needed what only the river-women could offer.

And the awakened had something their traditional counterparts lacked: mobility.

Unbound by the Covenant's restrictions, they could travel, adapt, and respond. They established new trade routes. Built new relationships.

What began as a strategy to survive their community's rejection had evolved into genuine independence.

By the time the river circle's exotic goods had begun appearing in Jaraan's markets—oils, teas, tinctures no one could source locally—even the most traditional families began seeking out the awakened women's stalls.

Little by little, the town that had cast them out found itself in quiet dependence.

Jaraan, increasingly, needed them.

~

JARAAN DID NOT WELCOME this reversal of fortunes.

Traditional merchants watched their profits dwindle as buyers bypassed their stalls for the river's fairer prices and superior goods.

The river circle's success only deepened the resentment among the most traditional families, who saw this prosperity built outside Covenant structures as a fundamental threat to their way of life.

Elders Merek and Varden, long wary of the river circle's influence, began rallying support for a separatist settlement. After three days of debate, the Samiti reached a compromise: the traditionalists could depart, but trade and visitation would continue.

On the morning the first caravan left, Sahira stood on the eastern ridge, heart heavy. Nearly a third of Jaraan had chosen separation over coexistence.

Tavin and his parents were among the first to leave, and Sahira watched from a distance as he climbed into a wagon.

The exodus carried more than just the most rigid families. Some families left out of fear, others to escape debt, and still others hoping distance from the river might protect their children from its call.

With them went skilled hands: the blacksmith, two of three grain merchants, and Vareena, the midwife.

By afternoon, Jaraan felt strangely hollow. The morning's silence felt emptier. The wagons had taken people, but also traditions, skills, and connections that had bound the community together for generations.

And even though Sahira had known change would come at a cost, the ache of seeing Jaraan as an emptied town, still surprised her.

IN THE MONTHS THAT FOLLOWED, Elder Murat began receiving quiet visits.

Prominent families, ones who had publicly upheld the Covenant, privately suggested that a more comprehensive coexistence with the river circle might serve their interests.

And with a third of the population gone, Jaraan's markets faltered. The reduced population meant less demand for goods. Stalls once bustling now stood half-empty. Services lagged.

And the Samiti's tax revenues plummeted.

Then came the letter from the new traditionalist settlement.

Elder Murat read the letter three times. The winter had been harder than expected. They needed supplies, medicine, workers, tools. The separation that once felt like a solution now looked like a slow unraveling.

The letter made clear what Elder Murat had begun to suspect: Jaraan needed the awakened women's economic contributions more than either side had realized. Without the river circle's innovations and trade, both settlements were failing.

The numbers confirmed it: Jaraan's revenue had dropped nearly fifty percent. Meanwhile, the river circle's independent trade continued to flourish, drawing buyers from distant towns.

The economic split had become an existential threat.

Elder Murat called an emergency session.

It was time to try something else.

WEEKS LATER, Elder Murat convened the first Meeting of Balance.

Unlike the Samiti's usual gatherings with rows of elders on raised platforms, this one took place in a circle, beneath the open sky.

Six elders sat on one side.

Sahira and Kaya sat opposite them, their shoulders squared. Neither woman bowed.

Elder Murat looked at the women meaningfully. "We gather in seeking, not in judgment," she began, her voice heavy with authority. "The old ways preserved us through famine and flood. But now, they are questioned."

Sahira met her eyes. "And stillness cannot be the only answer."

Elder Varden's lips tightened. "We will not return to the chaos of the Old World. Stillness—control of women—is what prevents chaos."

Elder Murat closed her eyes. "I have lived seventy-seven years under the Covenant's ways. I know its strength. I also know its stillness. But silence and stillness no longer serve."

Kaya's body tensed beside Sahira. But her voice did not shake when she spoke. "Control is a prison. And we won't remain inside it."

"Then let us choose peace," Sahira said, gently touching Kaya's arm. "Before the river chooses otherwise." Her tone was even, but the threat beneath it shimmered like a submerged current.

Elder Murat's eyes closed briefly. The silence stretched. Then, with a slow breath, she nodded.

"Then we must name the terms of peace." She unrolled a fresh scroll and laid it flat. Then she reached for a pen and uncapped an inkwell.

"First, no woman shall be punished for awakening," said Elder Murat, holding the pen up and looking pointedly at Elder Varden.

The man nodded reluctantly.

Kaya leaned forward. "No. No woman will be punished for any act a man would not be punished for. No more purification."

Elder Varden scoffed at Kaya. "The Covenant's teachings on purity must still be honored. Our traditions preserved our people through the Flooding Years."

"Then let them be honored equally," Kaya said, arms folding across her chest, her gaze fixed on Elder Varden. "If purity is judged, judge men by it too."

Before Elder Varden could protest, Elder Murat cut in, holding up a hand. "She is right. Perhaps it is time to take a more careful eye to what men do. To consider all choices that shape virtue. Not just the ones made by women."

"That's all we ask," Sahira said softly.

"You ask much." Elder Varden muttered.

Kaya didn't flinch. "We ask less than what was taken."

Elder Varden opened his mouth, then closed it again.

A long silence followed her words.

Elder Laal, silent until now, cleared her throat. "Give them full guard protection in the markets."

Elder Murat looked at her with surprise.

"My daughter's health improved thanks to their medicines," she shrugged.

Elder Murat nodded, and then spoke. "Then let it be: First, no woman shall be punished for an awakening. Second, no woman shall be punished for any act unless men can be punished for the same act." She looked at Sahira directly. "And third, river trade will be permitted along the border stalls," she added. "*With* full guard protection, and formal recognition from the Samiti."

Sahira nodded once, and glanced at Kaya for approval. Kaya also nodded.

Elder Varden huffed, but remained otherwise silent.

"Good. It is agreed," Elder Murat said.

The Meeting of Balance marked a turning point. By the time summer's heat blanketed the valley, the new agreements had settled into a fragile peace.

And then came the first true test of this fragile balance.

The drought.

The wells had been dropping for months, but after three weeks with no rain at all—the longest dry spell in living memory, during what should have been the monsoon season, they were now dangerously low.

The Bakki shrank visibly, exposing rocks and riverbed untouched by sunlight in generations.

And then the late-summer monsoon season failed to arrive.

Those who went to the riverbank and tried to drink from what remained found only bitterness. Water that stung and sated no thirst.

Some said this had happened before, that it was just part of a dry cycle. Others whispered the river had moved or changed its course. The most fervent traditionalists blamed the awakened women, claiming their magic had poisoned the Bakki.

But no one could explain why the rains no longer fell.

Rationing grew strict, and tempers flared. A fight erupted at the eastern well when a woman was caught drawing extra water for her family. The next morning, Sahira found crude symbols painted on rocks around their encampment.

ELDER MURAT CONVENED an emergency session as tensions rose, with several elders demanding restrictions on the river circle's water access.

Elder Murat sat at the head of the table, lips dry, expression grim.

Sahira, Kaya, and Leela arrived to find the atmosphere as tense as during Sahira's trial.

"We face a threat that does not care for tradition," Elder Murat said.

"Then why do the river-touched still have access to water while those devoted to our Covenant suffer?" demanded Elder Varden, his voice cracking with thirst and fury.

"Elder Varden, weren't you planning to leave Jaraan to join the new settlement?" Elder Murat asked her tone clipped.

"Oh, I will. But I want to make sure that when this community finally collapses under the weight of its own foolishness, no one can say we didn't warn them," he smiled.

Instead of arguing, Sahira met Elder Varden's glare steadily. "Show them the maps, Kaya."

Kaya unrolled parchments: hand-drawn maps made from the river circle's collective memory that identified underground channels and lines that flowed beneath even the temple's construction, and laid them across the table.

"The wells on the west side of the Bakki have always been vulnerable during drought," Sahira explained. "Because of how water moves flows beneath the valley. The Bakki flows north to south, fed by springs in the mountains. If those mountain channels are blocked, the valley is already cut off."

Jaraan had prized conservation. The river circle, guided by Syfir's ideas, prioritized flow.

But the crisis at hand would require manual intervention.

Sahira pointed to the mountains drawn in faded ink. "If we don't clear them before the autumn rains do finally come, backed-up water could cause flooding." She looked around at the elders. "They need to be cleared. But only those who read the river's patterns will know where to go."

A tense silence followed.

Elder Murat looked around the table at the other elders' parched lips.

Three more wells had failed that morning. Crowds were gathering. Rumors were spreading. Elder Murat's gaze swept the council.

"Faced with empty wells and growing unrest," she said finally, "we must accept all the help we can."

Sahira nodded. "The river circle will help. But not as subjects of Jaraan."

"And not as servants," Kaya added.

Elder Varden sneered. "You'd allow—"

"Not allow," Elder Murat interrupted. "We *request* that the river-touched women aid the Covenant in clearing the obstructions."

ELDER MURAT HIKED up her robes and walked alongside young awakened women as they followed the Bakki north.

Sahira had been right. Fallen trees, rock slides, and debris had dammed the riverbed upstream from Jaraan.

Traditionalist men worked shoulder-to-shoulder with blue-marked girls. Covenant engineers hauled ropes and dug trenches, while the river-touched guided water through newly opened channels with the lightest gestures of their hands.

The work was tense. Traditional men kept their distance from blue-marked women, communicating only through intermediaries. But when a boulder shifted and nearly crushed a Covenant engineer, it was Leela who raised a current to shift its weight just enough.

After that, cooperation grew slightly smoother.

When the rains finally came, they fell on a valley that had survived together. Barely.

But the drought had revealed a new truth to Jaraan and the river circle: they were stronger together, even if that togetherness remained fragile, than they were divided.

NEFRET SUTEKH HAD BEEN IMPRISONED after Sahira's trial, but only for a season. She'd only ever tried to protect Jaraan, she claimed, and Ameera Raazaan's death was so long ago.

Upon release, she was stripped of the title Elder. To everyone's surprise, she chose to remain in the main settlement, though she kept mostly to herself.

Sahira encountered her unexpectedly months later, near the boundary market.

Nefret startled at the sight of her, straightening into the rigid posture of the Covenant.

"You need not leave," Sahira said from a distance.

"I doubt we have anything to say to one another," Nefret replied.

Sahira set down her basket, studying the woman who had killed her mother. Nefret looked diminished, aged beyond her years in the months since her confession.

"The markings on your neck," Sahira said quietly. "How long?"

Nefret froze. "Since I was younger than you," she admitted. "Even before I became a temple acolyte."

"And you used to hear it. The river."

Pain flickered across Nefret's face. "What does it matter?"

"It doesn't. I just want to understand."

Nefret pursed her lips. "I silenced it. Because I was strong enough to choose duty over desire." She lifted her chin. "Now I'm free. It's forgotten me."

"It didn't forget," Sahira said. "It speaks still. You would just have to listen. You could still live a different life."

"You think I want your river madness?" Nefret's laugh was bitter, broken. "Look around you, girl. See what your 'awakening' has brought us. Families torn apart. Children hiding in fear. A community fractured beyond repair."

Her voice rose, decades of suppressed rage finally erupting. "I built something here. Order from chaos. Safety from fear. And you've destroyed it all. Everything I spent my life building. Every girl who drowns in madness now, every family torn apart —that's your doing. I'm innocent."

"You took my mother from me. And yet here we both stand —her killer and her daughter," Sahira said quietly. "The river doesn't forget its daughters."

Nefret's eyes blazed. "Then let it remember this: I choose to be forgotten. I want no part of the world you've made." She turned sharply, but something made her pause. Perhaps a flicker of the girl she'd once been, who had also heard the river's call.

But then she straightened her spine, and walked away, her stride rigid as she disappeared into the crowd.

Sahira never spoke to her again.

~

THAT EVENING, Sahira waded into the river, relaxing into its familiar embrace.

"Sometimes I forget how much has changed," Leela said softly, wading out beside her.

Sahira nodded, turning to look behind them. Lamps flickered to life, their glow glinting off the irrigation channels that now connected every home to the main water line.

"Sometimes I worry it could all be undone overnight," Sahira said quietly.

Leela looked at her. "Do you ever regret it? The choices you made? The life you might've had?"

Sahira considered the question seriously. She could have chosen some middle path that kept her within the Covenant's embrace while secretly nurturing her true nature. Women throughout history had chosen that path. Living a prescribed life, finding freedom in small, hidden spaces. But she hadn't.

"No." Sahira reached out, then squeezed her cousin's hand.

"Me neither." Leela pulled her into a quick hug, then turned back toward their camp.

Tomorrow, they would wake to the same struggles: the same careful balancing act between progress and survival, the same exhausting work of building bridges that some people would always try to burn.

Their work would continue.

~

THE SUN WAS NEARLY SETTING. Sahira stood waist-deep in the river, breath shallow. The water rose around her, murmuring of memory and change. Behind her, the wind carried the faint sound of bells. There was no ribbon in her hair now—only loose strands, wild in the breeze.

With slow, deliberate steps, she let the river take her fully, submerging herself in its ancient embrace. She reemerged, cleansed by the river she called home.

She closed her eyes, lying back in the current, and reached with that other sense—the one that awakened fully in the Mouth of the Serpent. Across distance, across time, she felt him: moving steadily toward her, his being attuned to hers like twin currents of the same river.

Somewhere far off—but drawing closer—she knew he felt her.

She waded deeper, following the certainty that lived in her bones. The pull was undeniable. She followed the feeling and swam downstream toward the confluence where five tributaries joined the main current and became one.

The water shimmered there like liquid starlight.

And then through the water, she heard something impossible, and yet familiar.

Music.

A melody she hadn't heard in almost a year, played on an instrument she knew intimately.

Heart racing, she followed the sound, swam to the far bank and climbed out, the river dripping from her skin, her hair, her clothes.

Her feet moved before her mind understood why.

And then, she saw him—a single figure silhouetted against the setting sun. Even from a distance, she knew the set of his shoulders, the way he held his head.

He stepped closer, and the world tilted on its axis.

"Hello, my Zarouni girl."

# EPILOGUE

A young girl with dark hair and amber eyes stepped over a boulder, plucked a burdock stem from the riverbank, and splashed into the water with the ease of someone who had never been taught to resist its call.

Mehrina was eight years old.

Sahira marveled at her ease and at the blue marks that glowed brightly from beneath her sun-warmed skin.

"Is it almost time to eat?" Mehrina asked, her voice carrying a melody that hummed with the river's rhythm.

As if summoned by the question, Syfir let out a familiar whistle, signaling dinner was ready.

Sahira turned, and there he stood, barefoot and leaning against the door to their kitchen, stirring something hot and fragrant in a wide bowl, his sleeves pushed up over his blue-marked forearms. His curls were touched with silver now, eyes just beginning to crinkle. But the way he looked at Sahira hadn't changed. He winked.

"Let's eat!" Mehrina shrieked, launching herself toward her father's arms. Sahira started forward to stop Mehrina from knocking over the bowl, but Syfir, having already anticipated their daughter's enthusiasm, set the bowl safely aside before catching her mid-leap in the same fluid movement. He spun her once before setting her down.

They ate dinner together on the veranda—Sahira, Syfir, Mehrina, Leela—and Mehrina leaned against her father.

"Is it time for you to go again?" she asked, her voice soft, already knowing the answer.

"Soon," Syfir said gently, brushing her damp hair behind her ear. "But not yet." He turned to look at his wife, his eyes twinkling with promises kept and new ones waiting to be made.

CHANGE HAD COME SLOWLY over the decade, through small victories and occasional setbacks that gradually reshaped the landscape. Their river settlement had grown into what was now the Bakki Village, with thirty-three households and trade agreements with three neighboring settlements. Trade with Jaraan proper was also less strained than it had been ten years earlier.

Sahira's life had found rhythm in her work with awakened women, and in the school she'd built for girls like Mehrina, who carried the river's mark from their earliest years.

And Syfir was a part of the rhythm: tending gardens, maintaining Bakki Village's water filtration system, telling stories by firelight. And leaving—only to return with each new moon, carrying news from distant allies. Always returning home.

WHEN THE TIME came to depart again, Syfir packed his satchel as Mehrina clung to his leg, her small face solemn.

"Six sleeps?" she asked, holding up six fingers.

"Six sleeps," he promised, kneeling to press his forehead to hers. "And I'll bring back new stories."

She pressed three fingers to her heart, where a small blue

river token hung against her chest, and he mirrored her movement before kissing her softly on the head.

Then, Sahira held Mehrina in her arms as they watched him disappear down the trail that led south, past the far edges of their land. Sahira felt the familiar ache of his departure, tempered now by the certainty of his return.

In six days, they would stand in this same spot to welcome him home again. The moon would wax and wane. The river would rise and fall. And their family would remain complete.

LATER THAT EVENING, after Mehrina had fallen asleep, curled against Leela's side, Sahira made her way to the water's edge.

Sahira thought of Dasha, of her mother, of all who hadn't lived to see this peace, but who had paid for it.

She waded into the river. The current embraced her, as it always had. But now she could also sense distant waters. Rivers where girls spoke to water without fear, where no one hid their markings. And other, unknown rivers where women looked down at arms marked with the pale golden swirling patterns of the earth, with the silver swirls of sky and air.

Mehrina would get to grow up in the world Sahira, and her mother before her, had fought to create. But the work would never be finished. Freedom was something each generation would have to choose again and again.

"I am my mother's daughter," Sahira whispered to the river. "I am the river's daughter."

And the river rippled, as if in response.

Sahira looked back toward their home, where her own daughter dreamed without fear. "And she will be the bridge to whatever comes next."

The water carried her words onward, to distant shores, where the future was awakening.

# ACKNOWLEDGMENTS

Thank you first to my mom, Sonia, for reading and giving feedback on every draft of this book, and for making me read so much as a kid that my writing a novel one day was inevitable.

Thank you to everyone who read early versions of *The River's Daughter*, especially Naveen, who listened to the entire (PG version) of this story and got so excited that it made me excited too. Thank you to Andrea, Sojeong, and Palwasha for cheering for this project before it was done, and to my beta readers for pushing the story forward. Thank you to my ARC readers for your time and enthusiasm in helping bring this book to the world.

Thank you to my friend and illustrator, Sarah Khan Azamy, for your artistry, your love for this story, and for helping me bring Jaraan to life.

I'm thankful to my Nani and Mummyji for telling me saakhis and for passing down our culture of storytelling.

I'm grateful for the legend of Mirza Sahiba and for coming from a people who love *love*.

Thank you to my parents, Sonia and Pali, for teaching me to use my voice.

Thank you to my husband, David, our boys, Naveen and Ishaan (who thank God share my love of sci-fi & fantasy), and Charlie: you four fill real life with romance, beauty, and magic.

And finally, to you, the reader: thank you from the bottom of my heart for making space for this story in yours. Thank you, thank you, thank you.

# About the Author

**Punita Rice** is the author of *The River's Daughter*, a story about forbidden love, feminine rebellion, and river magic, inspired by the legend of Mirza Sahiba. This is her debut novel.

She holds a doctorate in education from Johns Hopkins University and is also the author of *South Asian American Experiences in Schools* (Rowman & Littlefield, 2019; re-releasing 2026). A former middle school social studies teacher and education researcher, her work has appeared in *Berkeley Review of Education, Education Week Teacher, Radio New Zealand, The Baltimore Sun*, and other publications. She has also written several children's books for her sons, called *The Adventures of Hunny & Sunny*.

Though she now works outside education, she remains passionate about storytelling, learning, and raising curious, thoughtful kids.

Punita lives in Maryland with her husband, their boys, and their dog, and spends her free time daydreaming about rivers, rebellion, and love stories from the past. You can find her online at **punitarice.com** or on Instagram or TikTok @punitarice.

instagram.com/punitarice
facebook.com/punitarice
tiktok.com/@punitarice